Inheriting Love's Secrets

by

Laura Freeman

Second Chances

Inheriting Love's Secrets

Cover Art by *Teddi Black*

The Wild Rose Press, Inc.
PO Box 708
Adams Basin, NY 14410-0708
Visit us at www.thewildrosepress.com

Publishing History
First Edition, 2026
Trade Paperback Print ISBN 978-1-5092-6417-9
Digital ISBN 978-1-5092-6418-6

Second Chances
Published in the United States of America

Dedication

To women who deserve a second chance after life knocks them down.

Chapter One

Deidre Pierce savored the last bite of cherry pie as the sweet fruit and flaky crust formed the perfect bite. She placed her empty plate on the blanket beneath the oak tree where the shade protected her fair skin from the hot July sun. The residents of Crooked River, Ohio, were celebrating the centennial birthday of the nation with a town picnic, lawn games, and an evening dance and fireworks.

July 4 was Deidre's birthday, and turning twenty-one meant she was no longer considered a poor orphan dependent on relatives. Her uncle, Logan Pierce, was the only one left in her father's family and had been her guardian since she was six years old. She was old enough to understand the circumstances surrounding her parents' deaths, but society frowned upon illicit affairs, illegitimate children, and murdered lovers. Few mentioned her unfortunate heritage.

Deidre and Caroline Bauer gathered the used plates decorated in a blue centennial pattern. "We better wash these," Deidre said.

Liny was nineteen and a cousin to Logan's wife, Jem. Her parents had been murdered the year after the Civil War ended. Although Deidre and Liny were not blood related, the loss of their parents bound them tighter than sisters.

They put on their bonnets and made their way

through the patchwork of blankets where families finished their meals. Lawn games had been set up on the town square, and the sound of mallets hitting wooden balls through wickets and the clanging of horseshoes against an iron rod echoed along with shouts and cheers of participants. Older children played baseball while the young children chased wooden hoops on the brick road or jumped rope.

Deidre didn't want to break or chip the new plates and carried the stack with both hands as they walked to the pump in front of the schoolhouse. "How do you like working on the *Irish Rose*? It's been so warm this summer."

Crooked River was a small town of farms, a mill, and brick builders along the Ohio-Erie Canal. Liny worked on the canal boat, the *Irish Rose*. Her blonde hair had turned nearly white, and she had a tan on her arms and face.

"I didn't have a choice." Liny carried several pie tins and an empty glass pitcher. "George and Will wanted to earn some money, and I'm responsible for my little brothers."

"They're not so little anymore." Deidre clutched her stack of dishes and stepped aside as a boy trying to catch a fly ball nearly ran into her.

"George is sixteen and can handle himself, but Will is fourteen and doesn't seem to know how to stay out of trouble. When I reprimand him, he reminds me I'm not his papa or mama." Liny's voice quivered. "He barely remembers our parents."

"He was only four." Deidre led the way to the water pump. A washbasin and towels had been left on a table for cleaning dishes. "I was six when my mother died, and

I barely remember anything about her. I feel like a big hole exists in my life. He probably feels the same."

"I hated when other children asked me why I was an orphan."

"Sometimes I told others my father was killed in the war instead of in 1855," Deidre said. "Some of them understood that. And I'd say my mother died of a broken heart. The lies were easier to live with than the truth."

"You exaggerate the truth because you have a good imagination."

"Aunt Jem thinks it's overly imaginative but doesn't complain when I keep my cousins entertained with interesting stories," Deidre said. "But I need to find a way to earn a living so I don't become a burden."

"We are not charity cases," Liny said. "We've always worked. Dr. Greystone may need help with his patients when I'm gone. You've helped him in the past."

"I'm a little rusty on my nursing skills, but I'll be happy to lend a hand."

"Unless you want to join me as a member of the crew on the *Irish Rose.*" Liny chewed on her lip.

"I was hoping my canal boat days were over." Deidre placed the dishes on the table and moved the pump handle up and down. "I enjoyed working with you, but the boats only run during the summer, and I want a job that will pay all year round."

"You wouldn't need to work if you married someone who would take care of you," Liny said.

"And be totally dependent on him?" She had spent her life relying on others. She craved independence.

Water poured from the pump. Liny washed the plates while Deidre dried them.

Deidre had seen the price women paid for depending

on men. "Haven't you learned anything from Second Chance?"

"Never say yes to the first man who proposes?" Liny hesitated in her answer.

"Never say yes to a stranger," Deidre said. "Insist on a long courtship and be wary of a man shopping for a wife."

"Isn't a man eager to wed a good thing for a woman who wants to be a bride?"

"When a man is looking to marry, he proposes to every woman he knows until one of them says yes," Deidre said. "Men have been proposing to me since I turned seventeen. At first, I was flattered, but then I realized they didn't love me. How could they? They barely knew me. That's when I realized a man chooses a wife for all the wrong reasons."

Liny handed her the last plate. "What do you mean?"

"A man may marry someone to replace his mother to cook and clean and take care of him. Another man may pick the most popular woman in town and brag about winning the prize. Only he doesn't know what to do once he's won her. Then there's the man who marries for money." Deidre shrugged. "I don't have to worry about that one."

Liny helped Deidre carry the clean dishes. "How many men have proposed to you?"

"I don't remember. Too many of them are forgettable." Deidre smiled at her. "Don't worry. Plenty of men will propose to you. Just don't say yes to the first one."

Liny bit her bottom lip and nodded. "I won't."

Deidre looked around. They were alone. "Are we

still on for tonight?"

"Captain Donovan will have the *Irish Rose* ready," she whispered. "Our disguises will be aboard."

"I hope we're back in time for the dance," Deidre said. "You're coming, aren't you?"

Liny nodded. "I'm determined to overcome my shyness and dance with anyone who asks."

"Good for you," Deidre said. "I'm hoping Nate Burroughs works up the courage to ask me to waltz. He's handsome and chivalrous on the outside, but I'd like to find out what goes on in that lawyer's brain of his."

"I didn't know you liked him," Liny said with a lilt in her voice. "Doesn't he work for Tyler Montgomery?"

"For the past two years. Everyone speaks well of him, but when I've encountered him, he's so serious and polite. The last time we met, I told an outrageous story to make him laugh, but all he did was grin as if mildly amused."

"Men are the strangest creatures," Liny said. "If I didn't want children, I wouldn't bother with them."

"And I know how illegitimate children are treated," Deidre said. The taunts and insults from her childhood penetrated her memories. She forced them back.

"Your reputation is impeccable," Liny said. "Only a fool would insult you."

"And we do not tolerate fools." She emphasized each word.

They returned to the oak tree. Logan and Jem had claimed the blanket and watched their five children play on the square.

"Thank you for cleaning the dishes." Aunt Jem packed them into a basket but set aside the pie tins. "These belong in the church. Would you mind returning them?"

The church had provided pie tins along with fruit and sugar for the celebration. Volunteers had prepared the crusts and baked the pies for the event. Deidre had made three cherry pies. She gathered the tins. "Happy to, Aunt Jem."

Her uncle stood. He was the younger brother of her father, Derek Pierce, but the family resemblance was strong. They shared light-brown hair that turned blond in the summer, warm brown eyes, and deep dimples. "Be careful tonight."

Deidre glanced around and nodded. "I'm grateful you trust us for this mission."

"It's hard to pass responsibilities on to the younger generation, but you volunteered." Aunt Jem stood next to her husband. "Mr. Crawford will have the ladder you need."

"Everyone will be distracted by the fireworks, and Captain Donovan will be close by to help if there's any trouble," Uncle Logan said with a dimpled smile.

The sun filtered through a sprinkling of white fluffy clouds in the western sky. "Should we leave now?" Deidre asked.

"You'll need time to change out of your new dress," Aunt Jem said.

Deidre smoothed the red-and-white patterned skirt draped tightly across the front and tucked into numerous folds that trailed down the back. "Thank you for the birthday gift."

"It was our pleasure." Her aunt hugged her. "I can't believe you're all grown up." She brushed a stray tear off her cheek.

Aunt Jem joined her husband on the blanket and

snuggled against him.

Liny stared at the couple, a smile on her face.

Deidre nudged her with an elbow. "We better run this errand and be on our way." She led the way to the church.

"I've read in romance novels that a man and woman can fall in love looking at each other for the first time," Liny said.

"Stop reading that nonsense." Deidre was more practical than to believe sparks flew across a room. "Aunt Jem nearly ran Uncle Logan over with her buggy on their first meeting."

Liny sighed. "That sounds romantic."

Deidre stared at her lovestruck cousin. "Some people would call it attempted murder."

"You should marry a lawyer." Liny laughed as she bumped her with her hip. "Don't you believe in true love? You said Nate Burroughs was handsome and chivalrous."

"And a shiny red apple can still contain a worm."

Their laughter ceased as they entered the church. The solemnness of the building demanded respect. Dishes had been placed on a long table in the foyer to be claimed by those who had donated food for the picnic. Deidre added the pie tins.

Liny stepped inside the empty sanctuary, and Deidre followed. Two rows of pews were placed on each side of the central aisle with other pews placed against the windows. A raised dais was at the far end with a wooden pulpit for the preacher. The round ceiling had the peculiar ability to enhance voices. Someone above them was speaking. She turned to Liny and whispered, "Someone's in the balcony."

"I bet it's a couple canoodling." Liny giggled and covered her mouth.

The door was open to the staircase leading upstairs. Deidre pointed. "Let's find out who."

Liny's face turned red. "Oh no. What if it's someone we know?"

"That's even better." Deidre grabbed her hand and led the way to the second floor.

Two men were talking in the front pew near the railing. She was ready to turn around when she recognized the voices of Nate Burroughs and Oscar Leland, a clerk who worked for Uncle Logan, the mayor of Crooked River. She raised her finger to her lips to prevent Liny from speaking. She lifted her skirt and crawled along the floor behind the final row of pews until she reached the aisle.

She sat on the floor, blocked by the pew, and listened. Liny scooted next to her and tucked her skirt around her.

"I think she will make an excellent wife. She has beauty, charm, and connections," Oscar said. "I plan to propose. I expect her to be flattered and say yes."

"You barely know her," Nate said. "What's the rush to tie yourself down to one woman?"

"A man doesn't need to limit his sampling." Oscar chuckled. "Even after he's married. I know how to be discreet."

"If you don't plan on being faithful, why marry at all?" Nate sounded angry.

"I want to advance my career, and the mayor has connections," Oscar said. "She would be an invaluable asset for my ambitions."

What mayor? Could Oscar be talking about Uncle

Logan? And who was the woman? Deidre listened with rapt attention to their conversation.

"You haven't heard about her family's scandal?" Nate asked in a hushed voice that promised salacious gossip.

"Scandal?" Oscar's voice betrayed surprise and interest. "I thought she was an orphan."

Liny grabbed her hand and tugged, nodding toward the doorway.

Deidre shook her head. She wanted to hear what Nate would share. She could see the back of the men's heads and shoulders from her spot near the aisle.

"You probably have nothing to worry about." Nate leaned back in the front pew. "But I heard a rumor about something in Washington City before the war."

"That was a long time ago." Oscar snapped his fingers. "No one will care."

"Scandals have a way of resurfacing at the least opportune times, but it's not like you have political ambitions for yourself," Nate said.

"My future career includes running for state congress and serving in Columbus." Oscar sounded worried. "I don't want an old scandal to thwart my plans, but how bad could it be? After all, Deidre couldn't have been more than a child."

Deidre bristled as she clenched her hands. She *was* the woman they were discussing. How dare they!

"That's part of the scandal." Nate lowered his voice, but the round ceiling made his words clear and easily heard. "Her father had an affair with a married woman. The husband shot and killed Derek Pierce, and Deidre was born six months later."

She knew the story of her parents' scandalous affair,

9

but Nate Burroughs didn't have the right to share it. Deidre rose, smacking the back of the pew with her palms to make her presence known. "How dare you, Nate Burroughs and Oscar Leland. Gossiping in church!"

Liny rose from her hiding place and stepped toward the door. Deidre grabbed her skirt before she could flee.

Nate and Oscar stood like soldiers at attention, their mouths agape.

"Deidre," Nate said. "I didn't know you were up here."

"Obviously or you wouldn't have slandered my family and me." Her voice rose in anger.

Nate stepped to the aisle separating the rows and advanced toward her. "I'm sorry."

"I refuse to accept your apology," she said. "I will despise both of you for the rest of my life. If our paths chance to cross in the future, I will be polite but nothing more. You are both pariahs to me."

Deidre pushed Liny toward the stairs but turned when she reached the doorway. "You should be ashamed of your behavior, *gentlemen*." She expressed as much sarcasm as she could with the final word.

"I truly am." Nate bowed his head. "You don't know how much."

They ran down the steps and out of the church.

Liny kept pace as they ran across the town square. "You showed him."

Deidre didn't dare speak. Her lip quivered, and tears pooled on her eyelids. Deep in her chest, an ache grew at all the injustice of having a name marked by scandal. She was proud of her parents no matter what others thought of them. They had defied society to be together. But had they loved her?

"We need to board the *Irish Rose*," Liny said. "The captain and my brothers will be waiting."

Deidre nodded, not trusting her voice, which was ready to break in despair. She had truly liked Nate. How could he be such a blackhearted scoundrel? And Oscar was like all the other men who had thought of her as an object to be used for their own ambitions. What about her value? What about her feelings?

Liny tugged on her arm. "We have to hurry."

Chapter Two

Nate dashed down the stairs and out the main doors to the stone steps of the church. He watched Deidre and Liny run down the street toward the canal. She didn't look back. He had hurt her beyond imagination and couldn't think of a way to make amends.

Oscar joined him and patted him on the back. "I'm glad you warned me about her. I thought she was a lady, but she's nothing but a—"

Nate didn't let him finish. He threw a punch to silence him.

Oscar fell to the ground and rubbed his jaw. "What was that for?"

"She is a lady, and if you say anything contrary, you'll get worse."

Oscar slowly rose, keeping his distance. "If I didn't know better, I'd think you were interested in her."

Nate didn't answer. Any hope of a romance was dashed. He wandered toward the square where families were cleaning up after the picnic and games. Members of the band headed to the gazebo with their instruments. Others gathered around the square where bricks made in Crooked River created a hard smooth surface for dancing.

He didn't feel like watching fireworks, dancing, or enjoying any celebration. He leaned against the family buggy parked beneath a shade tree, his hands gripping the window opening of the door, his head bowed in shame. Why couldn't he be like other men and spin tales filled with lies?

Too many of his rivals had honed the skills to spout flowery speeches of eloquent insincere declarations of love to gain a rich or influential wife. Oscar's biggest flaw was bragging about his conquests. When he confided that Deidre was his next target, Nate had panicked. He loved her. His feelings had been building the past two years, but his tongue, so skilled in a courtroom, drowned in mute admiration in her presence.

He had revealed family secrets forgotten by most in town. His hurtful gossip marked him as a rake who couldn't be trusted. He needed to rebuild his reputation, not only for Deidre, but as a lawyer who needed his clients' confidences.

"Nathaniel?"

Nate stiffened. The last person he wanted to speak to was his mother. If he ignored her, would she go away and leave him alone in his grief? But he couldn't hurt another woman, especially Amanda Burroughs, a widow who had sacrificed so much so her son could succeed. She would be ashamed of his latest actions, but he welcomed her chastisement. He turned and faced her, ready to pay the consequences for his behavior.

Her eyes widened and gazed into his soul. She softly touched his arm. "What's wrong, baby?"

Baby. He was twenty-six years old but felt like a child. He put his arms around his mother's narrow shoulders and hugged her close, drawing comfort from the woman who had raised him and knew him better than anyone else. "I hurt someone."

"Hurt? Are they injured?" She pulled away and

searched his face.

"Not physically." He stuffed his hands into his pockets to hide his bruised knuckles. "I said something cruel to Oscar Leland."

She pursed her lips. "I doubt you could injure his enormous pride."

His shoulders sagged. "I told him some gossip about Deidre Pierce."

"What?" Her shocked expression confirmed the seriousness of his offense.

"I reminded Oscar how Derek Pierce had an affair with Deidre's married mother."

Her brows crushed together in a frown. "Why would you share such a private revelation?"

"I thought it was common knowledge." Nate removed his bowler hat and ran his hands through his hair. "He bragged he was planning to marry her. I was trying to deter him."

"Why?"

"I…" He couldn't compound his transgression.

"Nathaniel." She spoke in that tone mothers used even with adult sons. "I thought you liked Deidre."

What could he say? He had been awestruck the first time he saw her after returning home from Harvard College with his law degree. It had been a summer day, and the wind blew her hat off. She laughed as she chased it down the street, her sun-streaked curls dancing on her shoulders. He caught it and handed it to her. He didn't say a word. He couldn't. All he did was stare, memorizing every delicate feature of her face. She thanked him and skipped away, the music of her voice dancing on his heart. His tongue had loosened since then but in the wrong way. "I think the world of her, but I have little to offer."

"You're a lawyer with a promising future," his mother said.

"The future is the problem. She's looking for a husband now." His voice broke. "She's beautiful and clever, and I could only hope she would look my way. I panicked. I was afraid Oscar might convince her to marry him." He paced to the end of the buggy, turned, and shrugged. "It could be years before I could properly take care of her."

"Men who wait until they can support a wife never marry," his mother said. "Your father and I had nothing to live on but love, and we survived."

"I don't have to worry about ever marrying Deidre Pierce now." Nate smacked his hat against his thigh. "She hates me."

"Then you won't be attending tonight's dance?"

He stared up at the evening sky of magenta and cyan. "I don't see any reason to stay."

"I need a favor." She glanced around. "You can't ask why, but I need you to borrow a ladder from Mr. Crawford on Howard Street in Akron."

What an odd request. "Tonight?"

"Yes." She placed her hand on his arm. "He'll have it ready and tell you where to take it."

Ladders had only one use at night. "Is someone eloping?"

"No, dear." Her voice had a hint of exasperation. "You may not believe this, but I have other talents besides fixing your dinner and sewing a button on your shirt."

"What do you mean?" He studied her face. "I'm a lawyer. If you're in trouble, I can help."

"I'm asking for your help now. Two other people will join you. When they're done, you can return the ladder." She pointed at the family buggy. "You need to be there before dark."

He paused before climbing into the seat. "I don't say it enough, but I appreciate all you do for me, Mother. I know it's been hard since Pa was killed and I left for school. I neglected you all those years, so I'll do whatever you ask."

"You didn't neglect me," she said. "I kept busy in your absence."

He gathered the reins in his hands. "Working as a maid?"

"Is that what you think?" She put her hands on her hips. "You're smart about the law and what's in books, Nathaniel, but you know nothing about women."

He couldn't argue that fact.

"I was the housekeeper at Ravens Roost. I ran the place. It was a privilege to be trusted with such a large responsibility."

He had never asked about her work. "Then why did you quit?"

"To take care of you," she said.

He backed the horse to turn the buggy toward the road. "I can take care of myself."

"Good because there might be an element of danger in what I'm asking you to do."

He restrained the horse. "What danger?"

"Go." She pointed at the road. "Mr. Crawford will be waiting."

Nate pondered their exchange as he urged the horse down the main road and headed south to Akron. He crossed the bridge that spanned the Cuyahoga River and turned onto Howard Street. He knew where Gus Crawford lived. He was a family friend who had looked after them when his father had joined the Twenty-Ninth Ohio Volunteer Infantry in late 1862. Lloyd Burroughs had been older than the young men who signed up with him to replace those who had died in the first two years of the war.

"I can't let boys do all the fighting," he had said.

Only his father hadn't returned home. A Rebel sharpshooter's bullet had ended his life in 1865, a few months before the end of the war. The boys had returned and grown into men. Ethan Donovan was captain of the *Irish Rose* canal boat, Harry Herbruck owned a farm on Portage Trail, and Zach Ravenswood owned Ravens Roost, a horse farm in the neighboring county. The same farm his mother had worked at while he attended preparatory school and college.

Not as a maid. The details about her position in the letters she wrote to him had been sparse. His mother's writing had focused on the town and other people. He knew so little about her life. He needed to sit down and have a long chat with the woman who had given birth to him.

The sky was darkening, and most of the businesses had closed for the holiday. People had gathered at churches, parks, and town greens to celebrate. Fireworks would begin soon. He passed through North Hill and descended the steep slope of Howard Street. Gus lived near Cuyahoga Street past the Little Cuyahoga River. He pulled on the reins and hopped out of the buggy.

He knocked on the front door of the shop where Gus made glass windows.

Gus stepped outside. A thick bandage covered his

17

hand. "Better take the buggy to the back."

Nate led the horse to a barn in the rear of the property. "How did you hurt your hand?"

"Cut it this afternoon. I didn't give your mother much time to find someone to replace me. I guess you'll do." He opened a tack box and handed him an old coat and large-brimmed hat. "Put these on. You don't want anyone to recognize you."

Nate discarded his good clothes, leaving them on the buggy seat, and put on the dirty coat. He tugged the floppy hat down to shield his face.

"It's good you've decided to join the organization," Gus said.

"What organization?" Was his mother part of a secret society? "What am I getting into?"

"Your mother didn't explain?"

Nate took pride in being well prepared and informed before entering a courtroom. Clandestine mysteries were foreign to him. "She said I was to pick up a ladder and you would tell me where to go with it."

His bushy eyebrows shadowed his eyes. "Perhaps I shouldn't say anything."

Nate crossed his arms. "I'm not doing anything until I have some answers."

"I don't have time to explain the entire enterprise."

He gathered facts, figures, and evidence when making a decision. He didn't like surprises. "Then give me the basics."

Gus nodded. "Two women are in trouble. You are to take a ladder to the back of the Merry Widow Saloon and help them climb out."

"They aren't eloping?" He realized the ridiculousness of his question as soon as it left his mouth.

"Obviously not."

"They're escaping." Gus squinted. "Don't you know what type of establishment the Merry Widow is?"

"You said it was a saloon."

"Gardner is the owner. He runs a gaming room and brothel at the establishment."

"That's against the law." He couldn't participate in something illegal. What had his mother gotten him into? "As a lawyer I have a reputation to protect."

"No one will want to go to court. The owner denies any wrongdoing, and the customers won't testify against him. The women can't say anything without being beaten and starved."

He shook his head. "I'm rescuing two prostitutes?"

"Hazel and Gwen were respectable young ladies, but their father loves to drink and gamble. When his debts were too large for him to pay, he indentured Hazel to the owner. Gardner said she would only serve drinks, but that turned out to be a lie. He forced himself on her and then took money from other men who degraded her."

Nate had worked for a lawyer in New York City during summer breaks when he wasn't attending classes at Harvard. He had seen the seedier side of life. He'd helped on a case involving a prostitute who had killed a man. She'd claimed self-defense. No one had believed her, but she'd shown him the scars from beatings and burns she'd received when she tried to escape her duties. "How long has she been a prisoner?"

"Months passed before we realized the situation. Then her father agreed to contract her younger sister Gwen to the owner. She arrived today. That's why we need to remove them tonight."

"My mother said two others would join me."

"They're late, and we can't wait. The best time to remove the girls is during the fireworks display. After the show is over, men will start arriving to continue the celebration. Until then Gardner will be the only one at the saloon. He keeps the women locked in their room on the second floor. That's why you need the ladder." Gus held a lantern with the wick turned low and showed him the equipment stored along the wall.

Nate balanced the long ladder in his hands and headed for the open doors of the barn.

"Cross this street and follow the alley to the back of the Merry Widow," Gus said.

"How will I know where the saloon is or what room the women are in?"

"A blue cloth will be over the light in the window. When you return the ladder, I'll tell you where to take the women." He nodded and pointed at two figures walking toward them. "Your partners have arrived."

"We're sorry to be late," a soft voice whispered in the shadows.

The voice was familiar but didn't match the bulky figure in a coat, trousers, and floppy hat outlined in the soft light of the lantern Gus held. "Deidre?"

Her hostile expression made it clear he had guessed correctly. Liny was dressed in a similar disguise.

"What are *you* doing here?" Deidre demanded.

"My mother drafted me for this mission," Nate said. "We better hurry."

Deidre crossed her arms and glared. "We don't need your help."

He adjusted the long ladder. "This is heavy. Besides, I owe you. Let me make amends for my bad behavior."

"Someone else can help." Deidre looked at Gus,

who raised his bandaged hand.

"We don't have time to debate the details of the case." Nate pointed to the sky. "The fireworks are beginning."

Deidre grabbed the front of the ladder, and Liny took the rear as they made their way to the alley behind the Merry Widow Saloon. A dog barked, and Liny shrieked, jerking the ladder and knocking over a stack of empty wooden crates.

Nate cringed, waiting for someone to yell out a window or investigate the disturbance. A bright flash filled the sky, and a loud boom from the fireworks scared the dog away.

He searched for the Merry Widow. All the backs of the buildings looked alike. He finally spotted a blue light glowing in a second-floor window. "This is it." He maneuvered the ladder and placed it against the sill.

A head poked out the open window.

"That's Hazel," Liny whispered.

"I'll go up and get her," Deidre said.

"No." Nate removed her hand from the ladder. "You hold it. I'll get them." He didn't want Deidre or Liny risking their lives entering the Merry Widow. Who knew if someone would discover them and harm them? This wasn't a game. He would have to make sure they knew the seriousness of the risks they were taking. "Be ready to run if there's any trouble."

He climbed the ladder and looked through the open window. Two women backed away. The one identified as Hazel held the lantern that had been on a small table by the window.

"I'm here to rescue you." A flash of a fireworks lit the sky, and he climbed inside to escape detection. In his rush, he knocked over the table but righted it. The bed was the central focus among a few items of furniture. It sagged, and the thin mattress was badly stained. A single blanket was folded down. A carpetbag was on the floor.

"Are you ready?" he whispered.

Hazel wore a gown that would have been used as a rag by most women. The sleeves were torn from their seams, and buttons were missing down the front. She removed the blue cloth from the lamp, which illuminated her face. One eye was puffy and dark from a bruise. Her lip was cut and swollen. Her hair hung loose in greasy tangles. He hid any reaction to the smell of an unwashed body.

Gwen stood in sharp contrast. Her dress was faded but intact. Her face showed no marks of a beating, and she smelled of soap. A single braid hung to her waist. She was young, but old men were eager to pay for a taste of youth.

The room was bathed in dark shadows except where faint light peeked through the cracks around the door.

"Does your door lock?"

"No."

He grabbed a rickety chair and propped it under the doorknob. "Where are your belongings?"

Hazel handed a pillowcase to Nate. "In here."

The bag was light. He tied a knot and dropped it out the window as the crack of fireworks lit up the sky and disguised any sound. Gwen handed him the carpetbag. He waited for the next burst of light and dropped it outside. He signaled them to the window. "Can you climb down in your skirts?"

"We can tie them up." Hazel bent over, grabbed the back of her gown, and pulled it forward and up, tying the

22

ends around her waist to form pantaloons. Gwen did the same.

"Where's Liny?" Hazel asked as they gathered at the window.

"She's holding the ladder. How do you know her?"

"We attended school together," Hazel said. "Years ago."

Gwen stood at the window, her hands braced on the sill. "How do I get out?"

"Swing your foot out and find the rung. Then swing out the other. I'll hold on to you until you're ready to climb down."

When Gwen had moved past a few rungs, he signaled Hazel to follow. She jerked at his touch, and he kept his distance as she made her way on her own.

He blew out the light before climbing out the window.

Someone pounded on the door. "Why is this door stuck?"

It had to be Gardner. Nate heard the sound of wood splintering and took two rungs at a time to descend. He jumped to the ground and pulled the ladder from the window. "We have to leave. Now."

"Come back here!" Gardner shouted from the window.

Nate spun the ladder lengthwise, the women grabbed on, and they ran. When they reached the Crawford residence, everyone dropped the ladder, gasping for breath.

"Why do I feel like Tom Sawyer?" Nate asked. "All we needed was a dead cat and a visit to the graveyard at midnight."

"I haven't read Twain's latest book," Deidre said.

"Don't say anything more and ruin it."

He held up his hands. "I understand. I hate it when someone spoils a book I plan to read. You can borrow my copy if you'd like."

"I have my own. It was a birthday present."

He knew it was her birthday. He'd bought a small bottle of cologne and had planned to give her the gift at the dance along with a declaration of his intentions to call upon her on Sunday. No chance of that happening now.

Gus joined them. "I see you rescued them."

Nate returned the ladder to its spot in the barn and removed his borrowed coat and hat. "Someone was coming through the door as I left."

"Did they see you?" Gus sounded worried.

He nodded toward the sisters. "No, but Gardner knows they're missing. He'll be looking for them."

"We'll take care of that," Deidre said.

"The *Irish Rose* is waiting," Liny said. "We should hurry."

"Get in my buggy, and I'll take you." Nate led the horse out of the barn. "It'll be faster." And safer if the owner of the Merry Widow had recruits looking for them on the streets.

Another flash lit the sky. "Let's get out of here." He fought the urge to help the women into the carriage. Hazel was afraid of men for good reason, and two of them were dressed as boys. It was crowded when he joined them. He slapped the reins on the back of the horse. "Where is the *Irish Rose* moored?"

"Just below Mustill Store," Liny said.

Deidre sat next to him. "Don't you dare think of sharing anything that's happened tonight with your friends. If you betray us, you'll feel the full fury of my wrath."

Nate swallowed. The last thing he wanted to do was alienate Deidre more. Each misstep would make it harder for her to forgive him, but Deidre had accepted his help in rescuing Hazel and Gwen. That was a start toward changing her mind about him.

"I swear you have my full confidentiality," he said. "And I take my oaths seriously."

Chapter Three

Deidre tried to create more than a breath of distance between herself and Nate, but the narrow seat squashed them in the closest of proximity. Every time he slapped the reins on the back of the horse, she felt the hard muscle of his arm against her own and couldn't deny the feelings stirred by his touch. She had to remember he was the enemy.

"Naughty Nate."

"What?"

Had he heard her quiet comment to herself? "I'm going to call you Naughty Nate because of your bad behavior."

He chuckled in a low baritone. "Naughty, huh? I've never been called that before."

"You're not supposed to like it." She crossed her arms and wondered how the name could be a compliment.

Nate turned onto North Street and crossed the canal to the western side. They passed Mustill Store, a two-story structure that sold meat, groceries, and provisions advertised in a large sign across the roof. Double doors were flanked by twin windows shuttered for the night.

North of the lock were several boats tied to the mooring posts and a dock. Most of the canal boats would be taken up the closely placed locks in the morning. Called the staircase, the steep section of land in Akron required fifteen locks to raise the water and boats high enough to continue to Summit Lake and Southern Ohio.

Akron boasted a population of ten thousand, double the size during the Civil War. Businesses included agricultural equipment, an oatmeal cereal company, coal mines, and clay products. It was a main stop for boats on the Ohio-Erie Canal that transported goods from Lake Erie in the north to the Ohio River in the south.

The *Irish Rose* had come down the locks during the day and was loaded with goods to be transported to Cleveland. The canal boat consisted of three separate cabins connected by a catwalk joining the roofs. The stable cabin was in the center where three mules were stored inside. They would be attached to a towline and pull the boat through the still canal waters as they plodded along the towpath that ran parallel to the canal. Liny's two younger brothers, George and Will, traded duties with one walking behind the mules on the towpath and the other staying on the boat to work the lines and pikes to help direct the narrow craft through the fifteen-foot-wide locks.

The shipping boat was owned by Liny's cousin Ethan Donovan. After serving in the Civil War, Ethan had inherited the *Irish Rose* from his grandfather and shipped goods up and down the canal during the summer. The open space between the cabins was filled with barrels and crates. Ohio was farm country and shipped corn, wheat, and other crops to the larger cities or to the mills that had been built along the canal route.

Nate jumped from the buggy and placed a weight on the ground to secure the horse.

Deidre climbed down and took the bags from Hazel and Gwen who stepped on the small metal step to the ground.

"I'll take the bags, and you can help the women board." Nate waited for her to hand them over.

Liny led the way across the gangplank from the edge of the canal to the roof of the center cabin.

Deidre encouraged the sisters to walk along the narrow catwalk to the bow cabin where George and Will were watching the fireworks.

"You missed a great show," Will said.

George plucked at Liny's sleeve. "What are you doing wearing my clothes?"

"We borrowed them," Liny said. "No harm done."

George nodded at Hazel and Gwen. "Who are they?"

"Doesn't matter because you never saw them," Deidre said in a voice that demanded no questioning.

Ethan had been sitting in the stern and strode forward to the center cabin. "Are these my passengers?"

"Yes," Liny said. "The ones I told you about."

"There might be someone looking for them," Nate warned.

"The fireworks are nearly over, and people will be returning home," Ethan said. "Better get them below before anyone sees them."

Deidre turned to Nate. "We don't need you anymore. You can leave."

"What about returning to the dance?" Liny asked. "He can take us in his buggy."

"I'd be honored," Nate said with a bow. "I'm here to help in any way I can."

"Wonderful." Deidre took the carpetbag and pillowcase from Nate's hand. "We need to change into our clothes. You can wait here."

Liny opened the trapdoor on the deck of the bow cabin and disappeared below.

Hazel and Gwen descended with Deidre following on the short ladder. A lantern hanging from the ceiling provided light in the small compartment. Bunk beds were built on each side to accommodate four people.

Liny pointed to the bottom beds. "Take those."

Deidre stripped off the borrowed jacket, trousers, and shirt and grabbed her gown from a hook where she had left it earlier.

Liny showed the sisters the water bucket, towels, and other items they might need.

"A bath." Hazel grabbed a bar of soap and sniffed. "It smells lovely." She undid the few buttons left on her gown, and it fell to the floor. A thin chemise barely concealed her slender frame and pale flesh. Bruises marred her skin, and a long gash crossed her back from a recent beating.

Liny and Gwen gasped.

Hazel turned, a dark bruise visible beneath her swollen eye. "I've forgotten how I look in the light." She snatched a towel and covered her soiled chemise. "I'm so ugly."

"No, you're not," Deidre said. "I only wish we could have rescued you sooner."

"I didn't know anyone was willing to help until Mr. Crawford spoke to me. He'd come in during the afternoon to buy a beer. He saw my black eye and asked who gave it to me. I told him how my pa sold me to Mr. Gardner to pay for his debts, and I had to do what he said."

"Sell? How could he sell you?" Liny asked.

"He's our pa." A sob echoed in her throat. "He can

make us work for anyone until we turn twenty-one, and he collects our pay."

Liny reached out to touch her but hesitated. "I didn't know Mr. Gardner beat you."

"I didn't mind the hard work cleaning the saloon, but Mr. Gardner expected more personal service." Hazel bowed her head, and her shoulders sagged.

"What do you mean?" Liny asked.

Deidre shook her head. "You don't have to explain."

"You need to know the truth." Sobs shook Hazel's body as tears fell down her cheeks. "Mr. Gardner barged into my room whenever he wanted. He hit me to force me to obey. Then he sent other men. I had to pretend to like it, or I didn't get fed. I don't deserve your help. I'm ruined goods, but I couldn't let him hurt Gwen the way he done me." She swiped at the tears with the back of her hand. "Gwen is sixteen. She don't know nothing about men. I had to protect her. I told Mr. Crawford to help her escape. I was hoping you could help me get her out of there before the men…you know." Her voice was angry with a hard edge to the final statement.

"Raped her," Deidre whispered. She had been told Hazel and Gwen needed to escape the saloon, but she hadn't known about the abuse.

Liny had a shocked expression. She must not have known either.

Hazel grabbed her sister's hand. "Only Mr. Crawford said he had a plan for both of us to leave."

"And now you're safe," Deidre said. "You've been given a second chance."

"But where will we go?" Hazel asked.

"Captain Donovan will take you down the canal to Peninsula, and you'll take a train from there," Liny said.

"You'll be far enough away that neither Mr. Gardner nor your father will find you. You'll be safe."

"Safe?" Hazel had disbelief in her voice. "I can't believe it. How can we thank you?"

"Our reward comes from helping you," Deidre said. "You don't owe us a thing."

"You should sleep until morning," Liny said. "The trapdoor has a bolt lock."

Deidre looked at her dress as she prepared to put it on. "You should have my dress."

Hazel touched the silky skirt and backed away. "I'd get lost in all that fabric, but I'm grateful for you offering. It's beautiful."

Deidre wanted to do something for her. "Then take my bonnet. I have another."

Hazel handled the lace-trimmed bonnet as if it were glass. "Are you sure?"

"I wish I could do more." Deidre finished dressing and handed Liny her dress. "Aren't you coming to the dance?"

"I think I should stay here." Liny nodded toward the sisters. "They might need another woman's care."

Hazel and Gwen needed friends. "I should stay, too."

"No. I work on the *Irish Rose*. You'd make others wonder why you're aboard. Besides, people will talk if the mayor's niece doesn't show up at the dance. They won't notice if I'm missing."

"I'll tell them you ate something that didn't agree with you." Deidre hugged her and turned to the sisters.

Gwen had tears in her eyes. "I'm so glad I don't have to work for Mr. Gardner."

"No woman should have to suffer a man's touch if

she doesn't want it," Deidre said.

Hazel shuddered. "I don't know if I can forget, and what man is going to want me when he knows what I've been?"

"You have to believe you're stronger than all of them." Deidre gave each of them a hug. "And a man worthy of your love will understand you had no choice. Take care of yourself and your sister."

Deidre climbed the ladder and closed the trapdoor as quietly as possible.

"Where's Liny?" George asked.

"She's staying below with her friends," Deidre said. "Don't bother them unless necessary. They're tired."

"We'll take care of them," Captain Donovan said. "No one boards the *Irish Rose* without my permission."

"Are you ready to leave?" Nate looked at her hair. "Didn't you have a bonnet on at the picnic?"

"I lost it," she lied.

"It's good to see you again, Nate," Captain Donovan said. "It was an honor to serve with your father."

Deidre had forgotten Nate's father had been killed in the war. She gathered her skirt and headed for the gangplank. "I'd like to return to Crooked River in time for a few dances."

"With me?" Nate's voice squeaked.

"No." She climbed into the buggy, ignoring the hand he offered to assist her.

He moved to the other side and took the reins. "Please, let me explain about what I said to Mr. Leland."

She held up her hand, surprised it didn't tremble. "No need. Your excuses will fall on deaf ears, but I'm glad I discovered your lack of regard toward me and my parentage."

"I spoke about the scandal to protect you from Mr. Leland."

"Protect?" Was he serious? "What sort of threat is Mr. Leland?"

"He would deceive you with promises of marriage. I know more than one lady considers him charming, but the marriage would be based on lies and advance his ambitions. I spoke ill of you to deter him from proposing." He clenched his fists. "I made sure he would not repeat what I said. If it is your desire, I can encourage him to call and resume his courtship."

Nate thought she needed rescuing? "Did I look as if I were in danger of accepting any proposal from him or any man? From my courtship experiences I have learned that some men are so enamored of their own accomplishments they do not think a woman can be skilled in anything but needlework."

He opened his mouth but uttered no words.

"Thank you for helping tonight, but you had no right to gossip about my parents. I'm still angry with you."

He maneuvered the buggy across the canal bridge and down the road guided by the lanterns hung on each side of the vehicle. "Not as angry as I am with myself."

"I was always taught that compliments should come from others, but I've had plenty of braggarts in my parlor. Mr. Leland did not conceal his arrogance and conceit. I didn't need you to point out his flaws."

"I should have known you would be too perceptive to be taken in by lies," he said. "Personally, I find myself lacking in your presence."

"What?" No man had admitted a shortcoming to impress her. "You've barely said a complete sentence to me in the past two years. How have you found your voice tonight?"

"My fear of saying the wrong thing silenced me, but now that I'm not competing for your favor, I can speak without weighing my words. But I know none that would impress you."

"It's not difficult for men to brag about their achievements," Deidre said. "Men have all the advantages with education, money, and power. Only a few women have become lawyers, doctors, or run a business, and they are ridiculed for their achievements. Women are mocked for wanting to vote and have the rights every man enjoys."

"Our culture and laws allow men to take unfair advantage to avoid competing with women." He pointed at two men pushing each other and arguing. "Do you brawl in the streets or wage wars of destruction? No. How can you support violence when you give life and nurture it to thrive? You have the capacity to love and forgive that puts men to shame."

Was he trying to charm her? "Are you seeking forgiveness?"

"No." He stared past her, his jaw set. "Hazel's room was little more than a prison cell. No one, especially an innocent young woman, deserves to be treated like that."

"You didn't see the bruises on her body," she whispered.

"I know a wounded animal when I see one," he said with anger in his voice. "Do you rescue women often?"

"I'm new to the cause, but the Beecher sisters have been rescuing women since the war ended. I wish I could rescue more. That's the focus of my life. Not a wedding ring."

They neared Crooked River. The twang of a banjo,

the beat of a drum, and the wail from a trumpet echoed from the gazebo, which was lit with lanterns in the center of the town's square. The stomping of dancers on the bricks kept beat with the music as the fiddler called out the dance moves. Others clapped along, and deeper in the shadows couples courted and canoodled on blankets.

Deidre took Nate's hand when he offered to help her down from the buggy. "I have made helping women my mission in life."

He kept her hand in his. "You can't use a partner?"

"I have learned that most men want to tell women what to do." She slipped from his grasp. "They don't want a partner. They want to be the boss. They want to *climb* the ladder."

His eyes widened. "You wanted to climb the ladder into Hazel's room?"

"I would have liked the choice, but you took charge."

"My instinct was to protect you, but a man can learn to listen."

"A man can pretend to listen and then does what he wants." She wasn't ready to forgive him all his sins. She walked to where ladies were gathered, waiting for someone to ask for a dance. She turned to search for Nate, but he was gone.

Chapter Four

Nate watched Deidre disappear into the crowd. He would never be worthy of her love, but he hoped friendship would blossom if he proved he could be trusted. *If.* He leaned against a tree and reviewed his evening. He'd slandered Deidre's family, his mother was working for a secret organization, and he had rescued two sisters from dire circumstances. The courtroom was boring by comparison.

"Why are you here all alone?" his mother asked.

He stood straight and glanced around for anyone in the area. "Mother, we need to talk."

"Not here. Why don't you drive me home unless you want to dance?" She looked toward the couples twirling to the music.

"There's no one I want to dance with." Except Deidre who would reject his invitation. "The buggy is over here."

The sound of the horse's hooves on the bricks echoed as the music faded. "Why didn't you tell me you were part of a group that rescues women?"

"Secrecy keeps them safe from men who want to find them. How did the elopement go?"

Code words. Another protection. "Two successful elopements. Do you plan to enlist me in the future for your romantic trysts?"

"It was one time." She rested her hand on his arm.

"The usual ladder handler had an accident."

"I saw his bandage." He clucked to the horse. "The man handles glass for a living. You'd think he'd know how not to cut himself."

"Accidents happen. But don't worry. You won't be involved again."

Did she think so little of him? "What if I choose to help?"

"You're a lawyer. You can't be caught in any scandal."

"No one would have recognized me in the old coat and hat I wore."

She lifted her chin. "I want to protect you."

"Mother, I should be protecting you."

She stared at him, a frown on her face. "Are you angry with me?"

"No." He took a deep breath and gathered his thoughts. "You're the last person I would hurt, but I feel like I've been kept in the dark all my life. If it was to protect me, I'm a grown man. I want answers. How long have you been helping women escape brothels?"

"It didn't start with brothels," she said in a quiet voice. "Remember Mrs. Kasey?"

The name didn't sound familiar. "No."

"It was after you left for preparatory school." She folded her hands and cleared her throat. "Her husband was killed in the war, and she had two young children. Mr. Montgomery helped her obtain her husband's pension, but eight dollars a month isn't much to live on. She married a man she thought would help support her children, but he liked to drink. When he lost his job because he was drunk, he drank more. He stole her pension money and beat her if she complained. She hid the bruises, but Dr. Greystone had to set her broken arm. I was working at Ravens Roost at that time, and Jules Greystone visited her sister, Cassie Ravenswood."

"They're the Beecher sisters," Nate said. "Dr. Sterling Beecher's daughters."

"He had six daughters."

All married to men he knew in various degrees. "Cory married my boss. What role does Tyler Montgomery play in this?"

"He helps with legal matters." His mother sighed. "After Mrs. Kasey's baby was a month old, we decided to rescue her and the children."

"You climbed a ladder?"

"Don't be ridiculous. When Mr. Kasey was at the saloon, we packed everything up in a wagon and took her to Ravens Roost." His mother smiled softly. "She was there for nearly a year before she moved in with a widow. Her children grew up without a father, but they don't have to worry about bruises, broken limbs, and fear."

"Did Mr. Kasey stop drinking?"

"He didn't, but too many women give their husbands an attempt at reform. The abuse often escalates, and death can be the result." She didn't hide the grief in her voice. "It isn't easy to convince the women to leave. We tell them they need to protect the children if not themselves."

"Under the law even if the wife files for divorce, the husband gains custody of the children if he wants them." Nate realized his caseload had been tilted with those types of lawsuits. "Has Mr. Montgomery been giving me family disputes on purpose?"

"I thought you should be exposed to the real world. You've seen so little of the hardships women and children bear."

"I worked in Boston and New York. I've seen plenty of abuse. How many women have you rescued here?"

"Not nearly enough. All the Beecher sisters have young children or other obligations. That's why Deidre and Liny volunteered. They're part of a new generation, but most of the cousins are too young for the work."

"I'll help, and I can recruit my friends. The girls shouldn't risk the danger."

"And you're going to protect them by taking over their cause?" His mother raised her voice. "By the time a hero becomes aware of the problem, it's too late. Men help, but this is a woman's fight, and the rescue work isn't as dangerous as the lives of those wanting to escape."

"Did you start risking your life when you worked at Ravens Roost?"

"I helped at the house by taking care of the women others rescued. Mr. Ravenswood offered his farm as a refuge. Still does."

He knew the name. "Why didn't Zach Ravenswood help my father when he was shot?"

"He tried. When a sniper shot your father, Mr. Ravenswood grabbed on to him and fell off the bridge with him. He broke his leg."

"And he came home." He tightened his grip on the reins. "Unlike Pa."

She placed her hand over his. "Are you still angry with Lloyd?"

"Angry with a dead man? How could I be mad at my father, the man who loved war more than me?"

"That's not true! He loved us and wanted the best for you. The bonuses he received for signing up paid for your education."

"I didn't want an education. I wanted Pa." Nate fought the anger that always rose like bile when he thought of his father's death.

"I wanted him back, too." She brushed away a tear. "I was angry with him for a long time."

"You?" He pulled on the reins as they reached their home. "I didn't hide my anger, but I never saw yours. He broke his promise to come home."

"He never planned to die. No one ever believes they'll die in a war, or they wouldn't join. Your father was older than most of the men. He had common sense. He said he'd know when to duck. But you can't duck a sharpshooter's bullet."

"But why go?" He remained seated, his breathing labored. "He had responsibilities here at home. How could he leave us?"

"He wrestled with his decision for over a year. I knew it was important for him to fight. He wanted to make the world a better place. I did, too, but we learned too late that war wasn't the answer." She took out her handkerchief and blew her nose. "We tell them they're brave heroes, send them off with a parade, and pray for a safe return. But war is ugly and flies in opposition to our Christian beliefs to love one another, even our enemies. It scars the body, mind, and heart. Even the men who returned home were changed."

"I talked with Ethan Donovan tonight. He was proud of Pa." He coughed to clear his throat. "He said if I wanted to hear about what they had experienced during the war, he'd share some stories."

"Ethan, Zach, and Harry served with Lloyd. You should talk to them."

"I'm not sure I'm ready." He laughed to hide his emotions. "I nearly cried when he said Father's name."

She rubbed his back. "At least read your father's letters. I saved them for you."

He'd read them during the war when he was a boy before he knew his father wouldn't return home. He raised his head. "I'd like that. It's about time I faced the past."

"I'll put the letters in your room while you take care of the horse."

Nate helped her out of the carriage and watched as she headed for the house. His mother had kept their home by working at Ravens Roost and renting the farmhouse to a couple who took care of the animals and planted the fields. They now lived in a cabin on the farm and continued to help his mother while he worked in Akron. She had always put him first. How could he not have noticed her sacrifice? He had a lot to learn about unconditional love.

He led the horse inside the barn and unhitched the buggy. He put the gelding in a stall and made sure he had oats and water before brushing him down.

He took the lantern left on the kitchen table and climbed to the second floor. His mother had left a stack of envelopes on the desk in his room. He opened his window. The distant sound of music and laughter drifted on the night air. He gathered up the correspondence and discovered his mother had sorted them in chronological order. He slid the oldest letter out and began to read.

****

July 4th had been on a Tuesday. It was Friday, and Nate had read through his father's letters. He had remembered the doting man but had never understood his personal beliefs until he read his own words now as an adult. He was gone physically, but his thoughts and experiences lived on paper. The torn and stained pages revealed the hardships he had endured. He had fought for something important, and Nate needed to fight for Deidre.

He needed to repair the damage his comments had made and make amends if he was going to have any future with her. He knew how to prepare for a case in court, but how did he win a woman's affection?

Tyler Montgomery entered Nate's office. They shared space on the second floor of a building on Main Street in downtown Akron. "Do you have the will finished?"

Nate had been pondering his future courting strategy. He couldn't afford to lose his job if he wanted to support a wife. He shuffled through the legal papers on his desk and handed his boss the will. "Mr. Johnson didn't leave his wife much."

Tyler looked out the window as he examined the documents. He was a big man who had gained the width in his shoulders from pounding steel as a blacksmith in his youth. A bit of gray was present in his raven hair. He had a commanding presence in and out of court. He turned and sighed. "Mr. Johnson left his wife a third of their real property, which is required by the law. He also named his brother as guardian of the children."

Nate had met Mrs. Johnson when calculating the assets of her husband's property. She was a quiet woman who had three children under the age of ten. "Can he take them away from her?"

"As a widow she has custody, but as legal guardian he can decide whether the children attend school or work for wages."

"A lot of factories back east employ children," Nate said. "I saw too many of them maimed from the machines."

"Mr. Johnson's brother appears to be a decent man, but many families need children to work and contribute earnings to the household. He may not have a choice."

Nate had followed the career of Tyler Montgomery, who had become a legend in the area. Early in his career, Tyler had argued for the rights of a black man to claim his wife even though she was a white man's slave. He supported women's rights, and even though he was from Virginia, he'd supported the abolitionists and an end to slavery. He had fought for the pension rights of families who had lost a loved one during the Civil War, including his mother.

Last night's rescue had confirmed the injustices and unfair treatment of women. Men guarded their property, wealth, and offspring using the laws they'd created. The ideal custom was for fathers to care for their children, husbands to care for their wives, and adults to care for their aging parents, but orphans, widows, and the elderly suffered when no one was around to protect them.

Tyler looked at the paperwork on Nate's desk. "Do you have anything pressing?"

Nate straightened. "Nothing urgent."

"Come into my office."

Nate followed Tyler who sat behind a large desk. Two padded leather chairs faced it. Bookshelves filled with law books were topped with family photographs in ornate frames. His window looked out on Main Street. He motioned for Nate to sit and opened a desk drawer. "Do you know Logan Pierce?"

Had Deidre complained about him? He slumped back into the seat. "Yes."

"I have a letter I need delivered in person. I was going to stop at his home, but I won't have time. I'm scheduled to be in court all afternoon." Tyler handed him the envelope he had taken from his desk. "Don't you and your mother live in Crooked River?"

"Yes, sir."

"Do you know where he lives?"

He nodded and held out his hand. "I'd be happy to deliver it." The letter gave him an excuse to call and hopefully find Deidre home.

Nate noted her name on the envelope but in care of Tyler Montgomery, Esq. The return address was from Kinsman, a town in western New York. "It's addressed to Miss Pierce. Do I give her the letter?"

"No." Tyler rose. "Logan will decide whether she sees it."

His curiosity was piqued, but he wasn't going to question his boss. He returned to his office to grab his bowler hat and headed down the outside stairs to Main Street. He hoped to find someone who would offer him a ride.

Akron was built on a hill, and everything sloped to the canal and Cuyahoga River. Howard Street was the shortest route but was a steep brick road to Crooked River. He almost decided to take Riverview Road, but it followed the curves of the water and took longer. He began to climb the hill, dodging wagons and buggies coming down the sharp incline. Those going up the hill didn't offer a ride. They didn't need the additional weight for their horses to pull.

He was halfway to the top and noticed a beer wagon

stopped near the top on the opposite side. The driver unloaded a keg and rolled it down two boards propped against the floor of the wagon and toward the saloon door. The remaining barrels seemed perilously stacked.

Nate recognized Logan Pierce walking down the hill on the same side as the beer wagon.

"Mayor Pierce!" he called out and waved to him as he crossed the street.

Logan waved back and stepped out into the street below the beer wagon.

Nate cursed his bad luck. He would have to deliver the letter now instead of taking it to his house. He would lose the chance of seeing Deidre.

They were a few feet apart when he heard a crash, a cry, and saw barrels rolling down the hill toward them. He jumped back, barely saving himself from being knocked over. Another barrel crashed into a metal hitching post and burst open, spilling beer onto the street.

Logan jumped out of the way of one barrel but slipped in the puddle of beer. He waved his arms to maintain his balance but couldn't avoid a barrel as it hit him from behind and knocked him to the ground.

Nate witnessed the collision and heard a crunching sound and scream of pain. He saw the last errant barrel heading for Logan's head and pulled him out of the pathway. He knelt by Logan's side. His trousers were torn to the knee, and his leg had an unnatural curve in the lower half.

Logan grimaced in pain and reached for his leg.

"Don't move." Nate looked at others who had gathered but stared like motionless statues. He took charge and pointed at a man holding the reins of his horse. "Get Dr. Greystone. Tell him to go to Logan

Pierce's house in Crooked River."

The man nodded and rode away on his errand.

"I have a wagon," another man volunteered.

"We'll need to brace his leg," Nate said.

The man who delivered the initial beer keg ran down the hill and stopped. "I was taking a barrel inside and wasn't gone a minute. What happened?"

Nate waved at the barrels scattered on the steep street. "They rolled away."

"That's impossible. I put the back up." He looked at his wagon. The board along the back was down, and none of the barrels remained inside. "At least I thought I put it back up."

Nate couldn't remember if the back had been raised or not. He had been distracted by the sight of Logan. He looked around. The noise of the accident had attracted more men and women, who stood and stared at the damage.

A man carried a stretcher from one of the stores. Nate gathered two staves from a broken barrel and placed one under Logan's curved leg. He matched the other barrel stave on top. "I need a piece of cloth."

A man handed him his handkerchief, and Nate used his own to secure the staves above and below the bend of Logan's limb. The men loaded Crooked River's mayor onto the stretcher and lifted him into the wagon bed. Nate rode in the back next to him.

Logan was pale, and his skin had a sheen to it. He groaned when the wagon wheel hit a hole where the bricks were missing in the road. "That last barrel was heading straight for me. Thank you for pulling me out of the way."

"I wish I had reacted sooner." Nate stared at his

twisted leg.

"Get me home to my wife," Logan said. "Jem will know what to do."

Everyone knew the Beecher sisters had been nurses for their father, Dr. Sterling Beecher. Most of them had taken care of the wounded during the war. "I sent for Dr. Greystone."

"Thank you." He squinted. "You called my name from across the street. Aren't you Amanda Burrough's boy?"

"Nate, sir. I work for Tyler Montgomery." He searched his coat. "I have a letter for Miss Pierce that Mr. Montgomery wanted delivered."

"We're here," the driver announced as he stopped in front of the Pierce house.

Nate left the letter in his pocket. It could wait. He jumped down and knocked on the front door while the other two men unloaded the stretcher and Logan.

Deidre answered and frowned. "What are you doing here?"

He stepped aside so she could see the other men carrying Logan toward the door.

"What happened?" She rushed past him and examined her uncle. "What did you do to him?"

Nate raised his hands. "I did nothing. Runaway beer barrels hit him."

A girl of about fourteen with reddish-brown hair worn in twin braids screamed and ran past Deidre. "Daddy!" Chauncy Pierce was the eldest of Logan and Jem's children.

"Calm down, Chauncy." Logan took her hand. "I'll be fine."

"He has a broken leg." Nate turned to Deidre. "I tied

staves to it before we loaded him into the wagon."

"That was clever," Deidre said.

"I have my moments." He looked toward the door. "Where can we place him? I sent a rider to fetch Dr. Greystone."

"Aunt Jem!" Deidre called as she led the way into the house.

Jem appeared on the landing with a little girl in her arms. "What is it, Deidre?"

Chauncy gripped her father's hand. "Daddy's dying."

"Don't exaggerate," Deidre said calmly. "He has a broken leg."

"Take Ellie." Jem handed Deidre the little girl with blonde curls and brown eyes. She examined her husband calmly. She looked at the brace and then at Nate. "Did you do this?"

"I thought the leg should be immobilized. I hope I didn't make matters worse."

"No, you did the right thing," Jem said.

He removed his hat. "Nate Burroughs, ma'am."

"Carry him upstairs to the room at the end of the hall." Jem led the way.

"Let's give them some room." Nate stepped toward the edge of the foyer.

Chauncy was crying, and Deidre handed him Ellie. She gathered her cousin into her arms and comforted her.

"Your daddy is going to be fine." Deidre wiped Chauncy's tears with a lace-trimmed handkerchief.

Nate held Ellie with both hands gripping her tiny body as they stared at one another. What did she think of a stranger holding her? She drooled as her mouth lifted in a smile and revealed dimples.

He looked at Deidre. "I think she likes me."

"Give her time."

Chapter Five

Deidre had calmed Chauncy down, and her own heart rate had returned to normal. She turned her attention to Nate. "How did beer barrels hit Uncle Logan?"

"The barrels were stacked in the back of a wagon and began rolling down Howard Street. You know how steep it is. Everyone scattered, but your uncle slipped on spilled beer and fell. I heard the bones break when he hit the brick pavers."

Her eyes widened. "What were you doing there?"

"I was on my way to deliver a letter to Mayor Pierce when I saw him on the street." Nate adjusted Ellie in his arms to reach for the letter.

"Which pocket?" Deidre asked.

He nodded to his right.

She stuck her hand into his pocket and retrieved the letter. "It's for me."

"Not yet. Mr. Montgomery told me to deliver it to your uncle personally."

Deidre examined the letter. She ran her fingertips along the sealed opening. "Why?"

"I think he wanted your uncle to review it." Nate reached for the envelope, but she moved it away.

Ellie grabbed onto his ear and tugged.

"What is she doing?"

"Take Ellie before Mr. Burroughs drops her,"

Deidre said.

Chauncy cooed some words, and Ellie leaned toward her, falling from him and into her sister's arms.

"I wouldn't drop her," Nate said.

The two men who had carried Logan upstairs descended with the stretcher. "Mrs. Pierce says to boil a pot of water." One of them looked at Nate. "Are you coming with us?"

"I'll stay here," Nate said. "I have some business to complete."

"Romantic business?" One of the men winked before he departed through the door.

Chauncy looked from Deidre to Nate. "Are you one of Deidre's beaus?"

"Not likely," Deidre said. "You better put Ellie in her crib. It's time for her nap."

"If he's not your beau, why do you want to be alone with him?" Chauncy smiled, exposing the dimples all the Pierce children possessed.

"I'm sure you'll find out when you eavesdrop." She watched Chauncy carry Ellie upstairs before she examined the letter.

Nate snatched the envelope. "Your uncle is to read the letter and decide whether you need to know its contents."

"I'm twenty-one now. I have a right to read it, but I'll wait until after Dr. Greystone arrives. Put it here on the side table. I have water to boil." She headed down the hallway and glanced back to watch him place the letter on the narrow table in the hallway.

"Make sure he reads it before you do. Those were Mr. Montgomery's instructions," Nate called out in a loud voice.

She heard the front door open and close. She hurried back to the foyer and reached for the envelope.

"Tsk, tsk, tsk." Nate stood near the door on the inside of the house.

She tapped her fingers on top of the envelope. "I thought you left."

"I made a promise to make sure your uncle sees it first, and I always keep my word."

"I'll take it upstairs and read it to him if it's so important." She lifted the envelope. "Are you waiting for a reply?"

He hesitated. "I can wait for one."

"That won't be necessary." She opened the door. "You better inform Mr. Montgomery about my uncle's accident. If Uncle Logan has a reply, I'll send a note. Good-bye, Mr. Burroughs."

He tipped his hat. "I am forever at your service, Miss Pierce."

Good riddance. Deidre closed the door and hurried to the kitchen. She raised and lowered the handle to the pump until water flowed and filled a large pot. She loaded wood and lit the small bundle of tinder on top to start a fire in the stove. She paced back and forth as she waited for the flames to heat the water.

Steam finally rose from the pot. She held the envelope over the rising moisture until it loosened the glue and she was able to slide open the top fold.

The letter was from her grandfather's lawyer, Abraham Niles. She hadn't seen her mother's father, Emerson Kinsman, since she was six years old when Logan had become her legal guardian. Her grandfather was celebrating his eightieth birthday and had invited his five grandchildren and their spouses for a week-long visit to his home in western New York.

A handwritten note was included addressed to Logan. The shaky handwriting had to belong to her grandfather. *I know we have had our differences in the past, but I hope you will not deny me my last chance to see my granddaughter. You are invited to attend with her and will be treated with the utmost respect.* She reread the message. She would finally have a chance to meet her mother's relatives.

"What are you reading?"

Deidre jumped, the letter shaking in her hands.

Chauncy was her shadow. At fourteen she was too young to attend the formal dances and parties that promoted courting and marriage, but Deidre shared all the details about the fancy decorations, beautiful gowns, and delicious food. She sometimes shared tidbits and gossip about the guests but had not told her about Nate's bad behavior. Chauncy was not good at keeping secrets.

After her heart stopped racing, she showed Chauncy the envelope. "It's a letter addressed to me."

"Why does it have Uncle Tyler's name on it?"

"It's from a lawyer. Legal stuff."

Someone knocked on the front door and called out from the foyer. "Hello. It's Dr. Greystone."

She recognized the voice and turned to Chauncy. "Show Uncle Roe upstairs. Tell Mother I'll bring the hot water."

Deidre sealed the letter and shoved it into her apron pocket. Uncle Logan wouldn't be able to go anywhere for at least six weeks, and her grandfather's birthday was the twentieth, according to the letter. How was she going to convince her aunt and uncle to let her go alone?

Deidre transferred the hot water in the pot to two

pitchers and carried them into the bedroom. Jem had undressed Logan and placed a nightshirt on him. His legs were exposed on the sheet covering the mattress. They were bruised, scraped, and his left leg was bent in an unnaturally soft curve that the staves had hidden. Jem used the water to wash his wounds as Dr. Greystone examined the patient.

Roe Greystone was married to Jem's youngest sister, Jules. He had served under Confederate Colonel Chauncy LaDonte. The same man who had saved Logan's life after the battle of Bull Run. Logan and Jem had named their firstborn after him in gratitude even though she was a girl.

"Is Daddy going to be all right?" Chauncy asked.

"Has your mother taught you anything about nursing?" Dr. Greystone asked.

Her cousin's eyes widened. "A little."

He stepped aside. "What do you observe about our patient, then?"

Chauncy pointed at the bend above his ankle. "His leg is crooked."

"Which means he broke both bones in his lower leg," Dr. Greystone said. "Do you know what they're called?"

"Femur and tibia?"

"Not femur but it starts with an f," he coaxed.

"Fibula?"

"That's right." Dr. Greystone felt the bones in the leg that was straight. "This one appears unbroken, but I'm putting on a brace to make sure nothing moves." He examined the staves. "Do you mind if I take these? I can cut them down to the proper size and use them on a future patient."

"Go ahead," Jem said. "I don't think Mr. Burroughs wants them back."

"He may want the handkerchiefs." Deidre gathered the two squares of cotton.

"Then you should wash and press them before returning them," Jem said.

Wonderful. She couldn't give a simple task to someone else without her aunt becoming curious.

"Deidre, can you show Chauncy how to wrap the splints?" Dr. Greystone removed smooth pieces of wood and cloth strips from his bag. "I'll need four."

Deidre separated the strips of fabric to add padding to the wooden splints. She wrapped the first splint with the fabric as Chauncy watched and then let her wrap the other three.

Because of his youth and good looks, Dr. Greystone always had a female nurse with him on visits to women. Deidre had worked for him for three years as his nurse alongside Liny, who lived with Roe and Jules. It was a tradition for the women in the family to learn nursing and midwife skills. And everyone spent at least one summer on the *Irish Rose*, working on the canal.

Her work experience had taught her confidence and some odd skills like knot tying and wrapping a wound but nothing she could use in a career that would give her the independence she craved or the freedom to help others.

Jem finished washing her husband. "What do you want me to do?"

"I need you to sit behind Logan and hold him in place."

"I don't need to be held like a screaming child," Logan said.

"You sit behind me when I give birth and help me push." Jem removed her shoes.

His dimples deepened. "I'm not having a baby."

"You're going to wish you were when he's done tugging."

Deidre had helped with setting broken bones. She hoped Uncle Logan's screams didn't frighten Chauncy.

Jem positioned herself behind her husband and put her arms around his chest. "Now isn't this cozy?"

"Your arms don't reach all the way around."

Jem looked at Deidre. "Hand me a towel." She used it to fill in the gap so that Logan was secure.

Dr. Greystone placed strips of cloth beneath the good leg and took two splints from Chauncy. He placed them on each side. "Hold these while I tie them."

Deidre did as she was instructed, and Roe secured the braces.

"Now the other one." Roe placed the strips of cloth beneath his leg. "I'll need to pull the bones and set them straight. Have those splints ready when I call for them."

"Should Chauncy leave the room?" Deidre looked at her aunt.

"Please don't make me," Chauncy said.

"Why don't you stand by me?" Jem motioned for Chauncy to move toward the head of the bed.

Dr. Greystone gripped Logan's ankle with one hand and placed his other below his knee. He looked at the women. "Ready?"

Deidre had the splints ready and nodded.

Roe pulled and twisted until the bones were realigned. Logan screamed as he gripped the mattress. Chauncy jumped.

Deidre placed the splints against Logan's

straightened leg, and Roe wrapped the strips of cloth around his lower limb and tied them off to secure the braces and hold the broken bones in place.

Jem crawled out from behind Logan who panted to catch his breath. She hugged Chauncy. "You did great."

She visibly shook. "Maybe I don't want to be a nurse."

"It isn't as difficult if the patient is someone else besides your father," Jem said. "We hate to see the ones we love in pain."

Logan, who was visibly pale, held out his trembling hand to Chauncy. "You can be my nurse anytime, honey."

She placed her hand into his fingers, which curled around hers. "I love you. I would never hurt you."

His breathing had relaxed. "That's my girl."

Dr. Greystone removed a bottle from his bag. "Give him this pain medicine and keep him in bed. It'll take six to eight weeks to heal."

"What about my job?" Logan asked.

"You can work from your home," the doctor said.

"I'm the mayor," Logan said. "What if I use crutches?"

"You put weight on that leg before I say you can, and you'll need crutches for the rest of your life," Dr. Greystone said. "I had nightmares for years after the war from amputating arms and legs. Do as I say so you can remain whole and I can sleep at night."

"I'll keep him in bed," Jem said.

"I'll check on him every week," Dr. Greystone said as he packed his bag. "This first week he needs total rest. If the bones begin to knit properly, I'll think about crutches. But only for short periods of time."

"Can I carry your bag?" Chauncy lifted it from the chair.

"You can see me to the door, and I look forward to you working for me when you're ready."

Jem moved some pillows to support Logan in a semi-sitting position and covered him with a blanket.

Deidre handed her uncle the letter. "One of Tyler's lawyers delivered this for you."

"You mean Nate Burroughs?" Logan asked. "He saved my life."

"How?" Her voice was filled with disbelief.

"He pulled me out of the way of the last barrel, or I would have a broken head in addition to my leg."

Deidre pictured Nate as a hero rescuing Logan and quickly dismissed it.

Jem handed her husband a letter opener. Logan slit the envelope, removed the letter, and read it silently.

"Who is it from?" Jem asked, looking from Logan to Deidre.

Logan continued reading. "Emerson Kinsman and his lawyer."

Jem gasped and snatched the letter from Logan's hand. "Hannah's father? What does he want?"

"My grandfather?" Deidre asked as innocently as she could.

They both turned and stared. Lying was not her forte.

Jem examined the seal of the envelope, lifting a loose section. "Did you steam this open, young lady?"

"It was addressed to me," Deidre said with a hint of defiance. "I have a right to know what's in it."

Jem finished reading and handed the letter to her. "Yes, but you don't have to sneak a peek. I don't like secrets either. I'm sure Logan would have given you the invitation once he realized it concerned you."

Tears perched on her eyelids. She felt ashamed for not trusting her aunt and uncle. They had been nothing but kind to her. Deidre read carefully through the message again. "I guess I should write a reply and explain why I won't be attending."

"Do you want to go?" Logan's eyes widened as he shifted his weight.

She didn't want to hurt their feelings, but she needed to be honest. "I love you both. I hope you know that, and I will be forever grateful that you took me in."

"You're family," Logan said. "You're Derek's daughter."

"Yes, and I imagine you were alike in many ways even though I never met him, but I don't remember much about my mother. It would be nice to meet some of her family. Even if they're horrible people." She waited for a response in the silence that followed.

"Let me see that again." Jem pointed at the letter in Deidre's hand.

She handed it to her aunt.

"He is eighty." She turned to Logan. "It may be her only chance to meet Emerson. Hannah's brothers are dead, and it's only the grandchildren."

She had an ally with Jem. "I am twenty-one," Deidre reminded them.

"She can't go alone," Logan said. "Hannah's father reluctantly took her in. He valued money and wasn't close to any of his children. Who knows how he'll treat his grandchildren?"

"But he sent the invitation," Jem said. "And I traveled to Washington City alone when I was Deidre's age."

"I was on the same train." He looked at his wife, and his dimples deepened. They had been enemies when they first met, but had shared the details on how they joined forces on the train. Deidre recognized Logan was weakening.

"I could see if Liny can go," Deidre suggested.

"Liny is too young to be a companion." Logan held out his hand for the letter, which his wife gave him. He examined the pages. "We need someone older. Someone I can trust to protect you."

"What about the young man who saved your life?" Jem asked.

"Nate Burroughs?" Deidre asked in disbelief. The last person she needed learning more about her family was that tattletale.

"He works for Tyler." Logan's brow wrinkled as he waved the letter in the air. "The lawyer mentions some legal matters. Mr. Burroughs could review any papers and protect Deidre's interests."

Jem nodded in response.

They were leaving her out of the conversation. "I doubt my grandfather would leave anything to me," Deidre said.

Jem shook her head. "He mentions grandsons and granddaughters being invited."

"If I know Emerson, he'll size up his heirs," Logan said. "She might need a man who knows wills and inheritance."

They wanted Nate to accompany her? She opened her mouth to protest but stopped. Nate owed her. She could use his guilt to her advantage. He'd have to do whatever she told him.

Chapter Six

Nate knocked on the door at the Pierce home. He couldn't believe his luck. Tyler had informed him that he would escort Deidre to her grandfather's home and remain with her for a week to celebrate the old man's birthday. A week. He would have plenty of opportunities to convince her to forgive him. Perhaps friendship could blossom to something more, but he had to escape the guise of villain first.

Chauncy answered the door. "Hello, Mr. Burroughs."

He made a slight bow. "Hello, Miss Pierce."

Her dimples deepened. "Please come in."

If only charming Deidre was as easy as charming her young cousin.

A trunk sat inside the foyer with a bonnet on top. He'd packed all the belongings he thought necessary in a small leather valise. It was only a week.

"My father wishes to speak to you." Chauncy pointed up the staircase. "You better be on your best behavior with Deidre."

Did the girl know about the gossip he had shared with Oscar? He hoped not. He would have a hard enough time convincing Deidre he wasn't a rake. How would he convince her entire family? But if they knew, why had they asked him to escort her? He was debating the possibilities when Deidre appeared in the hallway.

"I've already received my instructions." She nodded at the door she had exited. "Uncle Logan is waiting to give you yours."

He wasn't sure what to expect. The man had requested he escort his niece. He had to trust him, but why had he chosen him? He knocked and entered.

Logan was in bed, his back supported by pillows and a quilt over his lower body. He had a portable secretary beside him with several letters on top. "Sit down." He pointed to a chair. "Did Mr. Montgomery explain the situation?"

"Miss Pierce wants to visit her grandfather and her cousins in Kinsman, New York. You need someone to accompany her and handle any legal matters."

"I'm not sure how much you know about Deidre's family. I want to explain the situation you'll be facing."

He gulped. Deidre hadn't revealed his bad behavior. What did that mean? "Yes, sir."

"The family has been estranged for some time, and I suspect her grandfather is planning more than a birthday party. It could be a friendly gesture on Emerson Kinsman's part, but I haven't seen him in fifteen years, and he swore to take Deidre from me. Frankly, I don't trust the man. How much do you know about my brother Derek?"

Nate kept the information to the barest facts. "He was a secretary for Salmon Chase when he was elected in 1849 to the United States Senate. Derek served as an escort for Hannah Smith at Washington City social events. Senator Lewis Smith killed him but was acquitted of any crime."

"Derek and Hannah fell in love and forgot to be discreet. Lewis Smith didn't care about their affair, but she asked for a divorce. The scandal would have ruined his political ambitions, so he shot Derek in January of 1855." Logan's voice caught in his throat. "He claimed he was defending the sanctity of his home, and charges were dropped. The newspapers praised his actions until they found out about his mistresses and illegitimate children. Hannah returned to her father's home and lived with her parents, but relations were strained after her mother's death. When Hannah became ill, she worried about leaving Deidre in her elderly father's care. Hannah named me guardian before her death, and I've honored her wishes. Deidre has lived with me and my wife since she was six years old."

Logan handed him a letter. He read through the contents. It was addressed to Deidre and must have been the one he delivered.

"Emerson Kinsman is Deidre's grandfather." Logan pointed at the letter. "He's a wealthy and powerful man who appears to be gathering his heirs for a final farewell. Deidre knows about her parents' affair, and Lewis Smith died four years ago. I don't expect any surprises, but I know little about Hannah's relatives. Deidre has an active imagination. She's built up her mother's family into a fairy-tale story. I expect you to remain levelheaded. Mr. Montgomery says you believe in facts."

"I look at the evidence in a case and base my decision on the truth. Do you know how Mr. Kinsman feels about Deidre?"

"Emerson didn't approve of Hannah's affair, but he allowed her to return home after Derek's death and provided for her and Deidre for nearly seven years," Logan said. "Hannah made her decision about Deidre's guardianship to protect her from Lewis Smith in case her father died. As Hannah's husband, he had a claim on any child born within their marriage even though he knew Deidre wasn't his daughter. Hannah named Derek as Deidre's father even though it labeled her illegitimate. I don't know how Mr. Kinsman felt about that stain on his family, but I wish to believe his current interest in Deidre is sincere."

"He's eighty. What do you think he plans?"

"I don't know. That is why I chose you," Logan said. "Besides saving my life, you are a lawyer. Don't allow her to sign any documents unless you read them first. Because she is twenty-one, her signature would be binding. Tyler said you're knowledgeable about wills and trusts. You've handled several cases for him."

"Yes." Nate would protect her with his life. "I can recognize trouble and circumvent if necessary."

"Deidre has always wanted to know more about her family. It's natural, but we don't choose our relatives. She has high expectations, and I fear she will be disappointed when they don't measure up."

Like him. "How many cousins does she have?"

Logan searched his papers and handed him a list of names. "She has four cousins. Three are married. I want you to form your own opinion about them and intercede if she is heading for trouble."

"Deidre may not like that."

"You're not there to be her friend," Logan said. "You're there to guide her against any bad decisions."

"I'll do my best." He rose from the chair. He couldn't alienate her any more than he had already done.

"One more thing," Logan said.

Nate turned.

"You're a young man and may have a personal

interest in my niece, but this is a business arrangement," Logan said. "I expect you to conduct yourself professionally and avoid any romantic entanglements."

He had thrown ice water on any opportunity to win over Deidre. "I don't see that as a problem, sir."

Logan raised an eyebrow but didn't inquire as to why. Nate hurried down the stairs.

Deidre was outside hugging her aunt and cousins and saying good-bye. She wore a blue skirt with matching jacket over a white blouse. Her outfit had no ruffles or gathers but displayed her trim figure. Her bonnet was white and blue striped with a fullness in the crown to cover her hair and a narrow brim to shade her face. Her trunk had been added to his leather bag in the rented carriage. She carried a large cloth bag embroidered with flowers.

Jem hugged him. She was friendly and kind, yet from stories he had heard, she possessed a strength forged by war and experiences his generation would never know. "Take care of her, Mr. Burroughs."

"I promise I will." He meant it.

"You know, Mr. Pierce and I traveled to Washington City together on a train," Jem said. "I refused to sit with him at first. I was angry with him, but feelings change."

Nate climbed into the carriage and sat next to Deidre. "What did you tell your aunt about me?" he whispered.

"Nothing." She tied her bonnet. "You weren't interesting enough to be a topic of conversation."

He let the blow slide off him. She was still angry, but if he succeeded in turning an enemy into a friend, he would call the trip a success.

The driver took them to the train depot, and Nate paid for the tickets with money Tyler had given him. Logan had added to the funds. He made sure her trunk and his valise were loaded into the baggage car. The conductor checked his pocket watch and helped them board the passenger car.

Deidre placed the cloth bag between them on the seat and removed a book. She opened it to a page marked with a wide ribbon.

He had hoped to talk to her on the trip, to explain himself more fully. "You don't want to talk?"

"No." She read, ignoring his presence.

He wasn't ready to give in. "What are you reading?"

She showed him the cover with two boys. One was painting a fence while the other sat on a barrel and ate an apple. *The Adventures of Tom Sawyer* was printed at the top.

"How far have you gotten?"

"Past the dead cat in the graveyard." She turned back to the page she had been reading and resumed her task.

The train trip was going to be a long, lonely ride. He pointed to the bag. "Did you bring any other books?"

"I brought *Little Women* and *Around the World in Eighty Days*. Would you like to read one of them?"

"I'm a fan of Jules Verne."

"So are a lot of people." She retrieved the Verne book from her bag, handed it to him, and continued her reading.

A couple of years had passed since he had read the story, and he was soon caught up in the travels of Phileas Fogg as he raced around the world. His reading was interrupted by scratching. Deidre wrote something in the margin of her book with a lead pencil.

"Are you defacing your new book?" He didn't hide his outrage.

She looked confused by his outburst. "It's my book."

"But others may want to read it. How can you write in it?"

"You never wrote in your textbooks from school?"

"My professors would have whipped me bloody for any mark in a law book."

"This is not a law book." She turned back to the first page. "I wrote my name in it to identify it as my property, Mr. Burroughs. And I leave little notes for those who borrow my books. Little inside jokes only we understand."

"It's criminal."

"You're a lawyer," she said with sarcasm. "What law says I cannot write in a book I own?"

He grabbed the novel from her hand and flipped through the pages. "Do you turn down the corners as well?"

"Like a dog's ear? I would never crease a page. I have a bookmarker." She pointed at the decorated ribbon marking the page she had written on.

He handed back the book. "Thank goodness for that small measure of respect for the written word."

She raised a dainty eyebrow. "Are all your books pristine?"

"Yes." He respected books. His collection was immaculate.

She searched her bag and found a ribbon like the one marking her page. "I would appreciate you using this to keep your place in my book."

"Thank you. I like to keep my books looking like new."

"Then they are not well loved. Books, dolls, and toys should be worn from use and love." She finished her note in the margin. "Besides, I only write in pencil and very little. I have lots of cousins who want to read my books."

"I know."

She tilted her head, her bonnet framing her face. "I bet you can't name them all."

"I have a list of your mother's relatives, and Logan is the only Pierce. The others aren't blood cousins."

"Blood doesn't make any difference," she said with an edge to her voice. "We consider all the relatives family."

"Then you're related to the Beechers, the Donovans, and the Bauers as well as the in-laws of Montgomery, Ellsworth, Mackinnon, Ravenswood, and Greystone."

She stared. "How do you know all of them? Even my cousins forget some."

He needed to hide how deep his interest was in her. "I work for Tyler Montgomery. His daughter Olivia quizzes me."

She smiled, revealing her dimples. "She and Chauncy are as thick as thieves. What family do you have?"

"My mother." *Who is full of secrets.* "Mr. Montgomery helped her receive my father's pension after he was killed in the war."

"What regiment?"

"The Twenty-Ninth Ohio Volunteer Infantry."

"Uncle Blake was their captain. Major," she corrected. "They lost a lot of good men. In what battle did your father die?"

"You don't know the story?"

She shrugged. She didn't have the same interest in his personal life as he had in hers.

"The Twenty-Ninth was marching north in 1865 from Savannah to Washington City. The war was all but over except for the parades. They were crossing a narrow bridge when a Rebel sharpshooter's bullet struck him. Zach Ravenswood grabbed on to him and fell over into the ravine below."

"I've heard the story about how Uncle Zach broke his leg, but I didn't know it was your father who was killed." Deidre furrowed her brow. "I thought the man's name was Pappy."

"That's what they called him because he was older. Pappy was Sergeant Lloyd Burroughs, my father."

"I'm sorry." She closed her book and turned to face him. "How old were you?"

"Almost fifteen. He promised to come home. It's the only promise he didn't keep."

"You sound angry."

"I was," he agreed. "But I've been reading the letters he wrote during the years he was gone. He described the men he served with, the hardships of war, and the slaves they freed. He was proud of abolishing slavery and helping those less fortunate. In his final letter he looked forward to seeing us and was grateful he had made it through the war so we could be together again."

"You loved your father very much." She studied her hands gripping her book. "I never knew my father."

He needed to change the subject. "What do you know about your grandfather?"

She frowned. "I remember bits and pieces from my

childhood. I was six years old when my mother died, and I can't remember much about her. I've always felt like a part of me was missing."

"I always wondered how my life would have turned out if my father had lived." Nate looked out the window. "I had forgotten so much about him, but the words in his letters conveyed his thoughts and dreams about his life and what he wished for me. I hope this trip gives you some answers."

"I'm glad you understand." Deidre removed a handkerchief from her bag. "My mother was sick before I left to live with Uncle Logan. She didn't want me to see her suffer before she died." She dabbed at her eye.

"She loved you enough to spare you the pain."

"In spite of my illegitimacy." She lowered her voice to a whisper.

He knew the ugly terms used for children born out of wedlock. If they weren't named in a will, they were often left out of any inheritance. Would Emerson Kinsman invite his granddaughter to his home only to snub her among the other heirs? "Children can't choose how they come into the world. And I had no right to share any information with Oscar Leland in order to sway his opinion of you."

"I already shared my thoughts on Mr. Leland." She opened her book to the marked page.

"I should have known you wouldn't be deceived by a liar."

"Do not think you can win me over with flattery, Mr. Burroughs."

"I know you would never consider me as a suitor after my bad behavior. Besides, I promised your uncle to keep our relationship on a professional level."

"Why do men think it is their obligation and right to control a woman's life? You were worried I would marry Mr. Leland, so you slandered my name. Now I find out my uncle thinks I will fall in love with you because we are sharing a ride to my grandfather's home. I can choose my own suitors. Mr. Leland is not one of them." She waved her book in the air as if to strike him. "And neither are you." Her hands shook as she found her place on the page and focused on her reading.

She lumped him into the same category as Oscar. A deceiver of women. That could make redemption more difficult.

He focused on the passing scenery and pointed out an animal, person, or building they passed. Deidre didn't appear to mind the interruption in her reading. She even closed her book to share in the landscape as the train journeyed from Ohio into Pennsylvania and New York. They shared a light meal from her bag, and he noted the names of the towns until they reached Kinsman.

The small square depot was located in the center of town with Main Street crossing the train tracks. Nate followed Deidre down the wooden steps placed at each exit.

He stretched his stiff joints and looked around for anyone to greet them. No one stepped forward. "I'll see if there's a message at the ticket window."

"Don't forget my trunk." Deidre pointed at the porter unloading belongings from the baggage car.

Nate had to wait in line. The agent informed him a carriage was waiting on the street behind the depot to take them to Kinsman Manor. Nate asked the porter to bring Deidre's trunk and his valise to the open carriage. An elderly man sat in the raised driver's seat above the padded leather seats. His head was bowed, his chin resting on his chest, a snore announcing to the world he was alive but asleep.

Nate loaded their bags from the porter's cart into the back-facing carriage seat.

The driver woke with a start. "Who are you?"

"I'm one of your passengers. I'll get Miss Pierce." He returned to the front of the depot to search for her when he heard a woman's scream.

Chapter Seven

Deidre placed her travel bag on the ground to remove her bonnet and used her combs to capture the loose strands of hair and pin them in place to repair the chignon at the crown of her head. A man bumped into her from behind, and she stumbled. She turned to see who it was, and he snatched her bag and ran away. She screamed as the figure disappeared into the crowd.

Nate appeared at her side. "What happened?"

Her finger jabbed the air as she pointed toward the main street in town where pedestrians crowded the sidewalks and street. "A man stole my bag."

Nate looked at the ground. "Did you have anything valuable in it?"

She didn't like his tone. "Everything!"

He rubbed his forehead, but she saw the grin partially hidden by his hand.

"What was inside besides your books?"

"My grandfather's invitation, a letter from Uncle Logan, combs, hairpins, two handkerchiefs, and the rest of my sandwich." She counted on her fingers. Her list didn't sound impressive, but they were her personal belongings. Why would a stranger want them?

"Any money?"

"No." She shook her head. "Aunt Jem said to keep my money in my corset or in a deep pocket."

He searched her figure.

"Stop looking as if you can find where it's hid." She replaced her bonnet. "Is the carriage here for us?"

"The driver is waiting behind the depot."

Deidre searched the signs hanging from the buildings along Main Street. "I see a general store. I would like to replace the items stolen before we head to my grandfather's house. The shop should have everything I need except for the sandwich and books."

Nate turned toward the depot. "I'll ask the driver to bring the carriage around."

She felt every ache and pain in her stiff body. "I'd prefer to walk after that long train ride."

"I'll have him meet us in front of the store."

"I'll go ahead."

He turned. "Wait. I won't be long."

She shrugged. "I don't have anything else a thief could steal."

He looked worried and wouldn't leave.

She waved her hand at him to scoot. "I'll wait until you return." She searched for her thief but spotted no one wearing a long loose coat or slouch hat like the man she'd seen running away.

Nate was true to his promise and returned so quickly she didn't know he had left.

The general store was smaller than the ones in Akron but larger than the small shop in Crooked River. She examined the day dresses, stockings, and undergarments to test Nate's patience. She placed a corset over her dress to watch him squirm and rock on his heels as he glanced everywhere else. But she felt guilty about wasting time and selected the items to replace those stolen. She added a large handbag to carry her belongings and placed everything on the counter. A sailor bonnet was on display, nothing more than a small-brimmed blue cap trimmed with a fluff of white feathers. She examined the delicate creation but put it back.

"Try it on," Nate said.

"It's impractical." A mirror on the store wall reflected her image, and she couldn't resist the temptation to see it on. She pinned the small creation on the slope of her hairstyle at a saucy angle. She turned to face him. "How do I look?"

His smile widened, and he gazed in admiration. "I like it."

"You're appealing to my vanity." She placed the cap back on its rack. "My cloth bonnet is more practical."

"We have summer hats." The clerk pointed to wide-brimmed straw hats with no decorations.

"Are you planning to plow a field?" Nate whispered.

She snatched the bonnet from the display and added it to her purchases on the counter. Her hand moved to her gown. The material clung to the tightly laced corset but was pulled back in folds over her hips. She reached into a hidden pocket among the gathered material and withdrew a small cloth bag to pay for her purchases.

Nate put his hand over hers. "Your uncle gave me money. I think stolen items fall under his funds."

"He gave you money?" Why hadn't he given her the money directly? "Why don't men trust women to handle their own finances?"

He opened a leather purse. "Do you want to take it?"

"No. It's better if we split the money in case there's another thief in our future." She placed her purchases inside her new handbag along with her old cloth bonnet and pinned her new hat in place. She approved of her image reflected in the mirror and stepped outside with a confidence in her gait. Silly how a piece of decorated cloth on her head could embolden her, but the tiny cap did nothing to protect her fair skin from the hot rays. "I should have bought a parasol."

Nate turned around and came out with the requested accessory in a matching blue color.

She opened it and shielded her face. "Wait until my uncle finds out how wasteful you are with his money."

"I bought the parasol with my own coin. Consider it a belated birthday present."

"Thank you." She looked across the street at the sheriff's office. "Do you think we should tell the officials about the theft?"

"I doubt the sheriff will spend much time investigating a stolen purse, but we should report it. Your thief may be robbing other women in town."

"And men," she added.

The sheriff's office was on the first floor of a two-story wooden building. The windows were small, and the door creaked when they entered. The interior was dark, lit by a small lantern hanging from the ceiling.

A man with thinning hair and a long white mustache sat at a desk marred with scratches and an ink stain. He looked up from studying a stack of papers on his desk and removed his spectacles. "How may I help you?"

Nate introduced himself and Deidre.

"I'm Sheriff Uriah Olsen." He stood, shook Nate's hand, and motioned for them to sit.

The chairs were wooden and worn from use. One leg on her chair was shorter and rocked if she leaned forward. "I wish to report a stolen purse. I was standing at the train depot, and a man snatched my purse from the ground where I had placed it."

Uriah squinted at the handbag in her hands.

"I purchased this one at the shop across the street along with the items stolen." She opened her bag and handed him the receipt. "I wanted to replace them in case you didn't recover my belongings."

He put on his glasses and read the list. "Can you describe the man?"

"No, he came from behind, bumped into me, and snatched my bag. I saw him run away. He wore a long coat and large hat."

Uriah looked at Nate. "Did you see him?"

"No, I was putting our luggage into a carriage. He was gone by the time I rejoined Miss Pierce."

Sheriff Olsen removed a piece of paper from his desk and copied the receipt before handing it to her. "Was anything else in the bag besides the items listed here?"

"Three books, a letter, and half a sandwich." She gave him the titles and described the purse. "I embroidered the flowers on it myself."

He snorted but made a note on his report. "I'm sure it was a local boy having a bit of mischievous fun."

"It wasn't fun for me," Deidre said. "And it had to be a large boy to be the same person I saw."

"I know it may appear to be a trivial crime, but you have a thief in town, and he may continue stealing," Nate said.

The sheriff stroked his long mustache into a curl at the end. "Are you in law enforcement, young man?"

"I'm a lawyer." Nate announced his occupation with a hint of arrogance.

The sheriff leaned back into his chair. "You don't say?"

"I represent this young lady." Nate motioned to Deidre.

"First client?" A chuckle escaped the lawman.

Nate rose and placed his hands on the edge of the desk. "I graduated from Harvard Law School and work for Tyler Montgomery of Akron, Ohio. If you wish to see my credentials, I can have them sent to you."

"Take it easy, sonny." The sheriff pointed to the chair. "Have a seat and tell me why such an esteemed lawyer has come to Kinsman."

The sheriff was mocking Nate. Deidre rose, and Nate remained standing.

"His name is Mr. Burroughs. He is my lawyer. And I am here to visit my grandfather, Emerson Kinsman." She spoke each sentence with the same tone her aunt used when one of her cousins misbehaved.

The sheriff looked startled and stood, staring at her. "Mr. Kinsman informed me his grandchildren would be visiting this week. I don't recall you. When was the last time you were here?"

"I lived at Kinsman Manor with my mother until I was six years old."

He put on his glasses. "You're Hannah's girl?"

"Yes, Deidre Pierce."

"Pierce? I thought your mother's name was Smith." His mustache twitched.

She took a deep breath to calm the anger rising within. "My father's name was Pierce. Mr. Smith murdered him."

The sheriff nodded as he stroked his mustache. "As I recall, he was acquitted of shooting an interloper."

Her hands shook as she gripped her bag. "My father was not an interloper."

Nate placed his hand on the small of her back. "Derek Pierce was a secretary to Salmon Chase, a man whose reputation was blameless. Lewis Smith had several mistresses and questionable business dealings. If he hadn't been a senator, he would have been charged with murder. As it was, he lost his seat in Congress and was an outcast from polite society."

"You think so?" Sheriff Olsen looked from one to the other. "Are you two married?"

"What does our relationship have to do with a theft?" Deidre asked.

"I have explained that I am her lawyer. If you imply anything else, I will consider it slander against our good names." Nate took her arm. "We have a carriage waiting. We'll be at Mr. Kinsman's home for the week if you find anything."

The sheriff followed them to the door. "Why should I waste my time looking for an old purse? You already replaced everything of value."

Deidre gripped Nate's arm harder than necessary as they headed for the carriage. "He seems incompetent."

"I agree, and I don't think you'll see your purse again."

"My new one is good enough, but I wish the thief hadn't taken my books."

"Books can be replaced. Your grandfather probably has a library full of them."

"He does. I remember a huge room filled with books on shelves from the ceiling to the floor. But one of mine was a birthday gift."

"*The Adventures of Tom Sawyer*?"

She nodded.

"I packed my copy. You can borrow it if you

promise not to write in it."

She raised her hand in an oath. "I would like to see how the story ends."

"Then let's not think about Sheriff Olsen." He helped her into the carriage and joined her. The driver urged the team forward, and they headed out of town.

Deidre played with the strings of her new purse. "Do you think my cousins know the sordid details about my father and mother?"

"Don't let your parents define who you are," Nate said.

"That's easy for you to say. Your father was a war hero."

"I didn't think of him as a hero. The most important man in my life was dead."

"Didn't reading his letters help?"

"They gave me peace. It's a strange feeling. I'm no longer angry. I'm proud of him." He chuckled as he shook his head. "I never thought I'd say that."

"I want to understand my family better. I hope we can be friends."

"People aren't always what we imagine."

Was he warning her about disappointment? "I plan to keep an open mind. I don't want to judge others the way they judge me."

"Then I'll help by gathering facts and form an educated opinion as an impartial observant."

"You approach the visit as a lawyer. I've come as a cousin wanting to know my family. I plan to be charming and gracious."

Chapter Eight

Nate relaxed as the carriage traveled down a winding road to Kinsman Manor to meet the relatives that awaited them. If anyone could charm the hardest heart, it was Deidre. He closed his eyes as he enjoyed the warmth of the sun on his face.

Suddenly, the warmth was gone, and when he opened his eyes, it was dark except for small triangles of light shining through the trusses of a covered bridge spanning the rushing water. He dismissed the anxious feeling the change had caused. He was a logical man.

When they exited the shadows, light shone on a stately stone mansion resting on a rise above gently rolling fields divided by low stone walls like the country homes in England. Carved lions rested on each side of a stone arch with the name *Kinsman* carved above.

Nate was duly impressed. "Does any of this seem familiar?"

"I remember the lions," she said as they passed through the arch. "I called them Leo and Lucy."

"Lucy?" He felt the corners of his mouth rise but didn't laugh.

She frowned. "I was six."

The mansion was built to impress with the symmetry of English manor homes. Two front sections were joined by arched walkways and attached to a larger section that spilled out on each side into two-story and single-story buildings. A balcony on the third floor held large ceramic urns and cupids who stood guard with their small bows.

"When was this place built?"

"My great-grandfather bought the land after the war of 1812, but it was years before he started building anything. Grandfather finished it."

"It must have been grand living here."

"It was so big I was afraid of getting lost," Deidre said. "It still looks overwhelming."

"Bad memories." He squeezed her hand. His touch was meant to be comforting, but a different reaction occurred as the warmth from her fingertips spread through his body. He reluctantly released her hand. She rubbed at it. Had she felt something, too?

The horses took the carriage around a circular drive and stopped at the main doors where a stone walkway led to the entrance. Nate stepped down and offered his hand to Deidre. The same excitement he had felt before surged as he took her hand.

Two men appeared from a side door and removed Deidre's trunk from the carriage seat from the opposite side. A third man removed Nate's personal leather valise.

Deidre took one step and stopped. "I forgot my new handbag." She rushed back toward the carriage.

He turned to aid her when he felt a rush of air and saw a shadow growing larger to his right. Instinct made him lunge as a loud crash echoed behind him. Something sharp stabbed him in the side of the leg.

Deidre had climbed into the carriage but turned at the sound. Her eyes grew wide as a scream escaped her lips.

He grabbed the wheel of the carriage and clenched

his teeth as pain radiated up his leg. He turned his head to see sections of a ceramic cupid broken on the ground, jagged pieces scattered on the pathway, and one thin shard stuck to the side of his shin through the cloth of his trousers.

"Don't move." She jumped from the carriage and knelt beside him.

He twisted around to examine the wound and saw blood on the fabric surrounding the shard. The warm flow of blood contrasted against his cold skin. "Pull it out," he said through gritted teeth as pain throbbed in his leg.

"Let's move you inside first. Can you stand on it?"

He shifted his weight to his damaged leg. Pain radiated from the wound. He grimaced. "I think I can manage."

She looked around. "Where are the servants?"

The ones carrying her trunk had disappeared. He looked at the man carrying his bag. "What's your name?"

"Max Doyle, sir." He was a stout man with curly brown hair showing beneath a tweed flat cap. He looked capable of helping Nate inside.

"I need some assistance."

Max handed the bag to Deidre who looked surprised.

"How long have you been a servant, Max?" Nate asked.

"I was hired as a worker in January." Max braced his body next to Nate's. "Should I carry you?"

"No, I can hop." He looked up at the balcony where another cupid was perched to the far right of the entrance. Balance was standard in architecture, so why was the cupid that had fallen directly over the doorway and not farther to the left? He turned to Deidre who had his valise in one hand and her handbag in the other. "Thank goodness you ran back to the carriage."

Her eyes widened as she stared up at the balcony. "You don't think it was an accident?"

"Of course it was an accident." Nate hopped through the open doorway. "But it was better I was hurt and not you."

"Then you think I was the target." Her skin paled.

She was jumping to irrational conclusions. He needed to reassure her. "No. The cupid was too close to the edge and toppled over. That's all."

She studied his face. Did she detect a hint of doubt in his words?

"Sit down." Deidre motioned to a bench in the foyer. The tall back had hooks for hats and coats. The bench had a hinge for lifting and storing items inside. "Extend your leg."

She removed his shoe. His white sock was stained red.

"I should have bought scissors at the store."

"I have a knife." Max removed a blade from the sheath on his belt.

She cut the hem and ripped the fabric to the shard.

"My trousers!" Nate examined the damage. "I need to wear these."

"How many pairs of trousers did you pack?"

His skin was warm where her fingertips touched his flesh. He needed to concentrate. "A pair that matches my tailcoat for dinners and a pair for every day."

"That's it?" She sounded incredulous.

He needed to defend his choices. "I was going to switch out the day trousers. I didn't count on having one pair shredded."

"Men. I'm going to talk to your mother about packing your bag."

"I packed my own bag." He reached for the shard.

"Don't touch." She smacked his hand away. "Do you have a handkerchief?"

He withdrew the square of white cloth from his pocket. "Here. It's the one you washed and pressed."

"This is going to hurt," she warned with a look of pain in her eyes.

"How bad?" He had led a charmed life with no serious injuries. In a fight, he gave better than he received. His motto was to avoid pain and blood loss when possible.

Max stepped closer.

Deidre folded back the fabric to expose his bloody flesh. A sharp pain radiated from his shin where the shard stuck out of the wound.

"Hold him."

Before he could protest, Max gripped his ankle and pressed down on his knee.

His natural instinct was to fight. "What are you doing?"

She blocked his view.

He heard a plop and felt warm liquid on his skin.

"Got it." She stood and showed him the ceramic shard she had removed. Blood dripped from the point.

A wave of nausea washed over him. "I'm going to be sick."

"Should I fetch a bucket?" a young woman in black skirt and a white apron asked as she stood nearby.

"I'll need water, a clean towel, and bandages," Deidre said.

"Yes, miss." She bobbed, turned, and left in a near run, repeating aloud the three items requested.

"I'm fine." Nate attempted to stand, but the wound throbbed in a rhythmic beat, and he felt lightheaded.

"Stay down," Deidre ordered.

"Should I hold him, miss?" Max asked.

She placed her hand on his shoulder. "Are you going to behave and do as I say?"

Nate rested against the bench and removed his hat. His hair was damp. He was sweating. "Do I have any choice?"

"It won't take long if you stay seated."

"I've never been impaled before." He examined his injury. The gash wasn't large, but blood dripped from the wound. "Shouldn't you fetch a doctor?"

"Women have been midwives and healers for centuries until they were accused of being witches." She pressed his handkerchief against the wound. "I think I can handle this."

He only knew of men who were doctors, surgeons, and pharmacists. "Do you think women should be doctors?"

Her gaze met his. "Yes."

"Then in your medical opinion, how bad is it?"

"You have a gash and some scrapes, but nothing appears broken. I'll wash and dress the wound. Does it still hurt?"

"I feel dizzy and warm." He waved his bowler hat in front of his face. "Are you sure it wasn't cupid's arrow that struck me?"

She placed the palm of her hand against his forehead. "You're delirious."

The young woman returned with a pan of water and

the other supplies. "I'm Wendy Knox. I assist Mrs. Knox, who is the housekeeper and my grandmother."

"I'm Deidre Pierce, and this is Nate Burroughs."

Wendy had dark hair and a sprinkling of freckles across her nose. "I thought your uncle was coming?"

"He sent Mr. Burroughs in his place." Deidre arranged the supplies.

"What happened?" She knelt beside Deidre. "I heard an awful crash, but I couldn't see what caused it."

"A little accident outside." Deidre kept her voice calm as she washed his leg.

"One of your cupids decided to test his wings." Nate flapped his arms. "He failed to take flight."

Wendy giggled but recovered when Max frowned at her. He didn't act like a servant.

"Did Nate Burroughs, Esq. make a joke?" Deidre asked.

He winced as she pressed against the wound. "I'm masking the pain with humor."

"The cut isn't deep, but I might need to put in a couple of stitches," Deidre said.

"No." He dropped his hat and leaned as far away from her as possible. "You can sew up my trousers but not me. I don't like being stabbed by needles. Just wrap it up."

"I don't like needles either," Wendy said.

Max picked up Nate's hat and handed it to him.

"That bag needs to be taken upstairs to Mr. Burrough's room." Wendy pointed at Nate's valise. "The key is in the door."

Max tipped his cap. "Yes, Miss Wendy."

"It's the last one in the south wing, and use the servants' stairs. Your boots are dirty."

He nodded and disappeared.

Nate tried to relax as Deidre bathed his wound. The water was cold but soothed the ache pulsing in his leg. He stared at the red water in the basin. Bright red. "That's a lot of blood." Did he sound worried?

"You'll be fine." Deidre plucked at a cotton cloth to create gauze and placed it over the wound. "If it makes you queasy, don't look."

He closed his eyes as his head swirled in circles. "I don't like seeing my blood outside my body. How long will it take?"

"I'm done." She tied off the bandage.

Nate examined the damage. His trousers had suffered a rip up the side and were stained with his blood. The bandage was clean and secure. His bloody sock and handkerchief floated in the basin. He slipped his bare foot into his shoe and tied it. "Good as new."

Deidre and Wendy gathered the medical supplies.

"I'll wash his handkerchief and sock, miss," Wendy said.

"It's probably his only pair." The two women exchanged smiles.

He rose to his feet, and his leg throbbed. He crept into the gallery, an open room with doorways to the other rooms. He looked around. "Did you say my room was on the second floor?"

"Yes," Wendy said. "That's where all the guests are staying."

Nate looked at the graceful staircase rising to the right and curving to the second floor above. It had a lot of steps. "Is Max coming back?"

"I'll see what he's doing." Wendy hurried off with her supplies.

"Where have you been? I heard a crash and wanted to find out what is happening!" The scratchy voice echoed from a room to the left off the gallery.

A man in a white coat pushed a wooden wheelchair toward them. The shriveled man in the wicker seat had to be Emerson Kinsman.

Chapter Nine

Deidre studied the man in the wheelchair for anything familiar. This had to be her grandfather, but any family features were hidden beneath sagging skin and imperfections that flourished on the elderly. His gray pallor and shaking hands indicated his journey through life was nearing an end. Had he invited her and the others to celebrate his birthday or to say good-bye?

Nate stood beside her, favoring his injured leg. "I'm Nathaniel Burroughs, and this is your granddaughter, Deidre Pierce." He extended his hand.

"I'm Emerson Kinsman." His handshake was brief, and his hand fell to the arm of the wheelchair like a limp rag.

Deidre placed her hand on top of her grandfather's cold one. The veins rose in bumpy pathways through the paper-thin skin. A blanket covered his legs and lap. "Thank you for inviting me."

Emerson looked from Nate to Deidre. "I was expecting your uncle." His voice trembled, and he ended his sentence with a cough he covered with a stained handkerchief. The corner was embroidered with his initials.

"He could not make the trip personally and sends his regrets," Nate said. "I am here to represent Miss Pierce if any legal matters arise."

"You're a lawyer?"

He stood a little taller. "Yes, sir."

Deidre understood her grandfather's doubts. Nate's boyish good looks made him appear too young to be an experienced lawyer, but Uncle Tyler praised his work. Too bad he had a gossiping tongue.

Her grandfather looked from Nate to her and snorted.

Did he think there was something more to their relationship? "Mr. Burroughs was the only one who could come on such short notice."

"What happened to your leg, Mr. Burroughs?"

"One of your cupids fell from the sky when I approached the door. I was cut by a shard." He turned to Deidre. "I believe it was a warning to abandon any romantic entanglements."

"Cupid's arrow missed me as well," she said to remind him their relationship was purely business. But had the statue fallen by accident as he claimed, or was it something more sinister? Was there someone who didn't want her to be at Kinsman Manor?

"I hired workers from town to clean the house and grounds," Emerson said. "I'm sure someone moved the statue and did not place it in a secure position. It was your bad luck to be near the doorway when it fell but good luck no harm was done. I hope you can forget it."

"Accidents happen," Nate said. "I'm sure it hasn't dampened Deidre's enthusiasm to spend time with you."

"I want to be here," she said. "You don't know how long I've waited to visit."

Her grandfather squinted. "I invited your uncle to visit with you in the past, but he declined. Why did he change his mind this time, or are you here against his wishes?"

She didn't know about the past invitations. She didn't know the reason Uncle Logan hadn't allowed her to visit. "I'm sure my uncle had a good reason to not visit in the past. He fully supports this one."

"And yet he sent a lawyer with you."

"A young lady doesn't travel alone," Nate said.

"And you're the best he could do?"

It was an unwarranted insult. "Mr. Burroughs is capable of facing any challenge in his path with courage and ingenuity."

Nate's face registered surprise. "Thank you."

Why was she defending the rogue? But his genuine smile sent a surge of pleasure to her core.

Her grandfather's dark eyes peered out from sagging eyelids. "We can talk at dinner, which is at three. That should give you time to unpack and dress. I hope you have formal attire."

Nate nodded. "Yes, sir."

Her grandfather was rude, insulting, and arrogant. No wonder Uncle Logan had never mentioned a visit. Sometimes the fantasy was better than reality.

"Don't stand there, Bruce. You have to bathe and dress me for dinner."

Bruce was a large man with closely clipped hair and a wide face. "Yes, sir." He bent over the handles on the back of the wheelchair and pushed her grandfather to the room he had exited.

She stared after him. "He's dying."

"I'm no doctor, but I would agree," Nate said. "I'm sorry."

"I'm glad I visited before the funeral. Do you think he was telling the truth about inviting me to visit in the past?"

"He has no reason to lie. Maybe your uncle couldn't bring you."

Her grandfather's correspondence had gone to Uncle Tyler, and she had been kept in the dark about him. "Or he didn't like him."

"Emerson didn't think much of me." Nate hobbled toward the stairs.

"That gives you an advantage. He underestimates you."

"Which makes it easier for me to remain in the shadows." He winked. "My task is to observe and gather information so you can make informed decisions."

She looked around, but the gallery was empty. "Do we have to find our own rooms?"

"Mine is at the end of the hall." He stared at the tall staircase and paused. "On the second floor."

An elderly woman emerged from behind the staircase and toddled toward them. She wore all black with a white lace collar. "I'm Mrs. Knox, the housekeeper. You must be our guests. I'll show you to your rooms."

Had she heard their comments and magically appeared? Deidre looked at the staircase. Mrs. Knox would never make it past the first few steps. "Perhaps Wendy could show us?"

"Wendy?" Her eyes widened. "She's my granddaughter. A lovely girl, but she's always fluttering about. But then what can you expect from a child?"

"Child?" Nate asked. "That's not the Wendy we met."

Mrs. Knox frowned. "It's the one I know."

"Mrs. Knox?" Deidre studied the elderly woman's features. "Do I know you?"

"We just met." Mrs. Knox turned, her movements more up and down than forward.

"You were the housekeeper when I lived here with my mother." The face had more wrinkles, and the gray hair had gone completely white, but it was the same woman she remembered.

Mrs. Knox looked confused. "You lived here?"

"I'm Deidre Pierce."

"Pierce?" Mrs. Knox shook her head. "I remember a Deidre Smith. She had dirty blonde hair and dimples." She stared. "You have dimples just like her."

"I am her." Deidre looked at Nate and shrugged. What was wrong with the woman?

"Deidre!" Mrs. Knox smiled. "You've come home. Your mother will be so happy to see you."

Deidre touched the old woman's arm. "My mother is dead, Mrs. Knox. She died when I was six years old."

She paused on the first step. "That's right. You left to live with your uncle." She looked at Nate. "Are you Mr. Pierce?"

He looked confused. "No, I'm Nate Burroughs."

She bobbed her head. "Pleasure to meet you, Mr. Burroughs."

He twirled his hat in his hands. "I'm sure we can find our rooms."

"Nonsense." Mrs. Knox reached into her skirt pocket and retrieved a round ring of keys. "How will you unlock the door without this?" She selected a key. "No, that one is for the cellar." She searched through several more. "These keys are all wrong."

"Grandmother," Wendy called as she hurried across the gallery to the stairs where Mrs. Knox gripped the railing and attempted to lift her leg to the second step.

"You're not allowed to climb the stairs."

"But it's the only way to reach the second floor." She shook her ring of keys. "None of these are the ones I need."

"All the guests' rooms have been unlocked," Wendy said. "Cook is baking rolls for dinner. You better make sure she doesn't burn them. I'll show our guests upstairs."

Mrs. Knox smiled and nodded as Wendy helped her down from the marble step to the floor. They watched her toddle past the staircase to sliding glass doors leading to a side wing.

"I'm sorry about my grandmother," Wendy said. "She's often confused. Mr. Kinsman has been kind to keep her on in spite of her age and shortcomings. But don't worry. He's hired extra staff to help out this week. We normally don't have any guests."

"Are you part of the regular staff?" Deidre asked.

"Yes." She lifted a triangular ring with keys from her apron pocket. "I've taken over most of my grandmother's duties, but we let her think she's still head housekeeper."

"That's kind of you."

"She won't relinquish her duties willingly, so we humor her." Wendy led the way but paused as Nate struggled in the rear. "Can you make it, Mr. Burroughs?"

He gripped the smooth wood of the wide banister and pulled his body upward. "I may be slow, but I can make it."

"Let me help." Deidre put her arm around Nate's waist and tucked her shoulder beneath his free arm. His weight shifted, and he wavered on the step.

"You better keep a tight grip on the railing, or we

may both topple down the stairs."

He stuck his hat on his head and used his free hand to grip her waist. "I'm grateful for your help."

She kept a slow but steady pace up the stairs. She attempted to ignore his close proximity and the stirrings his touch aroused with each step. Most of the men she knew restricted contact to hand holding and a quick grasp and release during dancing. Nate's prolonged caress was unnerving as a tingling sensation spread throughout her body. She couldn't explain the physical reaction but was determined to control any response. "We're almost at the top."

She squeezed out of his grip but kept her arm around his waist as he limped down the hall.

Wendy opened a door on the right. "This is your room, Miss Pierce, and your young man is next door."

"He's not my young man." Deidre released him. "Leave your trousers outside, and I'll see they are soaked and mended."

"I know how to sew," Nate said. "I can mend my own trousers."

"You can sew?" She didn't bother to hide the shock in her voice. Most men balked at sewing, cooking, or cleaning. "I thought your mother took care of you."

He squared his shoulders. "I take care of my mother, not the other way around."

Wendy stared at them arguing. "We were expecting your uncle to accompany you when we assigned the rooms. Is it proper for you to have a young man next door? Should we move him?"

It would serve Nate right to be moved, but after her purse snatching and the cupid crashing inches from them, she wanted him nearby. Besides, she didn't know any of the other guests on the floor. "No. Mr. Burroughs is a gentleman. He won't enter my room uninvited."

Wendy pointed at the key on the inside of the door's lock. "You can lock your door, and I have the only spare." She patted her pocket. "If you change your mind, there are plenty of rooms on the third floor."

"More stairs?" Nate asked with worry in his voice. "This room will be fine."

"You should rest," Deidre said.

"I'll try." He opened his door and hobbled inside.

Poor Nate. She had invited him to accompany her so she would have an advantage by reminding him of his debt, but he had suffered insults and injuries instead. She entered her room, and Wendy pulled back the drapes, which had been drawn to keep the room cool on a warm day. The four-poster bed was near the empty fireplace, which was shared with Nate's room. She could hear his bed creak. On the other side of her bed was a nightstand with an oil lamp and clock. A chaise lounge was placed near the window, and a dresser, washstand, and dressing table with an ornate mirror were along the far wall. The furnishings were white with gold accents. Floral wallpaper covered the walls, and the oak floor had yellowed with age.

She looked out the window facing the back of the house. A brick walkway wandered through an intricate garden and framed an open lawn. She had played in the yard under her mother's watchful eye. The memory was comforting.

"Shall I help you unpack?" Wendy asked as she stood by the trunk the men had hauled upstairs.

"Is there time to have one of my dresses pressed?"

"I'll see to it."

Deidre opened the trunk and sorted through the day gowns and evening wear. She selected a pale pink silk. "I think I'll wear this." She wanted to make a good first impression.

Wendy took the dress and petticoat and opened the door.

"Wait. You said there were empty rooms on the third floor. Do you have the key to my mother's room?"

Wendy's eyes widened. "Your mother stayed on the third floor?"

"I stayed in the nursery, and she was next door. My grandfather wouldn't let a baby stay on this floor, so she moved upstairs to be with me. I'd like to see our old rooms."

Wendy studied the keys on her ring. "I might be able to find the keys on my grandmother's ring." She giggled. "We give her keys to rooms no longer used. When I get a chance, I'll sneak the keys away from her."

Deidre stepped closer. "Do you think your grandmother remembers my mother enough to share memories with me?"

"She remembers things from the first day she started working here, but on bad days she doesn't even remember I'm her granddaughter. She's more lucid in the mornings. You should talk to her after breakfast if you want to ask her about your mother."

Deidre followed Wendy to the door. "Mr. Burroughs may need his suit pressed."

Wendy knocked on his door. "He isn't answering, miss."

Deidre tried the door. It opened. The drapes had not been pulled, but enough light filtered through to illuminate a body in bed. Covers were pulled to his waist but his back was bare. His arm was thrown carelessly over the pillow and a snore escaped as his hair fell across his forehead. He looked like one of her young cousins napping except for the finely sculpted muscles in his shoulders and biceps. How did he fall asleep so fast?

His bag was on the bench at the end of the bed. She opened it and found his formal clothes and handed them to Wendy. She picked up his damaged trousers discarded on the floor and glanced back at Nate collapsed under a single cover. Was he wearing anything underneath?

"Makes you want to peek under the covers," Wendy murmured.

Had she read her mind? "Wendy, you need a husband." She tiptoed out of the room and quietly closed the door.

"I can soak those, miss." Wendy held out her hand.

"I'd appreciate it. I can mend them when they're dry."

"Oh, I can mend them, miss. He's such a handsome man and a lawyer. I bet he has many young ladies chasing him."

An anxious pang of jealousy stabbed at her heart. "I made the tear. I can mend it."

"As you wish, miss." She took the clothing and headed toward the end of the hall where the servants' stairs were located.

Chapter Ten

Deidre placed her belongings into the dresser drawers and hung her dresses on hooks to remove the wrinkles. She examined a gown she could wear if Wendy didn't return soon with her pink silk. She brushed out her hair while she waited.

Just when she was about to don another gown, someone knocked.

"It's me, miss."

She opened her door, and Wendy carried in her gown.

"I'm sorry it took so long, but the other ladies had dresses they wanted pressed. None of them brought their own maids."

Aunt Jem had a woman come in once a week to help with laundry, and they had a cook for the main meal, but a maid was deemed unnecessary with other women to help with dressing. Most of her day gowns buttoned up the front, but most evening wear was fastened in the back.

Deidre put on the skirt, which was straight in the front but draped in folds over a bustle with layers of contrasting dark pink fabric trimmed in rows of lace. Embroidered pink forget-me-not flowers formed a ring near the hem.

The separate bodice maintained the straight silhouette of the front but dipped to reveal her shoulders and the swell of her breasts. Wendy fastened the tiny buttons in back that began on her hips and rose to the middle of her back.

She dressed modestly during the day, but evening wear was more daring. She wasn't ashamed of her appearance and blamed any sinful thoughts on the men who stared. They needed to control their lustful desires and foolish behavior over a trivial display of flesh.

"You look lovely, miss. Shall I do your hair?"

Her hair was as silky as a baby's fine tresses and often slipped from her combs. She sat at the dressing table and watched in the mirror as Wendy divided her hair and braided each section before arranging the plaits in intricate braids that crowned her head and allowed a cascade of curls to fall down her back and shoulders. She tugged a few small tendrils free to curl and frame her face.

Deidre normally wore her hair in simple styles she could do herself. She admired the intricate plaits. "You're good at this."

"I worked at a dress shop when I was a girl, and the ladies would want their hair styled after trying on gowns. I've been working here for nearly four years, but every time I learn one job, someone dies and I have to learn another." She covered her mouth with her hand. "Oh, I shouldn't have said that, miss."

Deidre turned to face Wendy. "Are most of the manor's employees as elderly as Mrs. Knox?"

"She's the most senior," Wendy said. "Mr. Kinsman doesn't terminate anyone, but some of the newer hires are closer to my age."

Wendy had her hands full. "Will they stay on after we leave?"

"Mr. Kinsman hasn't said, miss."

Wendy seemed open to discussing any topic. "How long has my grandfather been ill?"

"He took a fall about a year ago, and he went through several nurses before Mr. Bruce showed up. He don't mind the harsh words Mr. Kinsman uses. When he could sit in a wheelchair, they moved him into the study on the first floor. The master suite has furnishings, but nobody uses it. We didn't put any guests in it. Of course, this is the first time he's had overnight company since his accident."

"He's called us together before he dies." Deidre dismissed the morbid thoughts. "I hope I can get to know him this week."

"You never know when it's someone's time." Wendy made the cross with her hand. "He could live to be a hundred."

She knew better but laughed. "That would be nice."

Wendy looked around on the dressing table. "Do you have any jewelry to wear, miss?"

"I have a pearl necklace." It was a gift from Uncle Logan when she had graduated from high school. She removed a box from her trunk and was glad she hadn't carried it in her stolen purse.

Wendy fastened the string of pearls around her neck.

"Have you met my cousins?"

"Some of them arrived last night and the rest this morning, but they've kept to their rooms," Wendy said. "I only caught a glimpse when they called for food or wanted clothing pressed. I better hurry back to the kitchen. Mr. Kinsman likes meals served promptly. You don't want to be late."

Wendy opened the door, and Nate stood in the

hallway, his hand raised as if he were going to knock. He wore black trousers with a matching tailcoat that was cut to fit tighter around the waist. The double-breasted vest was gray with a matching tie knotted over a white shirt. He looked entirely too handsome for a bookish lawyer.

Would her cousins think she was a wanton creature unable to curb her lust and passions because of her parentage and think Nate her lover? Her grandfather already had suspicions, and Wendy had offered to move Nate to a different room. If she possessed a fiery nature, it had yet to be released.

Most men bored her, and Nate had disappointed her. Should she give him a second chance? She didn't want to fuel any speculation and prove her relatives' suspicions. She was a moral person at heart but had learned not to judge others. Women like Hazel deserved understanding and compassion.

"You look beautiful," Nate whispered, his eyes never leaving her face.

"Thank you."

He ran his fingers along the lapel of his coat. "Someone pressed my suit while I was napping."

"That would be Wendy." She looked for her, but like well-trained servants, she had quietly disappeared. Deidre took his arm. "How is your leg?"

"Sore and stiff but functional."

"Wendy washed the blood out of your trousers and returned them to me to sew."

"I can mend them if I can borrow a sewing kit."

She shook her head as a soft laugh escaped. "I'll repair the damage since I caused it."

"I can sew a button on," he said in a defensive tone. "But the only thing I've stitched is a hole in my sock."

"That's called darning."

"I called it something else, which I can't repeat in front of a lady." He lifted his hand. "I kept pricking my finger."

"That's why you wear a thimble." How much did he know about sewing? "You used a darning egg, didn't you?"

"Egg?" He shook his head. "What for?"

His sewing skill was limited. "Shall we join the others?" Butterflies fluttered in her belly as they descended the staircase. She needed to control her nerves and took slow, deep breaths that matched Nate's careful steps as he gripped the railing. His leg must have hurt more than he admitted.

"Your uncle said your grandmother, uncles, and aunts have all died," Nate said. "He gave me a list of your cousins' names and their spouses, which I memorized. Now I need to put faces to them."

"Uncle Logan provided me with their names and what he knew about them. Bart and Roland are the sons of my mother's eldest brother. Charlie and Annabelle are the children of her other brother."

"All of them are married except for Charlie," Nate said with confidence. "And you."

She paused as they reached the main floor. What had her cousins heard about her? "I wonder if they'll like me."

He patted her hand, which still rested on his arm. "The question is whether you'll like them."

The dining room was in front with an entrance from the gallery. Crystal chandeliers were lit with wax candles and hung from the coffered ceiling trimmed with crown molding. The walls were papered in a pale-green pattern with lantern sconces spaced at regular intervals. The polished oak floor reflected the candlelight.

A long rectangular table was set for ten. Covered dishes were arranged on a sideboard with servants standing nearby, ready to serve. Her grandfather sat at the head of the table in his wheelchair. He made the introductions and assigned seats. Women and men were seated in alternating seats with Deidre to her grandfather's right. James Glasgow sat next to her with his wife Annabelle across from him. Between Annabelle and her grandfather was Roland. Bruce remained standing by her grandfather's chair. He placed a large napkin around his neck.

"I don't need a bib," her grandfather complained but didn't remove the cloth. "Stop hovering. I can feed myself. You're always around when I don't need you and absent when I do."

Bruce appeared unaffected by the harsh criticism. His face was hard to read.

Roland examined the silverware and ran his finger along the delicate white porcelain plates trimmed in gold leaf. He lifted the crystal goblet, and a servant stepped forward to fill it with wine.

Annabelle placed her napkin on her lap and watched as the servant filled her glass.

Deidre was used to boisterous conversations at the table, but no one spoke, not even her grandfather who should have introduced the topic. She looked for a family resemblance in the two cousins across from her, but they shared no obvious traits. Annabelle had delicate features and straight brown hair she wore in a single braid wrapped on top like a crown. Roland had a high forehead and hawkish nose framed with long side whiskers. He might have resembled their grandfather at the same age.

She laid her napkin across her lap as the servant placed a bowl of clam chowder before her. She looked at her grandfather, who remained silent, and decided to speak. "The invitation said you were celebrating your eightieth birthday, Grandfather. Congratulations."

"A man my age knows when the end is near. I've gathered my family to see if any of you are worthy of the Kinsman name." He raised his spoon, but it shook so badly most of the contents spilled back into the bowl before reaching his lips. "Drat."

"Shall I help you?" Annabelle asked in a high lilting voice.

"Did I ask for your help?" he barked as his face turned crimson.

Annabelle jumped back and stared into her bowl, her spoon shaking in her fingers.

Deidre didn't like her grandfather's behavior, but the elderly often forgot to filter their comments. She tore off a large piece of bread from the loaf on the bread board placed in the center of the table. "The key to eating soup is to sop it up with bread." She dunked the bread into her bowl and took a bite.

"That might do the trick." Her grandfather reached for the bread but struggled to tear a chunk from the loaf.

Annabelle reached toward the cutting board.

He pulled the bread toward him. "Wait your turn."

Annabelle withdrew her hand, hunkering down with her head bent over her bowl like a beaten dog.

Emerson severed a piece and dunked it into his soup. He chewed and swallowed before turning to Deidre. "You must know how to feed invalids and decrepit old men."

Deidre had witnessed his bullying behavior toward Annabelle. "I know how to serve young children. My Aunt Jem has many relatives." She offered the bread board to Annabelle. "One of the first lessons was good manners."

Annabelle met her gaze but shook her head. "I don't want any." She swirled her spoon in her soup but didn't eat.

"Don't pout, Annabelle," James said. "A man must maintain his pride. He doesn't want a woman pawing over him like he's a weakling."

She looked hurt by her husband's reprimand. "I was only trying to help Grandfather."

"Your cousin offered a more dignified solution than feeding him like an infant," James said. "Now smile and show him you can be gracious."

Annabelle forced a smile and held it longer than anything spontaneous. "I'm sorry if I embarrassed you, Grandfather."

He grunted. "Your husband is right about one thing. I'm proud. Sometimes to my own detriment. How long have you been married?"

"Five months." James stroked the short growth of whiskers on his chin. "Her mother died shortly after we met, and we waited to be married."

"James was so comforting to me and Charlie," Annabelle said, glancing in her brother's direction.

"How did you meet?" Deidre asked.

"It was at a party," Annabelle said with a smile that was more natural than the previous one.

"I believe Miss Pierce asked me the question, my dear," James said in a low but firm voice.

"I interrupted." Annabelle turned her attention to her

bowl. "I'm sorry."

"I'm sure you both know how you met," Deidre said. "You were both there."

Annabelle looked up, glancing from Deidre to her husband.

"It was a Valentine's Day party, and I chose her card," James said. "I knew Annabelle was the girl for me as soon as we met. We were married exactly one year later."

Annabelle smiled at her husband with all the adoration of a new bride.

"Did you know she would be coming into money?" Emerson asked.

Her grandfather's rudeness extended beyond his table manners. Money was rarely the topic of polite conversation.

James clenched his napkin in his fist on his lap. "Her parents left her and Charlie a house and small inheritance." He dipped his spoon into the clam chowder. "But I support my wife with my job purchasing land for the railroad."

"The railroad?" Emerson asked. "Do we need any more tracks across this country?"

"Since the transcontinental railroad was completed, the demand for more tracks to ship goods has expanded," James said.

"Did you invest in any stock?"

"Only a little," James said. "I do not have the luxury of risking my funds."

"You have done better than my blood relatives." Emerson surveyed his family members. "Between bad investments and a lack of motivation for hard work, I can see the hands outstretched around the table waiting for me to die."

Deidre gasped at his blunt assessment. Maybe a few family members were hoping to inherit soon, but it seemed rude to mention it.

"That's not true," Roland said. "I attended college, but I haven't had time to establish myself."

"Did you graduate from college?" Emerson asked.

"No." Roland raised his chin. "I didn't see Latin and a liberal education as necessary for success."

"And what prosperity have you found?"

"I've tried several ventures, but nothing meets my standards." Roland's voice quivered slightly.

"Standards?" Emerson shouted. "I shoveled manure when I was young. A man starts at the bottom, learns a trade, acquires some skills, and if he's lucky, amounts to something. How have you supported a wife and yourself?"

"I sold some land." His voice was barely above a whisper.

"What land?" Emerson demanded.

He looked at his wife seated next to James. "Faith's family left her a few properties in Niagara Falls. It provided income while I looked for work."

"Is that why you married her?" Emerson sneered the comment.

"No. She believes in me." Roland squared his shoulders. "She's my champion."

"That's admirable," James said. "But I prefer to provide for my wife and not depend on her income."

"Then you won't mind if your wife doesn't inherit?" Roland asked with a slight smile on his lips.

"She's family," James said. "She has every right to inherit the same as the men in the family."

"Will you be managing her money for her?" Emerson asked.

James examined the cuff of his shirt. "As her husband, I would oversee any property or funds she would inherit."

"If I were to inherit anything, I would oversee my own finances," Deidre said.

Everyone stared at her as she raised her spoon to her lips.

"Do you think you could manage such a large responsibility?" her grandfather asked.

Deidre met his gaze. "Yes, I do."

James laughed as he looked at the other men. "And how long have you handled your own affairs?"

"I only recently turned twenty-one," Deidre said. "But as an orphan I have been making my own decisions for some time."

"Over pennies given you for sewing or cooking?" he mocked.

"I have worked as a nurse, teacher, tutor, and canal boat worker," Deidre said. "I contributed a portion to my family to repay their generosity, but I know how to make my earnings last."

"If you're going to manage your inheritance, why did you bring a lawyer?" her grandfather asked.

"My uncle Logan did not want me to travel alone," she said. "He thought a lawyer would be helpful if any legal matters arose."

"Is your uncle the brother of Derek Pierce?" Annabelle asked.

The eagerness in her voice warned Deidre to be wary. "Yes. Derek was my father."

"But he wasn't married to your mother." Roland

turned to their grandfather. "My parents did not approve of Aunt Hannah's choices."

"I would not be here without her choice," Deidre said.

"You've had a tragic life," Annabelle said with a hint of sympathy. "Didn't you live here after your father…"

"After he was murdered?" she asked in a firm, controlled voice. If she had learned one thing from Nate's gossip, it was to face the truth and not run from it.

"Murdered?" James asked with surprise.

"What do you call it when an armed man shoots one who is unarmed?" Deidre asked.

"But he had good reason," Roland said. "They used to stone people who committed adultery in the past."

"Violence is never a solution to a problem." Deidre turned to Annabelle. "After my father's death, my mother returned to Kinsman Manor, and I lived here until I was six."

"Is that when your mother died?" Annabelle asked.

"Yes." Deidre looked at her grandfather. "I don't remember much. I was hoping Mrs. Knox could tell me about my mother, but she becomes confused at times."

"Mrs. Knox is loony." James twirled his finger around his ear.

"That's a cruel thing to say," Deidre said. "She's elderly."

"Am I loony?" Emerson looked at James.

"Of course not." James studied his napkin on his lap.

"Mrs. Knox has been a loyal employee for many years," Emerson said. "I hope she can remember a few things about your mother. If not, I can share my memories."

Deidre couldn't fathom his mercurial behavior, but she was grateful for his offer. "Thank you, Grandfather."

Chapter Eleven

Nate was seated at the other end of the table. Bart sat to his left opposite his grandfather in a position of importance for the eldest grandchild. His wife, Wilma, sat to Nate's right. Opposite her was Faith, the wife of Roland, and between her and Bart was Charlie, the brother of Annabelle.

Nate attempted to listen to the conversation at the other end of the table, but Bart's booming voice drowned out Deidre and her companions as he bragged about his business investments. By his estimate he had made more than his grandfather but had plans for the money he should inherit as the eldest heir. He did his utmost to impress the others. Nate turned his attention to the pecan pie being served.

"I'll make a fortune from my investments in Riverton Mining." Bart nodded at the others who appeared to be impressed. "I had to borrow for the initial purchase, but I expect to triple the value by the end of the year."

"Riverton Mining?" Nate repeated. He had helped on a case suing the investment company for fraud. The mining company was a fake, and investors had lost everything.

"Yes," Bart said. "Have you heard of them?"

He looked more closely at Bart. His full beard hid most of his face, making it difficult to read his features.

Although his suit was quality, the fabric had a shine where it had been pressed too many times. A stain was visible on his lapel. Bart was lying about his wealth. He was a man who needed his inheritance and soon. "I've heard the name." He knew not to embarrass someone publicly.

"I can't wait for the money to arrive," Wilma said. "Bart won't let me buy any new gowns until we can go to New York City and buy the latest fashions."

She wore a gown that declared wealth with rows of gathers, silk ribbons, and lace. Was Wilma lying as well to cover up their financial situation, or was she in the dark about her husband's dubious business dealings?

"I have some gowns you can borrow if you need one," Faith said.

"I would have to hire a seamstress to take in the excess fabric." Wilma had hardly touched her food or dessert. She was as thin as a rail while Faith was full-figured, but it was unkind for the thinner woman to make a comment about Faith's weight. She was hardly fat.

Faith took a bite, smacked her lips, and left the rest of her pie untouched.

Wilma had a smug look on her face when she turned her sharp features toward Nate. "What do you do for a living?"

"I'm a lawyer."

"I could have gone to law school, but I was already successful with my business investments. Why waste time in a classroom?" Bart licked his fingers after eating the last of the pie crust crumbs.

"I wish Roland had become a lawyer or a minister or something." Faith looked at the other end of the table. Her husband either didn't hear her complaint or ignored it. "He can't make up his mind. He never finishes what he starts."

"What new project is he pursuing now?" Bart asked.

Faith let out a long sigh. "He wants to invest in hot air balloons."

Bart leaned toward her. "Is there a market for those?"

"Do you see them up in the air?" Faith asked with a heavy layer of sarcasm.

"I predict air travel will increase in the future," Charlie said. It was the first words he had spoken since dinner was served. Like Nate, he was clean-shaven.

"What do you know about hot air balloons?" Faith asked.

"I read," Charlie said. "I'm a fan of Jules Verne. Have you read any of his books?"

"Reading strains my eyes." Faith blinked several times.

"Verne is full of fanciful ideas and nonsense," Bart said. "Underwater ships and a manned projectile shot to the moon. You should invest your money in tangible items, not silly ideas. If you inherit anything," he added in a low voice.

Charlie's eyes widened. "Why wouldn't I?"

Bart leaned back and brushed crumbs from his beard. "Grandfather has his favorites."

"And you're one of them." Wilma smiled at her husband.

"I enjoy Verne," Nate said. "Have you read *Around the World in Eighty Days*?"

"It didn't have enough science in it for me," Charlie said. "But I liked the story."

Emerson tapped on his goblet with his knife. "Let us

adjourn to the library."

Everyone followed as Bruce wheeled Emerson from the dining room, into the gallery, and past the staircase to the library located in the rear of the house. The drapes were opened to reveal a wall of windows that overlooked the flower gardens.

Shelves of books lined the other walls from ceiling to floor. Ladders on rollers at the top and wheels on the bottom moved along the bookcases to reach the highest levels. Two tables were arranged side by side and a third placed perpendicular in the center of the room. Comfortable leather chairs and a settee were arranged near the windows. A glass door opened to the garden where benches provided additional seats for reading.

"It's so cozy," Annabelle said.

Charlie clapped his hands and walked around in circles, gazing at all the books. "This is my favorite room."

"Deidre enjoys reading, too," Nate said as his gaze met hers.

"I share your passion, Charlie," she said before turning to Nate. "Mr. Burroughs prefers pristine law books."

"Mr. Kinsman would like to address you," Bruce announced in a rumbling voice as he motioned for everyone to gather around.

"I invited all of you to decide how I will distribute my wealth," Emerson said. "You could receive a dollar or a fortune or something in between. I'll know how much after spending time with each of you this week."

"I accepted your invitation to become acquainted with my mother's family and learn more about everyone," Deidre said. "I look forward to spending time with all of you."

"Then you'll enjoy the activities I've planned to celebrate my birthday," Emerson said. "Everyone will participate."

"What sort of activities, Grandfather?" Roland asked.

"You'll find out tomorrow. Tonight, I want to look into the past. I hired an artist to paint your parents when they were newly married." Emerson pointed to the nearest portrait by the room's entrance. "Bart and Roland, this was your father and mother before you were born."

"What happened to them?" James asked.

"They traveled to France in 1870," Bart said. "The ship sank in a storm."

Emerson moved to another portrait on the same wall. "These are your parents, Charlie and Annabelle."

"Father died two years ago from *morbus cordis*, and mother died last year in her sleep." Annabelle looked at her husband. "We're hoping this year is happier."

"We're off to a good start." James took her hand and kissed it.

Emerson signaled Bruce to wheel him across the room where the portrait of a young woman was placed above the fireplace.

"This is a portrait of Hannah." Emerson turned to Deidre. "It was done when you were a baby and both living here."

Deidre stared, tears pooling in her eyes. "I remember that face."

Nate saw the resemblance between mother and daughter even though Deidre's dimples marked her as a Pierce. "She was beautiful." And sad. The artist had captured the grief experienced in her short life.

"Before disease ravaged her." Emerson looked at Deidre. "Hannah was right to send you away before she died. You should always remember her like this."

Deidre studied the portrait. "I will."

"Why isn't her husband in the portrait?" Bart asked. "Wasn't he in Congress?"

A silence punctuated his question.

"Lewis Smith wasn't my father," Deidre said with only a slight quiver in her voice. "I told the others about how my mother fell in love with Derek Pierce, but he was shot and killed by her estranged husband."

"A family scandal?" Faith looked at Roland with a gaping smile. "Why didn't you tell me?"

"You enjoy vicious gossip?" Nate asked.

"We're all family, aren't we?" Faith asked. "Do share the details."

"Good manners would dictate that you don't discuss it," James said. "But it was a long time ago. Can you share anything?"

"I don't mind people knowing the truth. I want you to share stories about your own lives. I shouldn't hesitate to share mine." She waited for Faith to stop giggling. "I don't know all the details. My mother married Lewis Smith when she was young. He was unfaithful and abused her."

"How do you know?" James asked.

"I can vouch for his unsavory character," Emerson said. "Hannah was young and flattered by the attentions of Lewis Smith. I should have done my due diligence and had him investigated before agreeing to the marriage, but he promised to help me with my business dealings. My greed made me encourage Hannah to accept his proposal. After the wedding I discovered his life was a lie. He was a rake and had more than one child out of wedlock. He promised to reform, but that pledge was quickly broken."

"How did she meet Derek Pierce?" Annabelle asked.

"My father worked for Salmon Chase who had been elected as a senator from Ohio. Secretaries and clerks escorted the wives of congressmen to social events when their husbands couldn't," Deidre said. "They met at a party and fell in love."

"And her husband shot him," Faith said with a clap of her hands. "And I thought this week would be boring."

"Did Lewis go to jail?" Charlie asked.

"He was acquitted." She looked toward Nate. "Lawyers make a lot of money arguing why guilty men should be set free."

Nate shrugged. "He claimed he was protecting the sanctity of his home."

"Hannah returned here a broken woman, but when you were born, a smile returned to her face," Emerson said. "A baby's laughter can soften the hardest heart."

Nate studied Emerson who coughed when he met his gaze. Did the old man have a heart after all?

"You need to rest, sir," Bruce said loudly enough for everyone to hear.

Emerson waved at the gardens. "You can walk about the grounds, socialize in the parlor, or retire to your rooms. Food left over from dinner will be placed in the dining room for supper around seven. You can serve yourself."

"May I borrow a book?" Charlie asked as he examined one left on the table. "You have quite a collection."

"I have an agreement with the schoolteacher in town," Emerson said. "He orders books to keep my library stocked with new editions, and I pay for textbooks for his students. He dropped a stack off earlier today. You and the others may read any that pique your interest."

"Thank you, Grandfather," Charlie said as he scanned the shelves.

Nate looked at Deidre. "I don't know if Deidre should borrow any."

"I promise not to write in any of them." She made a face at him. "Mr. Burroughs does not approve of my notes in the margins."

"Your mother liked to mark passages with comments." He frowned. "I gave her a journal to write her thoughts in so she would stop defacing my books. Now I search for the ones she wrote in."

"Sometimes we value material things too much and forget about people and their feelings," Nate said. "Someone told me a book wasn't loved if it wasn't worn."

Deidre cleared her throat.

"Well, I will take these." Charlie gathered a few books.

Nate searched through the titles of the books stacked next to a tall candlestick on the table in the middle of the room while Deidre talked to her relatives. Most of the titles were new publications, but he found *Little Women*, *The Adventures of Tom Sawyer*, and *Around the World in Eighty Days* on the bottom of the stack. He could replace the books stolen from Deidre.

He flipped through the pages of Twain's novel as he

waited for the others to leave the library. Small notes in pencil were written on several pages.

"Did Mr. Kinsman say these books arrived today?" he asked Charlie who hugged his collection to his chest.

"Yes," Charlie said. "Did you find some you like?"

"I found a couple of familiar titles," Nate said.

"Well, I'm off to my room to read," Charlie said. "I think I'm across the hall from you."

"You don't want to join us in the parlor?" Annabelle asked.

"I can't concentrate with everyone talking." Charlie gave her a peck on the cheek. "I'll see you tomorrow."

Nate flipped to the beginning of the novel and saw Deidre's name printed on the first page. "Deidre, a moment, please. Can you come here?"

She was talking to Annabelle and James but promised to join them in the parlor. "What is so important?" Her voice had a trace of impatience.

He handed her the book. "Look what I found among your grandfather's books."

She opened the cover. "It belongs to me." She looked at the other books in his hand. "Mine?"

He opened each book to reveal her name in neat print.

She looked at the table and remaining books stacked on it. "How did they get here?"

"Emerson said a schoolteacher delivered them. Do you think he's your thief?"

"A schoolteacher?" Deidre called to Wendy in the gallery. "What does the schoolteacher look like?"

"He's elderly with a limp," Wendy said. "I think he was wounded in the war."

Deidre shook her head. "That's not the man I saw

running away."

"Somehow the thief put your books with the schoolteacher's delivery," Nate said.

They entered the parlor, which was at the rear of the house and extended beyond the walls of the library and kitchen. Windows allowed a view of the gardens and countryside on three sides. Deidre lifted her books. "Let me put these in my room, and we can take a walk."

Nate looked at his leg. "A short walk."

"Go sit on a bench."

He found a metal bench outside and waited for Deidre to return. He looked at her relatives who were walking about the gardens or seated inside on comfortable sofas and chairs. Had one of them returned the books?

Deidre joined him, and he felt good enough to walk with her along the brick pathways laid out in a symmetrical pattern. She paused to sniff a blossom or name the flower.

She sighed as she gripped his arm. "Why would someone return my stolen books?"

"It's like an admission of guilt."

"Nobody knew but Grandfather that we would go to the library tonight," Deidre said.

Did someone want them to find the books? "A servant might have known his plans."

"Maybe he thought we wouldn't find the books among all the other ones," Deidre said.

"Then he should have put them on the shelf." His leg throbbed with each step, and he paused to rest on his good leg.

"You need to sit." She headed for the parlor door. "What do you think is going on?"

"I'm a lawyer not a detective." He plopped onto a soft sofa.

Deidre sat next to him. "Even Tom Sawyer played detective when he wanted to find answers."

"And look at the trouble he got into."

"I didn't read the ending," Deidre said. "I'll let you know what I think after I finish the book tonight."

Chapter Twelve

Deidre knocked lightly on Nate's door. She planned to go downstairs for breakfast but didn't know if he was an early riser like her or tended to sleep late like so many of the others. She'd listened for the last fifteen minutes for footsteps from any of the other rooms, but the hallway had remained silent and empty. Her stomach growled, unwilling to wait any longer.

"Are you awake?"

Nate opened the door. He was dressed in dark trousers, a patterned waistcoat, and a white shirt.

She handed him his trousers. "I repaired them last night. Did you change the bandage on your leg?"

"Per your instructions I wrapped the wound lightly with a clean bandage. No blood visible this morning, and it appears to have a scab forming." He disappeared into his room and returned wearing the same coat from yesterday.

"I envy your ability to pack so lightly. I filled my trunk with day dresses, evening gowns, and all the accessories and ran out of room."

"But your appearance is so much more impressive than mine."

"Flattery? I thought you were a man of facts and figures."

"I must be lightheaded from hunger. Has anyone else gone downstairs for breakfast?"

"I didn't hear anyone." She looked at the empty hallway. "And I couldn't wait any longer. My cousins appear to be late risers, but the Pierce family is up with the sun."

"More food for us." Nate tested his leg as he stepped down the stairs.

"How does it feel?"

"A little sore, but the patient will live."

She fought a laugh. He had a dry sense of humor, and she liked it. She would have to guard her heart against liking him too much. They came to the bottom of the staircase and entered the dining room to find it empty.

"Maybe they weren't expecting anyone this early," Nate said. "I can scramble an egg."

If his cooking was on the same level as his sewing skills, they could starve. Luckily, she was an excellent cook. "The kitchen is in the back."

They found Wendy with Max sipping coffee at a table in the kitchen nook between the main kitchen and a hallway leading to the servants' quarters. Benches served as seats. They both stood.

"I didn't know any of the guests would be up this early." Wendy wiped her hands on her apron. "The staff eats in here."

"As a working man, I eat breakfast early, dinner at noon, and supper when my work is done," Nate said. "Eating in the afternoon and late at night is for a rich man."

Deidre followed a similar schedule as Nate for her meals.

"It works better when the staff doesn't eat at the same time as Mr. Emerson and his guests," Wendy said.

"Follow me into the kitchen."

Max grabbed his flat cap. "I should do my chores."

Had they interrupted a tryst?

Wendy watched Max leave and turned toward the kitchen.

"Do you think there's anything left to eat?" Nate asked as he followed Wendy and Deidre through the swinging doors.

Cook stood by the larger of two stoves located next to a fireplace. Pots and pans hung from hooks, and a pantry with crocks and containers was stocked with supplies. A long worktable took up the middle space. "I've got plenty for you to eat if you don't like nothing fancy. What would you like?"

"I hate to put you to any trouble," Deidre said. "I can make something for the two of us."

"Nobody cooks in my kitchen if I'm on duty," Cook said. "How do you want your eggs made?"

"Over easy."

"Scrambled," Nate said. "And I like my bacon crisp."

"I've got some fried potatoes and biscuits," Cook said. "If you don't eat them, the hogs will."

"The hogs will be disappointed this morning," Nate said. "I'd like both."

Cook fixed the plates, and Wendy placed them in front of Nate and Deidre at the table in the nook.

"There's jam and butter on the table," Wendy said. "Do you prefer coffee or tea?"

"Coffee," Nate said.

"I like milk for breakfast," Deidre said.

Nate's chest shook as he chuckled.

"I'm surrounded by children at home," Deidre

defended. "Only Uncle Logan drinks coffee."

Nate raised his hands. "I was laughing because my mother makes me drink milk for breakfast."

Wendy returned with their drinks. "I'll be in the kitchen if you need anything."

Nate took several bites from his full plate and looked around at the empty room. "What did you learn about your cousins?"

Deidre was eager to share her newly gained knowledge. "Grandfather insinuated all of them needed money." She kept her voice low. "James invested in railroads. Is that wise?"

"Railroads have been expanding the last five years. It's a better business than Bart's choice." He bit into a crisp slice of bacon. "He bragged about some investments in mining, but I know the company is fraudulent because I worked on two lawsuits last month against them."

Deidre considered his comment and took a bite of her flaky biscuit. "Why would he lie about his wealth?"

"I have a feeling Wilma doesn't know how poor they are," he said. "She thinks he's taking her to New York on a shopping spree, and that's why she doesn't have any new gowns."

She shared her own observations. "Annabelle is sweet, but Faith loves gossip."

"Charlie loves to read," he said.

"He told me he was a fan of Jules Verne."

"He's a fan of science," Nate said. "He took a copy of *Hereditary Genius* and *Contributions to the Theory of Natural Selection* last night."

Wendy entered with a steaming pot. "Would you like more coffee?"

Nate held up his mug. "Thank you, Wendy. I hope we didn't put you off your routine."

"We don't mind," Wendy said. "Cook hates to waste food, and no one but you came down for breakfast."

"Do you know what my grandfather has planned for today?" Deidre asked.

"He's having the servants set up a croquet course on the lawn next to the garden. Do you know how to play?"

"Everyone in Crooked River enjoys the game." Deidre looked at the ceiling. "Do you think I'll have time to visit my mother's room?"

"If everyone sleeps until noon," Wendy said.

Deidre looked around. "Where is your grandmother, or are the rooms unlocked?"

"The rooms are locked, but my grandmother doesn't have the keys." She removed two loose keys from her skirt pocket. "I removed the ones you'll need last night while she was asleep, and you can go up there whenever you like."

"Are there any servants staying on the third floor? I thought I heard footsteps above me last night." She turned to Nate. "Did you hear anything?"

Nate shook his head.

"No one should be up there. The rooms have been locked for years. Most servants stay in the quarters through that door." Wendy pointed to a doorway off the nook. "And some of the men sleep in the stables."

Deidre remembered visiting Mrs. Knox in the servants' quarters when her mother became ill and went away to visit the doctors.

"Why did you and your mother stay on the third floor?" Nate asked.

Deidre shook herself. "It was the nursery. My

mother wanted to take care of me and didn't hire a nurse. She had a room next to mine." She showed him the two keys Wendy had given her. The young housekeeper had silently disappeared.

"Did your grandfather treat you worse than servants?"

"The rich view family differently than the poor," Deidre said. "Children are not to be seen or heard except after they are fed and scrubbed for bed in wealthy households. Then they are paraded downstairs, and the patriarch pats them on the head. I remember being scared of Grandfather on my nightly visits. But after passing inspection, my mother would take me upstairs, tuck me into bed, and tell me a story until I fell asleep."

"I don't understand why someone would have children and not spend any time with them," Nate said. "My fondest memories are the times I spent with my father before he left for the war. He was always teaching me things. He'd have me sort nails and then teach me how to drive one into a board with one strike."

Was he bragging to impress her? "One?"

"Yes, none of that tap-tapping you girls do." He pretended to tap a hammer on a nail. "A hammer is a lever. It's meant to be swung from the end of the handle. One swing and the nail goes in." He swung high and hard and then pretended he had hit his thumb and stuck it into his mouth.

Deidre laughed at his antics. "I do not tap-tap except to set a nail. And I know how to drive a mule, use a pike to keep a canal boat from hitting the lock walls, and toss a rope. Captain Donovan treated the girls the same as boys when we worked on the *Irish Rose*. We were paid the same, too."

His eyebrows rose. "You worked on the canal like Liny and her brothers?"

"I worked a couple of summers. It's a family tradition. Aunt Jem and all her sisters worked on their grandfather's boat when they were younger."

"That's the advantage of having a large family. When I have children, I plan to spend as much time with them as possible. Why have them if you don't?"

Deidre's mouth dropped. Was he serious? "Most men think it's the woman's job to take care of the children. The man is the authoritarian who gives the orders, and the wife obeys."

"Blame Moses," Nate said. "He created a patriarch society where men owned the land, had a special relationship with God, and passed everything on to their sons. Women were expected to stay pure and produce the heir without any doubt who fathered the child."

"Which is why my mother was branded a fallen woman," Deidre said.

"I think a marriage should be a partnership. Why marry if you're going to treat your wife like a servant?"

Had she misjudged him? "Is that how you truly feel?"

"I wouldn't lie to you, Deidre." He crossed his heart. "I might lie when the occasion warrants to others but not to you."

"You didn't really lie to Oscar, but I prefer to be the one who tells others about my parents. It's gossip when others repeat it."

"And Faith would have enjoyed repeating it," he said. "You outsmarted her by making the information publicly known."

She finished her bacon. "Most people enjoy gossip.

At least Faith was honest to admit her vice."

"I have learned my lesson not to gossip or listen to it. I should never have believed Oscar when he said you would marry him."

"I have better sense than to say yes to Oscar or any man who would keep me from achieving my goals." She finished the last bite of her biscuit. "Every woman who needs a second chance should have one."

He frowned as he took a sip of his coffee. "As a lawyer I've seen my fair share of women who have been left destitute by husbands who swore undying love in the beginning only to abandon their families."

"Or fathers who sell their daughters to saloon owners," she added.

"I'm glad you let me assist in their rescue," he said. "I can't imagine the horrors Hazel endured. But don't you want to marry someday?"

"I want children, and that requires marriage, but I want to make sure I know the man I marry well enough not to have any doubts about what sort of husband and father he'll be."

"No surprises?"

"None that I would regret," she said.

A high-pitched scream echoed from across the gallery.

Cook ran into the room as the doors flapped behind her. "What was that?"

Deidre and Nate stood, looked at each other, and dashed into the gallery.

Wendy ran at them, and Deidre grabbed her in a bear hug. She was shaking, and her face was ashen.

"What's wrong?"

"She's dead!" Wendy burst into uncontrollable

sobs.

Deidre stroked her heaving back. "Who's dead?"

"My grandmother." She pulled away and wiped her tear-streaked face with her apron.

"Mrs. Knox?" Nate looked around. "Where?"

Wendy pointed behind her. "She was in the library dusting. It's one of the tasks she's allowed to do."

"Sit down." Deidre led her to the bottom step of the staircase, and Nate handed her his handkerchief.

Bruce came into the gallery. "We heard a scream. What happened?"

"Wendy said her grandmother is dead in the library," Deidre said.

"What's going on?" her grandfather shouted from his room. "Where's Bruce? I need someone to roll this contraption."

"That would be me." Bruce hurried to Emerson's room and returned with Emerson in his wheelchair.

"What was that screech? What is all this noise about?" her grandfather demanded.

"Wendy believes Mrs. Knox is dead in the library. I'm going to investigate." Nate turned to Deidre. "You should stay here with Wendy."

So much for treating women as partners. "I've worked as a nurse. I'm better suited to determine her condition."

"Bruce can stay with Wendy." Emerson pointed at Nate. "You can take me."

Nate pushed the chair, and Deidre held the library door open to allow them to enter. The curtains were open, but the light was dim since the windows faced west. Soft shadows played on the rows of books lining the walls on the other three sides.

Mrs. Knox was on her back on the floor opposite the doorway between a table and the bookshelves. A sliding ladder was behind her, and a chair was overturned nearby. A feather duster lay on the floor.

Deidre knelt beside Mrs. Knox and felt for a pulse at her wrist and then her neck. None. "She's dead, but the body is warm." A gash on her forehead had bled and stained her white hair. Her eyes stared up at the ceiling.

"Move me closer," Grandfather ordered Nate. "Mrs. Knox worked more than fifty years for me. Her heart must have given out. The woman was nearly as old as me."

Deidre pointed at the blood on the tabletop near the sharp edge. "There's blood on the table and her forehead. I don't think this was her heart."

"Then it was an accident," her grandfather said. "She was climbing that ladder, fell, and hit her head."

Deidre stared at the ladder behind Mrs. Knox. The housekeeper barely managed climbing the staircase. Why would she attempt to climb a steep ladder?

"Is there any family besides Wendy?" Nate asked.

"Wendy's father lives in town," Emerson said. "I'll have one of my men ride into town and notify him and Dr. Jennings."

"I'd have him ask the sheriff to come out," Deidre said. "In case it wasn't an accident."

Her grandfather's bushy eyebrows rose. "Why do you suspect foul play?"

"I have an active imagination," she excused. "It comes from telling stories to my young cousins."

"We should let the doctor determine how she died," Nate said. "I'm sure her death was from natural causes. No one had any motive for harming Mrs. Knox."

"Motive?" her grandfather asked.

"A reason for killing her," Nate said. "It's something lawyers look for when a crime has been committed."

"What crime?" Her grandfather looked from Nate to Deidre. "She fell, hit her head, and died. Keep your suspicions to yourself. I don't want my guests to become worried over nothing. People die every day. I'm going to die someday."

"As a lawyer, I stick to facts," Nate said.

"Pardon me for having a theory based on observation." Deidre crossed her arms and headed across the room for the garden door. The flowers were blooming and offered a sense of tranquility that was in battle with her emotions. Too often she had been countered by a male of her species, her own opinions dismissed without discussion. She turned at the sound of the wheelchair. Nate was turning her grandfather around so he could take him out.

Something drew her attention to the portrait of her mother over the fireplace. She gasped in horror. "Come here! You'll want to see this." Her voice trembled, and she fought tears welling in her eyes.

"What is it?" Her grandfather motioned for Nate to push him next to Deidre.

Nate looked at the portrait above the fireplace. "Who would do this?"

The initial shock had receded, and Deidre studied the damage. Someone had slashed her mother's portrait from left to right in a diagonal cut. The canvas was damaged by a deep gash, but the frame held the two parts in place. She looked around at the other portraits in the room. They were untouched. "It's the only one."

Nate put his arm around her shoulders. "I'm sorry."

Her grandfather smacked his hands on the arms of the chair. "Her face wasn't touched. I'll have it repaired."

"Thank you, Grandfather." Deidre withdrew a handkerchief from her pocket and wiped the tears from her face.

"We shouldn't touch anything," Nate said. "The sheriff will want to determine whether the damage to the portrait had anything to do with Mrs. Knox's death."

"You don't think Mrs. Knox did this?" Her grandfather waved at Hannah's portrait. "She was dusting."

"No, which makes Deidre's suspicions more likely," Nate said. "But not the facts."

Nate had agreed and yet disagreed with her. The man was utterly frustrating.

"Take me to the gallery," her grandfather ordered.

Deidre followed but paused to look back at the damaged portrait and Mrs. Knox. What had happened? And why?

Wendy stood when she saw them approaching. "Is she really dead?"

"I'm afraid so." Emerson turned to Bruce. "Have one of the men ride into town and bring back Dr. Jennings, Mr. Knox, and Sheriff Olsen."

"The sheriff?" Wendy asked. "Didn't my grandmother die of old age?"

"Likely, but someone slashed my mother's portrait." Deidre took Wendy's hand. She didn't want her to worry. She would keep her suspicions to herself. "The sheriff needs to know about the vandalism."

Wendy took a tentative step. "What should I do?"

"Why don't you go to your room and rest?" Deidre

said. "They'll bring your father here."

Wendy wiped her tears with the handkerchief Nate had loaned her.

"I'm sorry," her grandfather said. "I valued your grandmother and the care she took in running my household. She will be sorely missed."

"Thank you, sir." Wendy rushed from the room.

Her grandfather slumped in his chair. He looked exhausted. "Bruce, wheel me back into my room. I'm tired."

Deidre sat on the bottom step Wendy had vacated. "Why do you think someone did it?"

Nate sat beside her. "The portrait is old. It could have torn…"

"I'm not talking about the portrait. I'm talking about Mrs. Knox."

"The two may not be related," he said.

"Or Mrs. Knox surprised whomever was damaging the portrait, and he killed her."

Nate's eyebrows rose. "What evidence points to murder? She struck her head in a fall."

"Mrs. Knox did not climb any ladder." What about the blood? "Someone slammed her against the table."

He looked worried. "You have an unhealthy affinity for the morbid."

Did she? "If it is murder, Sheriff Olsen won't be much help." She rested her hand against her cheek. "We may have to do our own investigation if we want to find out the truth."

"What investigation?" he asked. "As far as I can tell, no crime has been committed but a torn portrait."

"What about my stolen purse and the cupid falling on you? And what if Uncle Logan's broken leg wasn't an accident? Too many things have happened for them not to be related."

"We don't want to jump to any conclusions and worry the others," he said. "Let's see what the doctor and sheriff determine."

Deidre agreed with not alarming the others. Nate needed facts and evidence. Voicing her opinion might also alert the killer. Was damaging the portrait a message? But what message?

Chapter Thirteen

Nate had tried to downplay Deidre's speculations. Some of the things she had voiced could be true, but they had no evidence. Yet. She had been upset when she saw her mother's damaged portrait, but she had not become hysterical. He admired her courage, but he needed to temper her curiosity with caution. If someone was out to do her harm, and he was sure she was the target, not him, he needed to protect her. She had gone to check on Wendy while he guarded the library.

Sheriff Olsen arrived with Dr. Jennings, a man who was settling into middle age with a touch of gray in his dark hair and a few lines around his eyes. He looked at Emerson who had joined them and shook his head. "I don't like your pallor, Mr. Kinsman. Let me have a look at you."

"I'm not the one dead."

"The dead can wait. Let's make sure you don't join them." He motioned for Bruce to push Emerson to his room. He turned to Nate. "I'll be with you in a minute."

"Who found the body?" Sheriff Olsen asked.

"Wendy Knox," Nate said. "Mrs. Knox's granddaughter."

The sheriff looked around the gallery. "Where is Wendy?"

"She's upset. She's in her room," Deidre said as she walked toward them. "Her father is with her."

"I'll wait to talk to them," the sheriff said. "Where are the other guests?"

"Sleeping," Nate said.

"Why aren't you asleep?"

"I'm an early riser." Nate pointed at Deidre. "We were having breakfast when we heard Wendy scream. She said her grandmother was dead. Mr. Kinsman joined us, and we found Mrs. Knox on the floor in the library."

The sheriff squinted. "Aren't you the lawyer who reported a theft in town?"

"Nate Burroughs and this is Deidre Pierce," he introduced again. "We met on Monday."

"I had my bag stolen," Deidre said. "Did you find it? It had embroidered flowers on it."

"You embroidered them yourself." The end of his mustache twitched. "I did not find it."

"That's odd because the books inside my bag showed up here in the library," she said.

"The library is supposed to have books." The sheriff looked confused.

"They were my books." Deidre emphasized each word. "The stolen ones."

Sheriff Olsen's mustache twitched twice. "If the books were returned, doesn't that mean they were only borrowed?"

Was the sheriff joking? "The thief did not have permission to borrow her books," Nate said.

"If he returned them, they aren't stolen." The sheriff wiped his hands against each other as if the matter was dismissed.

She released a huff of air. "I think it's odd they showed up here."

"We're not worried about the books," Nate

interrupted. "We're worried about Mrs. Knox. Did she die of natural causes, an accident, or did someone harm her?"

Sheriff Olsen squinted again. "Why would someone harm an old woman?"

"An attack is one of the possibilities." Nate stepped closer. "I'd be happy to help any way I can to resolve the incident."

"We don't have an *incident*, and I don't think an old woman's death requires a lawyer," Sheriff Olsen said. "This is a peaceful town. We don't want any trouble with foolish speculations by outsiders."

Nate threw up his hands and joined Deidre who had retreated to the staircase and was leaning on the railing. "I'm liking this man less and less."

"Join the club," Deidre said. "He certainly doesn't like women."

He rested his wounded leg on the bottom step. "I don't think he likes lawyers either."

Dr. Jennings closed the door to Emerson's room and walked across the gallery toward them. He looked around. "Where's the body?"

"Follow me." Nate led the way to the library.

Deidre followed with the doctor, but the sheriff stopped her at the doorway. "This might not be pleasant."

"I've already seen the body." Deidre turned to the doctor. "I worked for Dr. Roe Greystone as a nurse. He was a battlefield surgeon during the war."

"Any doctor who served during the war has good credentials, and I can always use the help of a nurse," Dr. Jennings said. "Come along."

"How is Mr. Kinsman?" Nate asked.

140

"He needs to rest." Dr. Jennings turned to the sheriff. "I don't want you questioning Mr. Kinsman until later. I gave him something to sleep."

"If her death was from natural causes, I won't have to question anyone." Sheriff Olsen looked in Nate's direction.

Dr. Jennings knelt by the body as the others circled him.

"Looks like she fell and hit her head," the sheriff said. "She has blood on her forehead."

"There's blood on the table, too." Nate pointed at the stain on the wooden surface.

"Let me examine the body and determine cause of death before you speculate on how she died." The doctor felt her arms, looked at her eyes, and examined her head.

The sheriff looked around. "How could someone read all these books?"

"One at a time," Deidre said.

Nate had never known a woman who invited a fight, but Deidre was not backing down from Sheriff Olsen.

His mustache twitched, but he said nothing. The sheriff picked up the feather duster. "What's this?"

"Mrs. Knox was dusting."

Sheriff Olsen ran his finger along the dusty shelf. "She wasn't very good at her job."

Deidre's eyes narrowed as she stared at the sheriff.

"You'll want to see this." Nate led the sheriff away to the damaged portrait.

"It's ripped," he stated the obvious.

"It wasn't ripped last night," Deidre said. "Don't you think the two are connected?"

The sheriff looked from the damaged portrait to the body. "You think Mrs. Knox ripped it?"

Her jaw dropped. "No."

Nate placed his hand on Deidre's back. This was not the time nor place for a scene. "The man can't see past his nose," he whispered.

She relaxed against his hand.

The sheriff walked from the fireplace to the body. "How did she die, Dr. Jennings?"

"Nothing is broken, but her forehead is cut and swollen," Dr. Jennings said. "The blow caused bleeding in the brain and killed her."

The sheriff climbed the lower steps on the ladder and jumped forward, nearly falling into the table. "I conclude she fell from this ladder and struck her head against the table. That makes Mrs. Knox's death an accident." He removed his handkerchief and wiped the bloodstain from the surface of the oak table. "She was old and clumsy."

"What about my mother's portrait?" Deidre pointed toward the fireplace.

"Anyone could have done the damage any time during the night." The sheriff pushed the ladder along the rows of bookshelves until it reached the fireplace and stopped. "Or Mrs. Knox was on the ladder dusting the portrait and tore the painting when she lost her balance."

"Then how did she get from the portrait to where she fell?" Deidre asked.

"The ladder moves." He demonstrated by climbing on the lower rungs and pushing himself from the portrait's location to the body of Mrs. Knox. "She lost her grip, fell, and hit the table."

"Accident? She was too old to climb ladders especially high enough to dust my mother's portrait." Deidre pointed toward the body. "It's more than ten feet from the portrait to where Mrs. Knox struck her head. And if she fell from the rungs, wouldn't she have struck the back of her head?"

"I'd keep your speculations to yourself," Sheriff Olsen said. "We wouldn't want any hysterics from the other women."

"You don't believe Mrs. Knox could have been murdered?" Deidre asked.

"We don't have killers in Kinsman, young lady," Sheriff Olsen said. "We're a peaceful town."

"But you have a thief, or did I imagine my bag being stolen?"

"It could show up like your books did," the sheriff said.

Nate had seen the expression on Deidre's face before. He had been the recipient. The sheriff was oblivious to the storm brewing. He turned her toward the body. "Let's see if the doctor has found anything more."

Dr. Jennings closed his bag. "Sorry to disappoint you, son. She struck her head and died." He stood. "I'll have Mr. Kinsman's men move the body to town. Mr. Knox can make funeral arrangements."

"I'll let him know." Sheriff Olsen followed the doctor out of the library.

Deidre crossed her arms and released a huff. "He thinks Mrs. Knox's death was an accident."

"He could be right." Nate didn't want her to jump to a wrong conclusion.

"You don't believe me either?" She knelt by the body.

"What are you doing?" He glanced at the open door.

"Her skirt is bunched on one side."

He paced back and forth. "I don't think she's going

to care how she looks."

She patted Mrs. Knox's pockets. "Her keys are missing."

"Maybe Wendy took them. Didn't she take the keys to your mother's room?"

"She took those two keys off the ring when Mrs. Knox was asleep. Wendy said her grandmother always carried keys to the rooms that were no longer used."

"Not anymore." He liked to write down facts and mull them over. He withdrew a notebook from his pocket and wrote down *missing keys, torn or cut portrait, blood on table, and steep ladder.*

Deidre peered over his shoulder. "What are you writing?"

"Facts. You might call them clues."

"Then you agree we should investigate and find out the truth."

"The sheriff isn't going to like us asking a lot of questions and scaring the other guests."

Her dimples deepened. "Then we'll be discreet."

Did she want him to treat the accident like a crime? He didn't want to dismiss her outright. She could be right.

"Let's *pretend* we're not investigating Mrs. Knox's death so we don't alert anyone who may be involved," he said. "A lawyer waits and listens for someone to reveal the truth."

"I can do that."

Nate withheld his opinion. Deidre was not the sort of person to hold her tongue.

Chapter Fourteen

Everyone else thought the death of Mrs. Knox was an accident, and Nate would stick to facts, but Deidre had her own theories. Would the housekeeper climb a ladder, and where were her keys?

She hurried to the servants' quarters and found Wendy in the hallway tying her bonnet. Her eyes were puffy, and she handed Deidre a wadded handkerchief.

"Please return this to Mr. Burroughs. My father and I are going to town to make arrangements."

Deidre tucked the handkerchief into her pocket. "Let me know when the funeral is. I want to pay my respects."

Wendy took her hands. "You barely knew her."

"I remember she was kind to me when I was a child." She hugged her. "Did you take your grandmother's keys from her pocket? I couldn't find them."

Wendy patted her own pocket. "No, but I have mine."

Her father stood in the doorway. "Are you ready, Wendy?"

She nodded. "Why would someone take useless keys?"

"Does anyone else but you know they're useless?" Deidre asked.

"Some of the older servants and you." She shrugged. "Most people don't care as long as they have a key to their room."

"Then there are two sets of keys to every lock."

"For the guests' rooms, but I have the only keys to any room that stores anything of value, and Grandma had keys to storage rooms and the third-floor bedrooms."

Keys to her mother's room. "May I see your keys?"

Wendy hesitated but handed her a key ring shaped like a triangle.

"Isn't your grandmother's key ring round?"

"Yes." Wendy nodded.

Deidre returned the key ring. "One more thing. Would your grandmother climb the ladders in the library?"

"I caught her once trying, but she couldn't lift her leg to the first rung. Why?"

"Just curious." She pointed toward the door. "Go now and take care of your grandmother."

Wendy and her father exited out the back door from the servants' quarters. Deidre headed for the dining room. Her cousins had finally risen and were sipping coffee and eating biscuits and gravy Cook had prepared.

Bruce rolled Emerson into the room. His color looked better. "Mrs. Knox died this morning," he announced. "She fell in the library and hit her head."

"The sheriff said it was an accident," Nate said as he looked at Deidre.

She kept her eyes downcast. Nate was right. It was better everyone thought Mrs. Knox's death wasn't a murder, especially the killer.

"We are saddened by her death and will pay our respects in the future," her grandfather said with a catch in his voice.

"She was a maid," Bart said. "Let the servants show

their respect for one of their own."

"She was the housekeeper," Deidre defended as she looked at the others. "She was kind to me when I lived here, and her granddaughter works for Grandfather. I would think we could show our appreciation for everything she did."

"Are we to sit around all day in mourning?" Faith asked.

"For once you are right, Faith," her grandfather said. "We cannot spend the traditional time mourning when the week is rushing by and soon our time together will end. We must make the most of the moments we have together. I planned a game of croquet at noon, and it will go forward. I expect everyone to participate."

Wilma clapped her hands. "I love playing games."

"I prefer to win." Bart leaned back into his chair.

Roland turned from examining a decorative vase on the sideboard. "Do you plan on cheating?"

"I don't have to cheat," Bart said. "Especially against you, little brother."

Deidre slipped out into the gallery as the others ate. The death of Mrs. Knox had been a slight inconvenience to them and nothing more. She had waited long enough to explore her mother's room. She headed for the stairs.

"Where are you going?" Nate asked from behind her.

She jumped at the sound of his voice. "I'm going to the third floor." She showed him the two keys Wendy had given her. "I want to do some exploring before the game begins."

"I think I should go with you considering there may be a killer in the house," he said.

"You don't believe Mrs. Knox was murdered." But

if the housekeeper's death wasn't an accident, she didn't want to put herself in a dangerous situation. "Come along. You can help search."

He favored his leg slightly but managed the stairs better than before.

Deidre stopped at an alcove in the hallway and lit a candle inside a glass case before they climbed the narrow staircase at the end of the hall. Dust coated the steps, and cobwebs decorated the corners. This part of the house had been home to children and servants and lacked any amenities reserved to impress guests. The hallway had no carpet runner, and a layer of soot covered the sconces on the plaster walls. Candles had not been replaced and several were burned down to stubs.

Nate ran his finger along a side table where a short candle in a brass holder was placed next to an empty vase. "Looks like nobody has been up here in years." He opened the glass door on Deidre's lantern and lit the candle.

She lowered her lantern toward the floor. "Is that a footprint?"

He knelt and examined the mark in the dust. "I think you're right."

"I know I heard footsteps above my room." She crossed the hallway and inserted the key into the nursery room she had occupied as a child. "I don't know what to expect. I'm afraid I'll be disappointed."

"I waited too long to read my father's letters. You may find nothing, but if she left you a letter or note, stepping inside is worth it."

She pushed on the door, but it was stuck against the frame. "The wood has swelled."

"Allow me." He handed her his candle. He rammed

the wooden surface with his shoulder, and the door suddenly gave way, and he stumbled inside.

He crashed into something. She lifted the lantern and waved it in the air. He was sprawled on the floor. A small rocking horse lay on its side.

"Are you all right?"

He sat with his knee in his hands. "What did I hit?"

She pointed at the wooden horse. "Rocky."

"It felt like a rock."

She placed the lights on a table and pulled back the curtains in the window, securing them with braided cords. Sunlight streamed into the room.

Nate rose slowly to his feet and righted the wooden horse. He patted its yarn mane. "Good boy."

Deidre handed him his candle and took her own lantern. She walked around the room. Her movements caused fine particles to fly up from the furnishings, and she sneezed. She ran her finger along the edge of the bed frame and left a clean mark. "I should have brought a rag."

He searched his pockets.

She retrieved his handkerchief from her pocket. "Wendy returned this." She ran it over several pieces of furniture, causing more dust particles to rise and float in the beams of sunlight. She sneezed again.

"Maybe you should send a maid up here to clean," he said.

She wasn't ready to allow a stranger into her past world. "This was my room." A pink-and-white quilt covered a child's bed to her left. A small white dresser had contained her clothes. She opened a drawer and found it empty. A braided rug covered the floor, and on the far side was a red toy box. She lifted the lid. A box of building blocks and a bilboquet remained inside.

A wave a sadness washed over her. Few memories remained. "I took all my clothes and toys with me when I moved to Ohio to live with Uncle Logan. I didn't leave much behind."

He picked up a wooden cube. "You didn't take your blocks?"

"I had outgrown them."

He examined the bilboquet. "What about the cup and ball?"

"I broke it." She showed him the damage. "You can't catch the ball without a string."

He returned the broken toy to the chest.

In the corner was a small table. A teapot rested in the center with tiny plates and cups placed in front of two chairs. "I left the tea set so we could enjoy it when I visited." She sniffled as her lip trembled. She was determined not to cry. "I never returned until this week."

Nate looked worried. "Is it too difficult to see all this?"

"I want to remember." She pushed the rocking chair. "My mother would wrap me in my favorite blanket and read to me while she rocked me to sleep. I felt so safe and loved. I thought I forgot all this, but it's like I was here yesterday."

"It was a traumatic time. Did you understand why you left your mother?"

"No. I knew she was sick, but I thought she was going to get well."

She opened the door to the adjoining room. "This door was never locked." Deidre pulled back the drapes and secured them to allow sunlight in. The bed was in the center with a dresser and writing desk on one side and a dressing table and wardrobe on the other.

She picked up a corn-husk doll from the dresser. It crumbled in her hands, and she carefully placed what remained back where she had taken it. "I remember this doll. Her name was Inga. Aunt Jem gave her to me when I met her and Uncle Logan. We had dinner at a restaurant, and I didn't eat the peas. I remember everyone being sad. When we met Uncle Logan the next time, it was almost Christmas, and I knew I would never see my mother again. She was so sick she remained in bed. I gave her Inga to keep her company."

"She placed her where she could see her." Nate looked around. "She was a loving, kind mother who would have taken care of you if she could."

His words were meant to be comforting.

"I want to believe that, but I felt guilty." Deidre picked up the comb and mirror from the dressing table. "Everyone gave me gifts and were so kind, but all I wanted was my mother."

Nate put his arm around her shoulders, and she leaned into his warm body, drawing strength from the closeness.

"I was afraid to cry. I thought they would think me ungrateful. I must have made myself forget her so I wouldn't be sad."

"You had a right to mourn, but it must have been difficult to understand death. You were a child."

Tears filled her eyes. "They told me my mother was in heaven with my father. I wanted to be in heaven with them."

"When my father was killed, I wanted to join the Union Army and fight." Nate clenched his fists. "Even when the war was over, I hated the Rebel sharpshooter who had shot him. I was angry a long time."

She pulled away and stared. "Do you think we're scarred because of losing them?"

"A little." Nate stared out the window. "The pain never entirely goes away, but you learn to live with it."

"I think it's like a wound." She searched through the clothing in the drawers in the dresser. Very little had been removed when the room was locked. "You can let it fester and destroy you or allow healing and cherish the good things."

"I hope to be a good father with what my pa and others taught me." Nate joined her. "What are you looking for?"

She opened a box on the shelf. "My mother's journal. When Grandfather mentioned it last night, I remembered her writing in it."

He opened a cupboard. "Chamber pot. Do you remember a hiding place or secret compartment?"

Deidre closed her eyes and slowly turned in a circle. "Yes." She opened her eyes and pointed at the wardrobe. She opened the doors and pulled out a drawer near the bottom.

"It's a Bible," Nate said. "Your mother wrote in the Bible? That's sacrilegious."

"Then you're not going to approve of what she actually did." She carried the large Bible to the bed and opened the black leather cover. Listed on the first page were the births and deaths of family members, including hers.

"Your mother's death wasn't recorded," he said.

"No. She probably had hidden the Bible by then."

"Why? What didn't she want anyone to know?"

She flipped to the center. A rectangle had been

carved out of the pages, and another book was hidden inside.

His mouth dropped to his chin. "That is worse than writing in a Bible."

"I knew you wouldn't approve." She removed the leather-bound journal and opened the cover. A letter fell to the bed. She flipped through a few pages. "She began writing in this before she married. Sometimes she wrote in it every day, and other times it would be months before I saw her take it from her hiding place. She said that someday I could read it and learn about her life."

"Then it's good you came and found it." Nate showed her the envelope he had retrieved from the blanket. "This is from a law firm."

"Uncle Logan said my mother gave him all the legal papers before she died. When is that dated?"

He opened the letter. "January 6, 1855."

"My father was killed mid-January." She leaned over his arm. "What does it say?"

"Something about an investigation into Lewis Smith. He had debts for more than three thousand dollars, had taken bribes from businessmen, and had fathered at least two illegitimate sons by different mothers." He whistled. "Your parents could have used this as a reason for a divorce."

"My father's death made it unnecessary." She stared out the window. She had never known Derek Pierce. Lewis Smith had taken her father from her.

Nate handed her the letter. "It proves your parents wanted to marry."

She gave it back. "You keep it and add it to the other legal papers Uncle Tyler is keeping."

He tucked the letter into the pocket inside his coat.

She clutched the journal to her chest. "You've studied criminal cases. Why do people resort to violence to solve problems? It's so futile."

"For a variety of reasons. Some people are filled with pain and disappointment. It consumes them until it turns to anger and violence, and they lash out at helpless victims to ease their anguish. Only it doesn't work." He turned away. "Prisons and cemeteries are filled with men who gave in to their darker emotions and took the lives of others."

She turned the pages of the journal. She stopped when she saw a familiar name. "She mentions Derek Pierce." She flipped through several more pages. "This is about me and goes on for years." She found a familiar date. "This was written the day I left."

Logan came for my little girl today. I couldn't even get out of bed, but she kissed me good-bye and gave me Inga. She thinks she will visit, but I won't last the winter. All my strength goes with her. I miss her terribly, but I know Logan and Jem will take care of her. That gives me the peace to let go.

She searched for the final page. *The morphine no longer eases the pain, and I long for eternal peace. Logan wrote that Deidre is making friends. I regret we were never the family we had hoped to be. I've made peace with God and hope I'll see my beloved Derek soon.*

"You're not going to have time to read it before the croquet match." Nate joined her at the window. "It looks like the others are heading out to the field. Why don't I make your excuses, and you can read your mother's journal?"

"No. Grandfather wants everyone present." She placed the book inside the Bible and closed it. "I'll read it later."

He lifted the Bible. "Let's put this in your room in a safe place."

"Why? It's a family Bible I found."

"Your dimples deepen when you lie." He raised one eyebrow as if worried. "I don't know whether to admire your deviousness or be alarmed."

She locked the door to the nursery before leading the way to the second floor.

Annabelle was knocking on Charlie's door.

He stepped out into the hall. "I was reading."

"It's time for the croquet game." Annabelle turned to Deidre. "Where have you two lovebirds been?"

"I found my mother's Bible in her room." Deidre flipped open to the list of births and deaths while Nate held it. "Mother recorded your name here."

Annabelle looked at the page. "It doesn't have my parents' dates of death."

"No, she died before they did," Deidre said. "I'll add them later. We wouldn't want to be late for the game, and I need my bonnet." She unlocked her door and took the Bible from Nate. "I won't be long."

"I can't play in the sun without something to shade my face," Annabelle called out as she hurried down the hallway.

Deidre searched her room for a good hiding place. She placed the Bible in the bottom drawer of the dresser and covered it with a shawl. She grabbed her wide-brimmed bonnet and locked her door.

Charlie strolled down the hall and joined Annabelle and James waiting by the staircase.

Nate locked his door. He had removed his coat but carried his bowler hat. He offered his hand.

She laced her fingers in his. "Let the games begin."
Poor Nate had a worried look on his face.

Chapter Fifteen

Nate gripped the railing as they headed down the stairs. He winced as he took a step.

Deidre stopped and looked at his leg. "Does the wound still hurt?"

He reached down and rubbed his knee. "I think I bruised my knee when I fell over your rocking horse."

A short laugh escaped. "Have you always been so accident prone?"

Was she serious? "Never." If the series of injuries were a warning to avoid Deidre, he planned to ignore them. He escorted her through the parlor and out to the yard beyond the flowers.

A canopy protected Emerson in his wheelchair. Pitchers of lemonade, cider, and water were placed on a table along with sandwiches, fruit, and pastries for lunch. The others had already served themselves.

The women were dressed alike in lightweight day gowns and broad-brimmed bonnets. The men had discarded their coats.

Two stakes had been driven into the ground with nine wickets arranged in a double-diamond pattern across the grass that had been recently mowed by the sheep who grazed in different fenced sections on the property. Six balls were lined up for the players.

"Are we playing partners or singles?" Bart asked.

"We are playing my rules," Emerson said. "It's a

variation of doubles, but no husbands and wives on the same team. You can keep score, Mr. Burroughs." Emerson handed him a small notebook. "One point for passing through a wicket and two points for hitting an opponent's ball."

Nate didn't like being sidelined. "I don't mind playing."

"I don't need to know your character." Emerson didn't invite argument. "Let's begin. Put the balls in that large bag and let the ladies draw the team color."

Nate did as he was instructed.

Annabelle stepped up to the bag and turned her head as she reached into the duffle bag, felt around, and withdrew the blue ball. "What does that mean?"

"Blue goes first." Emerson pointed at the stake with bands of colors painted on it that matched the balls' colors.

Wilma withdrew the black ball, and Faith chose the orange ball.

"I don't want to go last," Faith said.

"That's the most strategic position," Wilma said. "Do you want to trade?"

Faith clutched her orange ball. "No."

Deidre chose the green ball.

"Now put those four balls into the bag and let the men draw their partners," Emerson said.

Charlie was paired with Faith, Bart with Annabelle, James with Wilma, and Roland with Deidre. Nate wrote each team down in his notebook.

"Let the women go first, and then the men can take their turns," Emerson announced. "You go first, Annabelle."

"I'm not sure what to do." Annabelle looked at

James. "I wish you were my partner, darling."

"Don't complain, dearest," James said. "Your grandfather is watching your behavior. Don't give him any reason to judge you lacking."

Annabelle glanced at Emerson who was watching his grandchildren, his fingertips steepled.

"I'm not sure of the rules," Charlie said. "Is there a manual I can read?"

"Have Faith show you," Roland said. "She's very competitive."

Faith stuck out her tongue at her husband. "You're going to regret those words."

Annabelle placed her ball in front of the stake. She stood to the side and swung her mallet. The ball barely made it through the first wicket, giving her another shot. She passed through the second wicket but swung and missed, leaving her ball in a dangerous position in front of the second wicket.

"That's great," Bart said. "I'm paired with the worst player. It's not fair."

Nate watched Emerson's reaction. What did he think about their conversations? His eyebrow rose a bit, and his lips twitched. How was he judging them? What did he respect in others? He had been a tightfisted businessman who showed little compassion or affection even to his family. Did he admire the same traits?

Wilma was next and hit Annabelle's ball. She sent it flying off to the left before hitting her ball toward the third wicket. "And that is how it's done."

"You should remember who holds the purse strings," Bart said. "Maybe I won't take you to New York City to shop."

Maybe? Nate made a notation in his scorebook.

When would Bart tell his wife there would be no shopping trip?

Wilma turned to Bart. "It's a game. You don't have to win at everything."

"You know I don't like to lose." Bart's tone had an edge of a threat.

"Games are meant to be fun." Wilma headed for the refreshment table.

"It's more fun if you win," Bart said.

Emerson squinted at his eldest grandson and pursed his lips. He didn't look pleased.

Deidre took her shot and, without any balls in the way, made it through the third wicket.

"Good job, cousin," Charlie said.

"You're on my team," Faith complained. "You don't cheer for our competitors." She lined her ball up and struck it through the two wickets and chose to knock Wilma's black ball with a thud. "Here goes your ball." She sent it flying. "That's two points for me."

"Are you having fun, my dear?" Bart asked his wife.

Wilma scowled and moved toward her ball, which had passed Annabelle's blue ball.

Faith hit her ball toward the third wicket but failed to go through it.

"Now it's the men's turn," Emerson said.

Bart lined up his shot and managed to get it near the third wicket.

James hit Bart's ball and chose to hit his ball through the third wicket and toward the center.

"I would have hit Deidre's ball if I had your shot," Bart said.

"Bragging about what you would have done doesn't net results." Roland hit the green ball at the black ball.

James groaned as his ball went flying, and Roland advanced through the fourth wicket.

Charlie took his time placing his mallet and overshot the wicket. "I must have miscalculated the angle."

"What calculations? You swing the mallet and hit the ball," Faith complained. "We're going to lose."

As the game progressed, tempers flared and complaints increased with the heat. Had Emerson chosen noon to play for a reason?

"I'm getting a blister." Wilma extended her hand. "Look."

"You have a dozen gloves," Bart said. "Why didn't you wear a pair?"

"It's too hot to wear gloves outside."

"Try not to grip the handle so tightly." Deidre swung her mallet loosely back and forth.

"I'm barely touching it," Wilma said. "My hands are more delicate than yours."

"I'm sure yours aren't as delicate as mine," Faith said.

Deidre examined her palms. "My calluses keep my hands from blistering."

"Calluses? That's dreadful. You should dip them in hot wax," Faith said. "A lady is known by the condition of her hands."

"I like mine to be useful," Deidre said. "I've earned every callus."

"Does she really have calluses?" Emerson asked Nate in a whisper.

"She worked on a canal boat," Nate said. "I bet she had splinters, too."

"You think that's admirable?" He sounded shocked.

"I respect a woman who isn't afraid to work and

doesn't sit around waiting to be rescued." He meant it. "She does the rescuing."

Emerson stared at Deidre. "Who does she rescue?"

"Those who can't rescue themselves," Nate said.

"And you don't mind?"

Nate's gaze rested on Deidre. "I plan to help her."

Emerson looked confused. "Why?"

"I once thought women were beneath a man's notice, but they are capable of so much more than we allow. We're fools to think ourselves superior."

"You sound like an old man who realizes he wasted time ignoring the things in life that mattered," Emerson said.

Nate took that as a compliment. "I'm glad I've learned the lesson before growing old."

Emerson grunted.

Roland was the first to reach the stake and pointed at Bart. "I won! I finally beat you. How does it feel coming in second?"

Bart looked down at Annabelle. "Maybe if I had a different partner, I would have won."

Annabelle burst into tears. "It's not my fault. I'm not good at games."

"You're not good at anything," Bart said.

"That's not very chivalrous." Deidre offered a handkerchief, but Annabelle had her own. "You'll improve your skills with practice."

She looked at her husband. "James doesn't like to play games."

"I did not have a frivolous childhood," James said. "I started working when I was ten. It's my labor that allows you to enjoy nonsense like lawn games."

"When I inherit my share of Grandfather's money, I

can support you, and we can play all the games we want." Annabelle's words were answered by silence.

"That's not funny," James said after a pregnant pause. "I support you, not the other way around. I would think if you inherited anything, you'd want my advice on managing investments. After all, you have no experience in finance."

"Doesn't a husband have the right to control his wife's wages, property, and children?" Roland looked at Nate.

"In the past a married woman had no control over any property she owned before the marriage and couldn't acquire any while married, but the New York Married Women's Property Act of 1860 gave women more rights," Nate said. "A wife can inherit money and transfer property separate from her husband, but New York overturned the guardianship of children in 1862."

Annabelle looked at James. "We don't have any children."

"When you do, your husband will decide what's best for them," Nate said. "He may need to hire out the children to work for others or learn a trade. Anything they earn will go to him."

"What about school?" Charlie asked.

"He would decide whether they continue their education," Nate said. "He makes decisions until the child turns twenty-one."

"That doesn't seem fair," Faith said. "Women give birth and raise the children. Why should a man decide what happens to them?"

"Because a man is educated and wiser about the world," Roland said. "Women are emotional and would neglect their household and children if they had too many decisions to make. Society would turn to chaos."

Wilma raised her mallet in the air. "That's not fair. Men make bad decisions, and they don't have any excuses but their own poor judgment."

Charlie looked at his sister. "I think Annabelle has good judgment."

"Nobody asked your opinion," Bart said. "Bachelor."

"He has a right to speak his mind," Annabelle said.

"This is not a good time to start a crusade." James turned on Nate. "You shouldn't have said anything about women's rights. You're not part of this family."

"Roland inquired about legal rights," Nate said. "I'm a lawyer. I told him what New York law allows."

"I don't want my wife getting any ideas." Bart crossed his arms. "I make the financial decisions in my family."

"Are your bad business decisions the reason she's wearing old clothes?" Roland asked.

Nate was standing behind Roland who suddenly ducked. He saw Bart lunge forward, heard the smack of a fist connect against his nose, felt the pain radiate, and saw his white shirt turn red as warm blood flowed from his injured body onto the once pristine fabric.

"Hey, that was a dirty trick!" Charlie raised his fists.

Roland lunged at Bart and wrestled him to the ground. Bart threw a couple of punches.

More than one woman shrieked, but it was Deidre's soothing voice Nate turned toward.

She pressed a handkerchief against his face. "Tilt your head back."

Blood flowed down his throat. "I'm drowning."

"Sit." She led him to a chair next to Emerson.

Deidre wrapped his nose with the blood-soaked handkerchief. Charlie and James were trying to break up the fight between the brothers. Faith was cheering on her husband.

"Stop this," Wilma shrieked. "It's only a game."

Emerson chuckled.

Nate turned to see a smile on Emerson's face. He was enjoying the ruckus. He looked at Nate. "Sorry about your nose."

"I've been told I'm injury prone."

"When I see evidence to the contrary, I'll apologize." Deidre borrowed a clean handkerchief from Annabelle and dropped the bloody one on the ground. "Let me find something cold to put on your face." She poured a glass of water from the pitcher on the table and brought it to him. "Put this against the side of your nose."

The cold felt good against his injury, but his pride had taken a beating. He'd learned to box under the rules of the Marquess of Queensberry while attending college. He had kept his face free from blood and broken bones. A sucker punch was embarrassing.

They watched Bart and Roland wrestle until they collapsed on the ground.

"It's time we escaped the sun. I'd like to take a nap before we dine." Emerson didn't wait for an answer as he signaled for Bruce to wheel him inside.

James and Charlie stood close enough for Nate to overhear.

"The old man is playing his cards close to his chest," James said. "I wonder what he learned from watching us play croquet."

"You don't think it was just a game?" Charlie asked.

"That wasn't a game." Annabelle took her

husband's arm. "Insults about the ladies and a brawl. They ought to be ashamed of their behavior."

"Bart and Roland have always fought," Charlie said. "They were always trying to prove who was better."

"Neither one in my opinion." Annabelle headed for the house.

Everyone but Deidre had left when Nate drank the water in his glass.

"Is it broken?"

She gently felt along the ridge. "It doesn't feel broken." She stepped to his side and stared at his profile. "But I'll have to wait until the swelling goes down to know for sure."

"I didn't realize so much blood would be spilled on this job to protect your interest." He stood and tested his balance.

"You weren't even playing croquet." Deidre looked toward the parlor door. "Did you hear James? Grandfather is sizing us up."

"I agree. But what is he looking for?"

"What do you mean?"

"Does he like Bart for taking chances or Roland for bragging? Does he prefer Charlie for reading or Annabelle for being sensitive?"

"What about me?"

"He can't find fault with you."

"You must be lightheaded." She put her arm around his waist. "You better clean up. I'll have Wendy soak the blood out of your shirt."

"I have another."

"It's only Tuesday. We're staying until Saturday."

"I hope the other games your grandfather has planned are less violent," Nate said.

"So do I," Deidre said. "I'm rather fond of your face when it isn't battered and bruised."

Fond? Maybe getting punched was worth it.

Chapter Sixteen

Dinner had been moved to four o'clock, but Deidre dressed for dinner in case time snuck up on her. She made herself comfortable on the chaise lounge by the window and read through the entries in her mother's journal, starting with her eighteenth birthday. Hannah had been lonely in Kinsman and longed to attend parties. Her father agreed to take her and her mother to New York City where he could make important political connections for his business interests, and Hannah could attend the parties and dances hosted by the residents.

She listed the men she met, how many dances they shared, and what she thought of them. A familiar name was written on the page. Lewis Smith had met her at a party where he claimed three dances. He was running for a seat in Congress and had complimented her about her ladylike manners and quiet reserve.

In the margin, her mother had written *LIE* in bold letters. Deidre flipped through the pages and noted several comments added to the writing. Hannah had edited her earlier writing, harshly criticizing the words of Lewis or her own naïve thoughts.

Lewis wouldn't have won the election without a wife, her mother had added to a page that included a happy announcement of Lewis winning his congressional seat. The writings turned darker after the marriage.

I don't know what I said to anger Lewis, but he hit me. I've never been struck by anyone, let alone by someone who claimed to love me. Hannah had written in a shaky script. *I was stunned and forgot to cry or protest. Later he apologized and insisted upon touching me. That it was his right as my husband. I feared to say no, but I couldn't fake my feelings of disgust. I pretended to be far away and scrubbed my body when I left the bed.*

A few weeks later she'd written again.

For no reason I can understand, he flies into rages, and the beatings are brutal. My body is left with bruises on my arms, back, and legs. He is careful not to mar my face and raise questions from others. My heart has died from the insults and raging complaints he heaps upon me. I can't believe I loved him. I am the most foolish of women. I believed his lies and declarations of love. But he kept this dark side well hidden from me and others.

A month later the passage was scribbled and uneven. *Lewis broke my arm, and I returned home while he was at the Capitol. I sit in my room overlooking the garden and feel safer than I have in a long time.*

Three months later she'd written again. *Lewis arrived to take me home from my safe haven at Kinsman Manor. Mother sympathizes with my pleas to remain but won't go against Father, who says it is my duty to stay with my husband. Lewis needed me to accompany him to a ball tonight. He forced me to wear a gown so immodest it shocked the other ladies and made me ashamed to be seen in public. He said I made him proud because other men envied him and wanted me in their beds. Was it a veiled threat to prostitute me? Once he was done with me, he left to be with his mistress. I hate him, but I fear him more.*

She read until a knock interrupted her. "Who is it?"

"Nate. Are you dressed?"

"You sound funny." She placed the journal inside the Bible on the bed and opened the door. Nate's nose and eyes were swollen.

"I can tell by the expression on your face you're shocked by my appearance."

"You need to put ice on it."

He lifted a bag. "Wendy brought me some."

"Is it time for dinner?" She closed the door and led him to a chair. "I need to fix my hair."

"No hurry." He looked at his watch. "We have forty-five minutes." He glanced at the door. "Shouldn't we keep that open?"

"Nobody is at this end of the hallway but Charlie." She sat at her dressing table.

He leaned his head back and placed the cloth bag on his face. "I was thinking about what James said about your grandfather testing you and your cousins. What do you think he wants to find out?"

"He wants to know more about us." She hoped. She added a few combs to her hair to hold it in place.

"But to what end? If he leaves you nothing, will you be disappointed?"

Was he worried her grandfather might leave her out of his will? "I didn't come here for any money. I wanted to celebrate Grandfather's birthday and become acquainted with my cousins."

"They're more focused on a possible inheritance than making friends."

She had to agree. "Every family has its faults, and you have to overlook them."

"Not always." He looked past her to the bed. "Have

you been reading your mother's writings?"

She lifted the journal from its hiding place. "I read about how Mother met Lewis. He was so charming and attentive before he proposed. Then he changed. He beat her."

"Why does a man hurt a woman?" Nate asked with outrage in his voice. "Especially if he loves her."

"Proclaims to love like Oscar Leland," she clarified.

He bowed his head. "Lying is bad enough, but beating a woman is far worse."

"Lewis didn't marry Hannah for love. He wanted to become a congressman, and Mother provided him with respectability he didn't possess. Once he won, he didn't worry about how he treated her."

He shook his head. "I'm sorry."

"She wanted to be loved, not used for another's ambitions." She reclaimed the chaise lounge. "The marriage was doomed from the start."

"When did she meet Derek Pierce?"

"I just read that part." She found the page. "She had been married about a year and was living in Washington City with Lewis. They had separate rooms, and he was gone most of the time. She was grateful the beatings were less frequent, and she was able to make a few friends in the city. An older woman invited her to a party, but she needed an escort."

"And Derek Pierce walked into her life." He leaned over her shoulder. "You're writing in the margins?"

"Mother did." She flipped through the pages and showed him some of the notes. "She commented on some of the things she had written earlier. Hard-earned wisdom she wanted to share."

He pointed at a page. "Why is Derek Pierce written

six times?"

"She was in love." Deidre giggled at her mother's enthusiasm. "For the first time in her life, she loved a man and he loved her. I've read this part twice."

She turned to the previous page. *"I met a man tonight who has filled my life with happiness. He works for Senator Salmon Chase. He's from Cincinnati, Ohio, and has a younger brother named Logan. I asked so many questions he must be dizzy from my inquiries. He hates his blond curls, but I long to run my fingers through his hair. His eyes are a dark brown but contain softer shades and a shot of gold. But the most wonderful trait he possesses are dimples that deepen when he smiles. And I smile in return. I never knew I could be so happy."*

She looked up. "Then she writes his name six times." She pointed at each one.

"Their romance continues through the winter months. She suspects she's pregnant." Deidre read. *"I thought Derek would be angry when I told him I was going to have his baby, but he's overjoyed. I reassured him that Lewis hasn't touched me in months, but that makes it more imperative we escape before he discovers our secret and realizes the child isn't his. Derek knows someone who can help with a divorce. We want to be together, the three of us."*

Her voice cracked. She had been wanted. She had been loved. "Then this." She showed him an article that had been cut out of a newspaper, announcing the shooting. "She doesn't write for several months."

She flipped through pages with newspaper clippings until she reached her mother's handwriting. *"Father only allowed me to return home because of my delicate condition and Mother's pleadings. He reminds me I disgraced the family. I've moved upstairs to the nursery where I've created my own world."* She turned another page. *"My daughter looks more and more like Derek with her pale hair and warm brown eyes. My heart swells every time I look at her. I'm so grateful I have a part of him with me. I don't mind that my father condemns me for my disgraceful behavior and sides with Lewis. I have taken my stance, not for me, but for Deidre. I will not reconcile with Lewis, although I don't know what I will do if Father throws us out. For now, Mother is my ally, but she gives in too easily to Father."*

"Did her father throw her out?" Nate asked.

"No." She turned several pages. This was written in 1859. *"Mother died two weeks ago. She had taken ill, and the doctor could do nothing for her. I began to pack my belongings, fearing the worst, but Father said I can stay and serve as hostess."*

"I remember sneaking out of my room and coming downstairs to watch the guests enter in their fancy gowns," Deidre said. "Mother was so beautiful. Several men proposed, but since she wasn't divorced, she couldn't accept any of them."

She read. *"My married status is a blessing in that I can remain faithful to Derek's memory. Besides, I am a terrible judge of men, or I wouldn't have married Lewis. Better to focus on Deidre. She is growing so fast. I will need to hire a tutor soon."*

"How old were you?"

She searched through the dates. "Four." She scanned several pages. "She begins to complain about unusual bleeding. The doctor said it was a woman's ailment."

"You don't have to share it with me."

"I want to share this." She turned to the last few entries. *"Lewis visited. He brought a boy with him. Freddy is about fourteen and a vicious little monster like his father. He wandered around the house, stealing items. Money and several pieces of jewelry are missing. But the worst part was when Freddy pushed Deidre down the stairs. My heart never pounded so fiercely. Luckily, she wasn't hurt. Just scared. I was so angry I slapped the boy and cut his cheek with my ring. He barely reacted. He has his father's eyes, cold as ice."*

Deidre looked up. "I was nearly six, but I don't remember being pushed down the stairs or a boy named Freddy."

"He could have been one of the sons mentioned in the letter from the law firm."

"Mother was desperate after that." She read the next page. *"I wrote to Logan about becoming Deidre's guardian and received no reply. He's in Washington working for Salmon Chase who is now the secretary of the treasury. I plan to travel to the Capitol. My cousin owns a hotel and says he can arrange a meeting with Logan. I have all the papers in order. I need him to agree. I think I can convince him if I can speak to him in person."*

"And he became your guardian."

She rose from the chair and placed the journal in its hiding place.

"You read all of it?"

She placed the Bible in the bottom drawer and closed it. "I skipped some passages and plan to read all of it when I have time, but I wanted to read the ones about Lewis and Derek first. They seemed the most important. The boy Freddy would be twenty-eight now, but I wouldn't recognize him even if he still has eyes like ice."

"The legal letter and the journal barely mention him. Your cousins are the ones with the most to gain." He touched his nose. "If I were to choose a troublemaker, Bart would be at the top of my list."

"That was an accident." She brushed his hair back and examined his face. "They have no reason to hate you. And they've made it clear I shouldn't inherit because I'm illegitimate."

"Your grandfather wouldn't have invited you if he didn't plan to include you in the will."

"I don't know whether to like him or hate him. He didn't treat my mother very nicely, and he was rude to Annabelle when she was only trying to help him. I hope he plans to include her in his will."

"Men can change." He pointed at his chest. "Even young ones."

"I do feel a little sympathy for you," she said. "First your leg, then a knee, and now your nose. If you're not accident prone, you're having a terrible run of bad luck."

"I have a history of neither. I happen to be in the wrong place at the wrong time. Let's join the others for dinner."

Deidre entered the hallway, and Nate followed.

Annabelle and James were standing by Charlie's door.

"I was giving her legal advice," Nate said in a guilty voice.

Deidre locked her door. "It was extremely good advice." Her voice boasted scandalous behavior.

Nate looked more shocked than the others.

Charlie joined them. "Did everyone have a good

time today?"

"Some more than others," Annabelle said.

"I don't think Mr. Burroughs with his numerous injuries could be having a good time." Deidre lifted his bag of ice. "Keep this on your nose."

"I'm sorry." Annabelle cringed as she stared at Nate. "No one could accuse you of having fun."

Chapter Seventeen

Nate paused by a large mirror hanging in the hallway at the top of the stairs. Who belonged to that distorted face staring back? His eyes had dark circles beneath, and his nose was swollen like a sausage.

He had hoped to impress Deidre on this trip and would horrify young children with his present features. He looked at the woman next to him. She was the beauty to his beast, and he found himself unworthy of her company. "How could they think we were having an affair when I look like this?"

"Your appearance is temporary," she said as they descended the stairs. "I remember how chivalrous you looked before all this."

"Chivalrous?"

She blushed. "You were like a beautiful apple that fell from the tree and ended up all bruised."

"Cut out the bruises, and you can still eat the fruit."

Her dimples showed. "I'll let you know if I want to take a bite."

"Why did you let your cousins think you had already eaten of the forbidden fruit?"

She laughed. "Your excuse for being in my room was ridiculous. *Legal advice?*"

"I panicked. I couldn't tell them we were discussing your mother's writings." He grabbed her hand. "You don't mind the gossip?"

"I've lived my life avoiding any misbehavior because of my parents, but they found love by embracing the scandal. Let others think what they want. I know my value."

She was precious to him.

They greeted the others assembled in the dining room, but acknowledgments were formal and short. Bruce wheeled Emerson to the head of the table. What if Deidre's grandfather didn't leave her anything? How would that affect her? She wanted to belong to a family, not be excluded, and an inheritance was a public acknowledgment of acceptance or being ostracized.

Emerson assigned new seats for dinner, and Nate was seated to the left of their host with Bart across from him.

"I'm sorry about the nose." Bart stared at his brother who was seated at the other end of the table. "But if Roland hadn't ducked, I wouldn't have hit you."

"Violence rarely solves anything." Nate placed his napkin on his lap.

"Don't you mean never?" asked Faith, who sat to Bart's right.

"Men solve problems with their fists," Bart said. "I was showing my brother who is the better man."

"I prefer to use my mind." Charlie seated Wilma next to Nate and took the seat next to her.

"No one ever won a war with their mind," Bart mocked.

"War isn't a solution," Nate said. "It forces leaders to compromise, which they should have done before violence erupted. Because our founding fathers ignored the issue of slavery, it festered."

"But President Lincoln freed the slaves with the

Emancipation Declaration," Wilma said.

"That proclamation freed slaves in the Confederacy but could only be enforced if the Union conquered those states in battle," Nate said. "The Thirteenth Amendment freed all slaves in the United States, but eleven years later, the hate still festers, and war may erupt again."

"I pray not," Faith said. "I know plenty about the conflict. My father died at Antietam. What do you know about war, Mr. Burroughs?"

"My father was killed by a Rebel sharpshooter months before the war ended," Nate said as a potato and broccoli soup was served.

"That's awful," Charlie said. "Sort of like a man hitting another who wasn't looking."

Charlie's comparison made Bart rise from his chair. "I apologized, didn't I?"

"Apologies have been given and accepted." Emerson turned to Nate. "What was your father's reason for fighting in the war?"

"He wanted to end slavery," Nate said. "And he didn't want the burden to be placed on young men alone."

"His life made a difference," Charlie said.

"Slaves were given their freedom and right to vote with the Fifteenth Amendment, but the Amnesty Act restored civil rights to Southerners no matter what they did during the war," Nate said. "Why should the sharpshooter who shot my father have his life restored when my father is dead?"

"Did you want him punished?" Charlie asked.

"I wanted him dead, but I was a boy. As a lawyer, I wanted him to earn his citizenship, to prove he realized slavery was wrong and that power was not their exclusive right. Too many Southerners are terrorizing former slaves now that they have their positions restored."

"But don't you believe that some men will never be equal to those who deem themselves rightful leaders?" Bart asked.

"And what makes them leaders?" Nate asked. "Men with money and power control the laws, businesses, and can influence public opinion to favor their decisions. It breeds abuse and corruption. It encourages violence and bullying to maintain power."

"Science supports race separation and that authority should be concentrated to those few who have the intelligence to make decisions," Charlie said. "Have you read *Hereditary Genius* by Galton? I just reread it."

"Yes, but he did not take into consideration the environment in which the possible genius is raised," Nate said. "A successful father can pave the way for his son. A lack of education suppresses a genius. Look at women. They do not have the same opportunities as men when it comes to schooling."

The soup was removed, and chicken fricassee with rice was served.

Deidre buttered a roll and raised her voice to be heard. "Do you believe a woman could be a genius?"

"I hope so," Nate said. "Her children would be exceptional."

"But women have not evolved like men," Charlie said. "You need to read *The Descent of Man, and Selection in Relation to Sex* by Darwin. Males differ from females in many traits. Males will compete for a female, and traits that give him an advantage will advance the race."

"But doesn't a woman determine what traits in a man she desires?" Deidre looked at the other women.

"That's why a man eliminates his competition," Bart said with a small jab of his fist.

"To the victor go the spoils." Emerson raised his glass.

"And why not? Men of valor conquer others to become the leaders," Bart said. "Kings of Europe were ordained by God to rule."

"That's a circular argument." Nate stabbed a piece of chicken. "Did God choose them, or did they use their military strength to take what they wanted and, by victory, claim it was God's will?"

"You don't believe some men are superior to others?" Charlie asked.

"All men possess talents and abilities," Nate said. "But is a man who sings better than a man who makes barrels? Is a lawyer better than a carpenter?"

"A man's worth is determined by how much he is paid." Bart rubbed his fingers together.

"But who determines that worth?" Nate felt like he was in a courtroom and warmed to his subject. "Like the kings of Europe, the rich pay themselves more and keep the poor struggling to earn a dollar a day. I've defended men who were maimed on the job and lost everything because they could no longer work. Women and children work in factories that leave them ill and crippled, but the owners don't care as long as they can replace them."

"They're lucky to have jobs," Bart said. "And a man who is smart enough to make money should keep it all."

"And what if he makes a mistake?" Nate had not asked Bart about his investment. "I know of men who invested in a company that turned out to be a scam. All the investors lost their money. Should he and his family suffer because of another's deception?"

"Was that the Riverton Mining Company?" Emerson asked in a clear voice.

Nate had not planned to reveal the company, but Emerson knew about his grandson's folly. Bart swiped his hand over his beard.

"The Riverton Mining Company?" Wilma glared at her husband. "That's the company you invested in. Is this true? Are we penniless?"

"I'll make the money back," Bart said.

"With what? You invested all your money and the little I had in that company." Wilma looked at Nate. "Are you sure it was a scam?"

Nate nodded. "Yes. We're trying to locate the men who sold the stock, but they used aliases."

"We're ruined." Wilma sobbed and used her napkin to wipe her tears.

Bart rose. "Look what you've done." He strode around the head of the table, bumping into Bruce. "Get out of my way."

Bart grabbed Wilma as she rose. "I swear I'll make it right."

"You lied about your business success?" Roland asked from the other end of the table. Everyone turned their attention to the couple.

"It was a minor setback." Bart seated Wilma and returned to his place.

"You have an excuse for everything," Roland said. "You wasted the money Father left us."

"No one forced you to invest with me."

"You guaranteed a profit." Roland slammed his fist on the table.

"If you knew anything about business, you would know it's unpredictable." Bart wiped his brow. "A man must take risks to make any gains."

"That's true." James nodded. "A man can make a fortune one day and lose it all the next."

"But a good businessman knows to diversify and not invest all his wealth into one venture." Emerson looked at Nate. "What have you invested in, Mr. Burroughs?"

"I invest in myself. I earn a modest salary, which has taught me to live within my means. I take care of my mother and employ a couple to run the farm where we live."

"Do you have plans to marry?" Emerson asked.

Nate made sure not to look at Deidre. "Marriage is a distant dream, but someday I hope a woman would look upon me favorably and become my wife and the mother of my children."

"Do you plan to have a large family, Mr. Burroughs?" Emerson asked.

Why was Emerson asking him personal questions? "I will take what God grants me."

"You do not give God credit for choosing a king, but you give him credit for children?" Bart asked. "Where is your logic?"

"I understand how a man can use violence to claim power, but I do not know how a child is created from nothing," Nate said. "I consider it a miracle, and therefore, God receives the credit."

"Well said," Emerson said. "Do you consider yourself a good lawyer?"

"I've won a majority of my cases, and I've learned from my mistakes." Nate looked at Deidre. "I plan not to repeat them."

"Would you give a man a great deal of money at one time or a small amount over time?" Emerson asked.

Emerson was drilling him with questions, but to what end? He was not an heir. "It depends upon the man. If he is experienced and responsible, then he could handle a large amount of wealth, but most men need to learn how to manage small amounts first."

"You have common sense, Mr. Burroughs," Emerson said. "A rarity among young men of today. They look to science to answer questions and latch on to any idea presented. I have met idiots born to men of wealth and success, and I've met men of talent and genius born to slaves. Wealthy men give their children every advantage to succeed, but they often fail. Why is that?"

"I don't have an answer," Nate said.

"I don't either, and I'm much older than you," Emerson said. "I am fatigued and will retire. Enjoy your desserts."

The servants served baked Alaska made of yellow cake, strawberry ice cream, and meringue.

"Mr. Burroughs, what do you think Grandfather meant by asking about how much money a man can handle?" Bart's booming voice interrupted Nate's eating.

He finished a bite. "I can't read his mind."

"You should have told him with age comes responsibility," Bart said. "I can handle a great deal of money."

"You've proven otherwise!" Roland shouted.

"I think wisdom is more important." Charlie raised his fork in the air. "I've read many books on investments and how to make money."

"Yet you have nothing to show for it," Roland said.

"I make a modest income," James said. "But I think we would all benefit from any inheritance Grandfather gives us."

Bart pointed at him. "You're not a blood relative."

"But my wife is." He turned to Annabelle. "She deserves to inherit."

"It's not up to us to slice the pie." Charlie took a bite. "Or cake. Grandfather will make that decision, and so far, he doesn't seem to be in favor of any of us."

"But he liked Mr. Burroughs," Wilma said.

"I can assure you I will not inherit," Nate said. "I would caution everyone not to jump to conclusions. I'm sure your grandfather will let you know his plans in due time."

"Mr. Burroughs relies on facts and evidence." Deidre dabbed her napkin to her mouth. "But I agree. I don't think Grandfather has made up his mind yet."

"What if he doesn't write a will?" Bart asked.

"Then the county surrogate court will divide his wealth and property equally among the heirs," Nate said.

Chapter Eighteen

Sleep eluded Deidre as she considered her relatives. Dinner had been civil, but Bart dominated the conversation even though he was seated at the other end of the table. Her grandfather had known about Bart's bad investment. What did he know about the others? About her? She couldn't understand why her grandfather had asked Nate question after question.

After a delicious dessert, they had retired to the parlor, and the women appeared to warm up to her as they talked about fashion and the latest hairstyles. The men focused on their achievements before arguing over baseball teams. After a supper of leftovers, they finally agreed to retire.

Her bed was too soft, and she tried to find a comfortable position for sleep. Did the ropes beneath her mattress creak? No, the sound came from above. She strained to hear the noises she had heard the night before. Footsteps. Someone was walking around above her. She listened, trying to track the steps. Her room was located beneath her mother's old room, but nothing of value remained. She had left the rooms unlocked so they could be cleaned.

The footsteps stopped. Wood scraped against wood. Was a drawer opened? Someone was searching her mother's room. Why would they have an interest in her mother's journal? Or were they searching for something else?

She listened until the noises ceased. She relaxed against her pillow and pulled the covers up to her shoulder as she turned on her side. She needed to sleep. Mrs. Knox's funeral was tomorrow.

Her door creaked as it slowly opened. She froze. She hadn't locked her door since she was in the room. Who would be rude enough to intrude uninvited?

The draperies were pulled back, and moonlight bathed the room in soft shadows. A form, dark against the soft gray, moved toward her. She squinted through narrow slits, trying to bring the fuzzy outline into focus so she could identify her intruder. She opened her mouth to call out but hesitated. *Let him think I am asleep.*

The figure moved to the table beside her bed where she had extinguished the lamp after enjoying a couple of chapters of *Little Women*. He wore dark gloves and picked up the book she had been reading.

Should she make herself known? How would he react? She stretched out her legs beneath the blanket and groaned, hoping it would scare the man off.

He turned toward her, the moonlight illuminating his face. Only it wasn't a face. He wore a mask made from a burlap sack with large uneven stitches where the mouth should be and holes cut out for eyes that couldn't be seen in the darkness.

She sat up and screamed at the hideous sight.

He swung his hand holding the book and knocked the oil lamp on the nightstand to the wooden floor. The chimney shattered. The intruder's shoes crunched on the broken glass as he dashed out the open door.

She swung her legs over the edge of the bed but realized glass shards were scattered on the floor. She crawled to the end of the bed and slipped on her robe before running into the hallway.

Charlie stood in the opposite doorway with a book in his hand. He rubbed his eyes. "I heard a scream and a crash. Are you all right?" He wore a long robe over a nightshirt, but his feet were bare.

The book in his hand was about plants. Wrong book and no shoes. He couldn't have been the man in her room. "Did you see anyone in the hall?"

Charlie looked confused. "No."

Nate opened his door, a lit lantern in his hand. He wore trousers with the suspenders hanging to the sides, untied shoes, and an open robe. "I heard a ruckus. What happened?"

Deidre stared at the sculptured muscles of his bare chest. His tousled hair made him appear boyish, but his poor face was a rainbow of colors. She wanted to kiss him out of sympathy. And maybe something more. She shook the invading thoughts away. "A man wearing a mask entered my room and stole my book."

Nate looked at Charlie and his book.

"*Little Women*," she said. "It has a blue cover with the title in a gold-framed circle."

"We have a book thief?" Charlie clutched his book to his chest.

"A man with strange tastes," Nate said. "Are you sure he was after your book?"

"It could have been a different *book* he was after." She hoped Nate understood her hint.

"You said he wore a mask?" Nate asked.

"It was made from a burlap sack, and he looked like a scarecrow. He had on a heavy coat, floppy hat, and work gloves." She waved her hand toward her cousin.

"Charlie couldn't have changed clothes that quickly, and I didn't see anyone else in the hall until you appeared."

Nate stepped toward her room.

"There's glass on the floor," she warned. "He knocked my lamp over when I frightened him. The chimney broke."

He looked at her bare feet. "Let me clean it up." He glanced over his shoulder at Charlie. "Do you want to chaperone?"

"I don't see the need. Besides, all this commotion interrupted my reading." Charlie entered his room.

Nate looked at the closed door. "I know you can't pick your relatives, but don't you think he should be more concerned about a bachelor being in your room at night?"

"I'm more concerned about the masked man in my room." Deidre shrugged. "Charlie is an intellectual. He can't be bothered with immorality."

He looked surprised. "Whose immorality?"

"I told everyone about my illegitimacy to clear the air of rumors, but James and Annabelle likely told Charlie they saw you coming out of my room."

"I explained that." He tied his robe. "I can live with a little tarnish, but I won't have your reputation ruined because of me."

His chivalry was making her mad. "Then give me your lantern, and I'll clean up the mess myself."

He entered her room. Glass crunched beneath his shoes as he placed the light on the table.

She pointed under the bed. "Hand me my slippers, please."

He tossed them at her feet. She slipped on her footwear.

"Stay back." He removed a shovel and broom from the fireplace tools. He swept the glass and dumped it into the ash bucket.

She tightened her sash and grabbed his lantern. "Let's search upstairs."

He replaced the tools by the fireplace. "You think he's hiding up there?"

"I heard footsteps above me before he entered my room. I think he was searching my mother's room."

He looked at his robe. "Don't you think we should get dressed?"

"We've already wasted time. He's probably gone, but we should still search." She closed and locked her door. "I'm going to keep it locked at all times now. You should do the same."

"Why?"

"A cupid falls and nearly hits you, stolen books show up in the library, Mrs. Knox is murdered, my mother's portrait is cut, and now someone enters my room." She headed for the servants' stairs. "If I wasn't a logical lawyer, I'd be terrified."

Nate locked his door and caught up to Deidre on the stairs. "Are you sure Lewis Smith is dead?"

She paused on the steps. "Yes. Uncle Logan told me about his death and confirmed it. Why do you ask?"

"Your uncle Logan told me your mother considered him a threat not only to her but you. That was the main reason she sent you to live with him. If your uncle confirmed Smith's death, he may have been watching his activities over the years."

"Or Uncle Tyler did. He handled my mother's legal matters."

"Did they know about Freddy?"

"They never mentioned him." The stairs creaked beneath her feet. "Do you think Freddy is a threat? He was only a boy."

"That boy would be a man now."

They reached the third floor, and she waved the lantern around. The hallway was deserted. "Our scarecrow has disappeared."

Nate glanced back at the stairs. "He could have gone downstairs instead of up."

"Those stairs go to the ballroom in the south wing. I would watch my mother and guests from the steps."

"The thief could be a relative or a servant who knows the house."

"Wendy said there were several new workers hired the past months to help make repairs and clean for this week's events."

He stroked his chin. "Young men?"

"The men who carried in my trunk were young." Why did age matter?

"I should talk to them," he said. "Find out more about them."

Her grandfather had given the servants Wednesday morning off. "Most of them should be at the funeral tomorrow. We could talk to them then."

He opened the door to the nursery. "We?"

"I wouldn't want you to upset one of them and add to your injuries." She gasped when they entered her childhood room.

Drawers and cupboards had been left open and items moved. The adjacent room belonging to Hannah was equally disturbed. "I thought I heard the scarecrow searching the rooms before he came to my room."

"The scarecrow?" he asked.

Deidre shrugged and closed a drawer. "It's what he looked like."

"Don't change anything. Let's leave it alone and pretend we don't know it's been disturbed."

"Do you think the person will come back?"

"I think the person is looking for your mother's journal. It's the only logical conclusion. But we need to figure out who he is and why it's so important to him."

She opened the drawer she had closed. They exited, and she turned toward the staircase they had used.

She realized Nate had turned the other way and wasn't following her. "Where are you going?"

"We should check the rest of the hallway." He took the lantern from her and waved it from side to side.

"What's that?" She pointed toward the floor.

He bent down. "It's your book."

She took it from him. "Then he passed this way to the staircase leading to the kitchen and servants' quarters."

"Why did he throw your book away after stealing it?"

"*Little Women* wasn't the one he wanted."

"What do you think is so important in your mother's journal?"

"I don't know. I read the parts I skimmed over initially, but nothing seems important to anyone but me."

"Maybe he's a Verne fan and stole the wrong book."

"Do you suspect Charlie? He was barefoot."

"And the only one in the hall," he said. "Everyone is a suspect until we rule them out."

She grabbed his hand. "You'll stay close, won't you?"

He squeezed her fingers. "Of course. You should

carry the lantern in case I need to use my fists."

"You know how to fight?"

"Don't let this swollen nose fool you. Bart caught me off guard." He stopped at the end of the hallway. "Your scarecrow is long gone."

They retraced their steps to the second floor. She kept her hand in his until they reached the stairs.

"I'd like to read the journal," he said. "Maybe I can figure out why the scarecrow wants it."

Deidre unlocked her door and retrieved the Bible. "Nate, what do you think all of this means?"

"I don't know, but we need to be careful. I don't know who we can trust."

Chapter Nineteen

Nate made sure a buggy was available for the ride into town Wednesday morning for the funeral.

A family might wait three days before a burial to make sure a person who had died was not in a coma. Coffins were sometimes equipped with bells in case a deceased person awoke and needed to signal a mistake had been made. But Mrs. Knox had died in July, and no one believed she would rise from the dead.

Nate and Deidre went to the Knox home, a single-story structure in town painted white with green shutters. Flower boxes were overflowing with blooming plants. The cheerful exterior was marred by a length of black cloth draped over the doorway to signal the death of a loved one. Wendy greeted them. She wore a black blouse instead of her white one. Others wore black or gray to signify they were in mourning.

The pine box was placed on wooden supports in the parlor where the body had been washed and prepared for burial by the family. The gash on her forehead had been covered by sweeping her hair over the wound. The journey of the soul was a mystery, and superstitions were followed to avoid another death. The curtains were closed, the clocks stopped, and mirrors covered. Photographs on a table had been turned face down.

Guests brought food for the family. Deidre had brought a ham, bread, and jam from Emerson. Nate volunteered to carry the coffin along with other men who were not part of the immediate family. The pine box was taken from the home and transported by wagon to the local church in town where friends and neighbors gathered to say good-bye. Nate searched the faces of those in attendance. He didn't know which ones were servants working for Emerson and who lived in the town. He recognized the sheriff who shook hands and maintained a steady flow of conversation with those in attendance.

He nodded when he saw Nate and shook his hand. He looked at Deidre. "Are you the only member of the Kinsman family in attendance?"

"Yes," Deidre said.

Was the sheriff judging the family? "Mr. Kinsman wanted to attend, but he's too ill," Nate said. The other family members had begged off on the morning service, choosing to sleep instead.

"I knew Mrs. Knox as a child. She was kind to me," Deidre said.

He stroked his mustache. "Nice of you to show your respects. No purse with embroidered flowers has shown up, but it could. You said the books showed up in the library at the manor?"

"Yes," Nate said.

"That's a bit odd."

"We think so," Deidre added.

"We appreciate you showing your respects." The sheriff headed to the back of the church.

"You didn't say anything about the scarecrow to the sheriff," Nate said.

"He'd want proof."

After the preacher had delivered his sermon and

family spoke in tribute of their matriarch, Nate and the other pallbearers carried the coffin to a wagon. Wendy, her father, and other members of the family rode in a carriage belonging to Emerson. Nate and Deidre followed in their buggy. They were trailed by others in carriages or wagons. Those on foot brought up the rear as they headed to the cemetery on a hillside at the edge of town.

A canopy covered the freshly dug grave site. A few chairs had been placed along the coffin. A freshly dug hole was covered with boards and canvas. If anyone spoke, it was in a whisper.

Nate had stopped at the telegraph office before going to the Knox home to send a message to Tyler and to mail the legal letter Deidre had found in the journal. Maybe Deidre's scarecrow had wanted the letter instead of the journal. Now was out of his grasp. He hoped Tyler or Logan might know what had happened to the young man named Freddy. Did he have a reason to come to Kinsman Manor? Was he among the young men gathered around the grave?

"Maybe we're looking for the wrong person," Nate said. "I read most of the entries last night and didn't find anything that would point to a motive."

Deidre stood next to Wendy who sobbed into her handkerchief. Although the wealthy followed long periods of mourning, the poor couldn't afford the luxury. Many of the servants in attendance would have to return to work. They wouldn't be paid otherwise. Even Wendy was planning to return with them after the service.

He scanned the crowd and noticed Max staring at Deidre. Could Max be the mysterious Freddy mentioned in the journal? He was about the right age and possessed a knife. Deidre had used it to cut Nate's trousers.

Their eyes met, and Max looked down, clasping his flat cap.

"What do you know about Max?" Nate whispered to Deidre.

"He works in the gardens and orchards. I've seen him deliver vegetables and fruits to the kitchen."

"Isn't a garden outside the library?"

"A flower garden." She looked startled. "Do you think Max is the scarecrow?"

"He's the right size and age. He has access to buildings that might contain burlap sacks."

"But he was carrying in your bag when the cupid fell. That would logically eliminate him."

She was trying to turn his own words against him. "Not if it was an accident the cupid fell."

She leaned toward Wendy. "What do you know about Max?"

Wendy stared at the man across from them. "Max?"

Max returned Wendy's gaze and nodded.

She looked at her feet. "He's a hard worker and awfully nice to come and pay respects to my grandmother."

"He's worked about six months at Kinsman Manor," Nate recalled.

"He helps out with any work that needs done," Wendy said.

Deidre looked from Max to Wendy. "I don't think he's the one."

Nate wasn't sure how she had concluded that. Was she using feminine intuition? Max seemed more likely to be the mysterious scarecrow than anyone else present.

The final eulogy was concluded, and everyone

voiced their condolences to the family members and left the cemetery. Max lingered near Wendy.

Nate pulled Deidre aside as the gravediggers lowered the body into the ground. "Why don't you suspect Max?"

"He's sweet on Wendy. Can't you tell?"

Nate looked at Max and Wendy standing close. His hand brushed against her fingertips. "When did you know?"

Deidre shrugged. "The first time we met them. She was ordering him about."

"What does that have to do with love?"

"He obeyed." She smiled. "A man who loves a woman does whatever she asks. He's been shadowing her all morning to take care of her. Look."

Nate saw Max give Wendy a flower from a bundle near the grave. He offered his handkerchief to her.

Deidre was right. Max couldn't take his eyes off Wendy. "He seemed a logical choice."

"You should rely more on instinct."

Max would know the other men working at the manor. The servants were boarding the Kinsman carriage. He stopped Max and Wendy. "Would you like to ride back with us? We have plenty of room."

"We'd hate to intrude," Wendy said.

Max brushed at his coat. "I'd be honored." He put on his flat cap and offered his arm to Wendy. "As long as I can drive."

Nate helped Deidre into the back.

Max helped Wendy board, took the reins, and urged the horse down the road.

Nate settled back into his seat. "So, Max, what made you want to work at Kinsman Manor?"

"My uncle lives in town. I came to visit, and he told me about workers needed at the Kinsman place. The pay was good, and I liked the people who worked there." He looked toward Wendy.

"You work in the gardens, don't you?" Deidre asked. "I've seen you deliver food to the kitchen."

"I do a little bit of everything," Max said. "There aren't many young men around. When they need a strong back, I volunteer."

"Why do you ask?" Wendy asked with a hint of suspicion in her voice.

"Some strange things have been happening since we arrived," Nate said. "You were there when the cupid fell. Last night a man in a scarecrow mask entered Deidre's room."

"You suspect Max?" Wendy's voice rose.

"No." Nate held up his hand. "But we think he might know the man. Do you know of anyone who wanders about the estate?"

"Someone who seems out of place," Deidre said.

"Or goes places he doesn't belong," Nate added.

"No." Max shook his head. "The servants are busy during the day, and most head into town at night unless they sleep at the manor."

"What about relatives?" Nate asked. "What do they do during the day?"

"Charlie and James like to visit the tool barn," Max said. "They tinker with things, but neither is mechanically minded. They make junk."

"Anyone else?"

"Roland and Bart like to ride the horses. They fancy themselves country gentlemen."

"What about the women?" Deidre looked at Wendy.

"They stroll through the gardens or sit in the parlor. I'd be bored being a fine lady like them." Wendy reddened. "I shouldn't have said that."

Deidre touched her shoulder. "I agree. I hate sitting around doing nothing."

"Looks like you've got your hands full keeping Mr. Burroughs alive," Max said.

"It's turning out to be a full-time job." Deidre laughed, and the others joined her.

Nate should have been mad being the butt of their joke, but if it took an injury for Deidre to be his nurse, he'd suffer humiliation on top of bodily harm.

They arrived at the manor house. Deidre and Nate stepped out at the main entrance. Nate looked up at the remaining cupid and made sure they were wide of any possible descent of the love god.

"We'll go around back," Wendy said without rising.

"That's not necessary," Deidre said.

"It's best," Wendy said. "I wouldn't want to lose my job by offending Mr. Kinsman."

"Besides, I have to put the horse in the barn." Max lifted the reins.

Deidre patted Wendy's hand. "If you need anything, don't hesitate to ask." She waved and turned to Nate. "Do you know of any law that requires servants to enter by the back door?"

"I think it's an English custom," he said. "A medieval lord flogged a servant for using the front door of the castle, and they have been using the rear entrance ever since."

When they entered Kinsman Manor, the other cousins were in the parlor playing cards and grumbling about waiting for dinner. Emerson had dozed off in his wheelchair. Bruce stood vigil.

"You're back," Wilma said. "I hope that means the servants have returned. I'm starving."

"You don't know how to cook?" Deidre asked in a barely veiled sarcastic tone.

"I supervise the meals." Wilma stood and squared her shoulders. "Menial tasks are for the hired help."

"I helped out in the kitchen when I was a girl," Faith said. "It taught me to appreciate servants when you can afford them."

"We should give them time to prepare something," Deidre said. "What card game are you playing?"

"Faro." James shuffled a deck. The cards with spades were arranged in two rows with the seven of spades at the end. "Do you know how to play?"

"Yes, but you already have enough players," Nate said.

"I've never played," Deidre said. "But I'd like to watch."

Nate and Deidre observed the others play a round of faro with James acting as banker. Each player placed their chips and pennies above the cards. Annabelle won the most chips.

Annabelle clapped her hands. "I've never won anything in my life."

"It is a game of chance," Charlie said. "Anyone can win. The odds of winning are calculated by the number of bets…"

"I like to think some talent is necessary," Annabelle said.

"You had beginner's luck," Roland said. "And your squeals distracted me."

Wendy stood in the doorway and announced dinner

was ready. Bruce rested a hand on Emerson's shoulder and shook him to wake him from his nap.

"What did I miss?" Emerson asked.

"I won at faro," Annabelle announced. "I do like playing games."

"Those you win." James claimed the winnings from her hand.

Emerson directed Bruce to push his chair into the dining room and took his position at the head of the table. Seating arrangements had been changed again. James was seated to the right of Emerson with Deidre next to him. Nate was seated across from Deidre with Annabelle to his right. Charlie sat at the other end of the table with Bart and Faith on his right and Wilma and Roland on his left.

At least Nate was on the same end as Deidre. He hated not hearing what she was saying.

The soup was served, and Emerson raised his hand. "I want to thank Deidre and Mr. Burroughs for attending Mrs. Knox's funeral."

"It's the least we could do," Deidre said.

"I value loyalty," Emerson said. "And my servants will be compensated for their years of service."

"Then you can't leave any of us out," Bart said. "We're your flesh and blood."

"We shall see." Emerson looked at his startled heirs. "Although it's only Wednesday, I've observed your character and what you value these past three days. I believe I've discovered enough to know who will benefit from an inheritance and who will squander it."

"I wouldn't squander it." Roland scowled. "Unlike my brother."

"Anyone can have an investment go bad," Bart said.

"You seem to have your fair share of them." Roland blew on his soup before tasting it.

Bart tapped his finger on the table. "An entrepreneur needs to take risks."

Nate was glad Bart was at the other end of the table. Too bad the brothers had to share their quarrels. He turned his attention to their host.

Emerson struggled eating his soup.

Annabelle reached out to touch Emerson's hand but pulled back and fumbled with her soup spoon. "Will your granddaughters be included in your will?"

"Illegitimate children do not inherit." James's voice flashed with anger.

Nate confronted him. "Perhaps in England when there is a title at stake, but Mr. Kinsman can name anyone as his heir."

"Is that true?" Charlie asked from the other end of the table.

"Mr. Burroughs is a lawyer," Emerson said. "If anyone would know, he would."

"I didn't mean Miss Pierce," James said. "You see, I'm illegitimate. I hardly knew my father. He left me nothing but bad memories."

"I'm sorry," Deidre said. "I treasure the memories of my mother, and I've learned a great deal about my father from my uncle. It helps to have answers."

"I kept my birth a secret, but I've done well." James fumbled with his napkin. "Annabelle is my family now."

Annabelle smiled at him and turned to her brother. "And Charlie. We're all family. I'm sure Grandfather thinks of us that way."

Emerson grunted. "What's left of family." He pointed at Deidre. "I heard you were on the third floor.

Did you find what you were looking for in your mother's room?"

The old man didn't miss much. "A family Bible," Nate said quickly.

"And my mother's journal," she added.

Nate dropped his fork on the floor. Had she misinterpreted his warning? The last thing they needed was for someone to know they had found the journal. "Ouch!" Someone had kicked him.

He met Deidre's gaze across the table. What was she up to? She flashed a dimpled smile.

"My injury must be acting up," Nate excused as he rubbed the new bruise.

"You found her journal?" James leaned forward. "Have you read it?"

"Yes," Deidre said. "She started writing about her life here at Kinsman Manor before she met Lewis Smith."

Annabelle shared a glance with James. "Did she write anything about her husband?"

"Yes. He was charming at first," Deidre said. "He wanted to impress the social elite in Washington. Once his position was secure, he neglected her, cheated on her, and beat her."

"I hope she didn't go into details," James said. "That would be shocking."

"She shared her experiences and thoughts about her life, but I'll cherish the passages she wrote about me," Deidre said.

"Did she write about the scandal?" Faith ignored the roast pork and seasoned potatoes on her plate and looked around Nate to see Deidre.

"She added newspaper clippings," Deidre said.

"Reporters discovered Lewis Smith had several mistresses and at least two illegitimate children. Along with his infidelities, my mother and father had gathered evidence of corruption and bribes. They were planning to expose his lies so he would agree to a divorce."

"Did she divorce him?" Wilma asked.

"My father's death made that unnecessary." Deidre turned to Emerson. "She didn't write for a long time after his murder."

"Hannah was like a ghost until you were born," Emerson said. "Then she embraced life again. You made her happy."

Tears glistened in Deidre's eyes. "I'm glad you shared that."

"I know Mr. Smith was acquitted, but what happened to him after the trial?" James asked.

"My mother wrote about a visit. He brought a boy with him." Deidre looked at Emerson again.

"The boy visited later, but Mr. Smith made several visits. Always for money."

"You paid him?" Nate asked.

"After his first visit, I hired a detective to look into his background and realized he was not only cruel to women but children. I didn't want to take any chances with their safety," Emerson said. "I initially fought Hannah's plan to have Logan Pierce become Deidre's guardian, but realized it was best."

"It must have been a difficult decision," Deidre said.

Emerson sighed. "I only wish I could have spared the life of your father. My detective also investigated the Pierce family and told me Derek was hardworking. Salmon Chase spoke highly of him and his service to him as his secretary. Your uncle Logan served Chase when he was secretary of the treasury during the war."

"He respected Mr. Chase, especially when President Lincoln appointed him as chief justice to the Supreme Court," Deidre said. "It was one of the reasons Uncle Logan became mayor of our town."

Her grandfather's bushy eyebrows shot up. "Is he a good mayor?"

Deidre laughed. "Yes. Even with a broken leg."

"Is that why he didn't accompany you?" Bruce asked.

Deidre looked startled by his question. "Yes. A barrel hit him."

"A wagon lost its load of beer," Nate said. "Mayor Pierce was knocked to the ground and broke his leg. I saw another barrel heading toward him and pulled him out of the way. I believe that was one of the reasons he chose me to replace him on this trip."

"Did you keep track of Mr. Smith?" James asked Emerson.

"I received reports from my detective. He lost his seat in Congress and made some bad investments. His friends abandoned him. He was drunk on his last visit. He wanted me to invest in one of his schemes. I said no. I heard he died four years ago after a long illness. His lifestyle finally caught up to him."

"That's sad," Annabelle said. "I mean Lewis Smith, for better or worse, was part of the family."

"I think it's fun to know a family's deep and darkest secrets," Faith said.

"Some secrets are better left unknown," Bart said.

"Do you have something to hide, brother?" Roland asked with a smirk. "Other than your bad financial decisions?"

"I consider it poor manners to discuss personal details," Bart said. "I'm sure poor Deidre agrees."

"I'm not ashamed of my life. I visited to find out about my mother," Deidre said. "Her journal provides me with a link I didn't have. Now that I've met you, I hope to correspond and visit in the future. But I have no interest in Lewis Smith. He's dead and buried and no longer a threat to me."

When they retired to the parlor to play cards, Nate pulled Deidre aside in the gallery. "Why did you tell everyone about the journal? Your relatives are prime suspects."

"I hope not." She glanced around. "I want the man in the mask to try to get it. What better way to prove guilt or innocence? When you see that it isn't a relative, you can apologize."

Nate stared. "Why are you asking for trouble?"

"Aren't you here to protect me?"

"Why are you making my job harder?"

Chapter Twenty

Deidre took Nate's arm, surprised by the hardness beneath his sleeve. Men grew into formidable towers of strength. Some protected women while others turned their power against those they proclaimed to love. She had witnessed the damage a fist could inflict. Others ignored the bruises and torn flesh, but her aunts had not. They had taught her to fight for those weaker when men failed to be honorable.

But Nate had proven himself to be brave. The damage to his handsome face was evidence of her family's violence. The swelling had receded, but a half-moon of purple shadowed his eye, and his skin sported a yellow tint.

"How do you feel?"

He grimaced. "I felt fine before someone kicked me in the shin."

"We should probably work on a less physical signal to communicate silence." She turned toward the parlor where her cousins were seated at several tables. "A game of cards should be harmless."

Bruce stepped in front of them and blocked their path. "Mr. Kinsman wishes for you to visit his room."

The others in the parlor turned toward the sectioned glass doors, which had been left open. Wilma and Annabelle hurried to the doorway.

"Does he want me to visit?" Annabelle asked.

"What about Bart?" Wilma glanced back at her husband.

"Not at this time," Bruce said. "You can continue with your game."

Deidre looked at the group gathered in the opening, watching and waiting. She shrugged. Why was her grandfather summoning her and Nate?

His room was in the front of the manor. They passed through the gallery and into the formal study, which had been converted to a bedroom. A few books and a Bible remained on the built-in shelves. Medicine bottles of blue and white glass filled the lower shelf. Medical devices were cluttered on top of a narrow table. A slop bucket was visible beneath the bed but within easy grabbing distance if needed. A pitcher left within a porcelain basin covered the surface of a washstand with towels draped over the narrow handles. The smell of bitter medicines and soiled linens hung in the air.

"It's easier for me to sleep down here than to be carried up and down the stairs," her grandfather said. The blanket shifted and exposed swollen legs. Bruce adjusted the cover and propped several pillows behind him so he could sit up.

"I want to make sure the others haven't upset you with their talk of illegitimacy," Emerson said. "My father was born on the wrong side of the blanket, and in England that meant he was disqualified from inheriting. He came to America where his natural-child status could be overlooked. He had a dream to build a grand manor house. He bought the land and named the town Kinsman, but it was years before he drew up the plans and started construction. He died before the house was finished, so I fulfilled his dream. I have every intention of including you with your cousins as heirs to the Kinsman estate."

"Thank you, but I didn't come for the money. I've had a good life with Uncle Logan and Aunt Jem, but I wanted to know more about my mother and her family. I was hoping to talk to Mrs. Knox." She looked at her grandfather. "What can you tell me?"

"You said you read Hannah's journal. Didn't she talk about herself?"

"Yes. She recorded events but not always the reasons behind them." Deidre hesitated. "She wrote that after Lewis beat her, she returned home, but you made her go back with her husband. I want to understand why you would do that."

"Sometimes we make decisions based on societal norms. I knew marriage could be difficult, but vows are made before God and men for better or worse." Her grandfather shook his head. "I gave Lewis a stern warning about treating Hannah like a beloved wife. I thought that would be enough, but he had no honor."

Bruce dropped a bottle. It crashed to the floor, but the thick glass prevented it from breaking.

Nate retrieved the container before it emptied. "I saved some."

Bruce nodded as he poured the contents into a glass and mixed it with water and honey. "You need to drink this, sir."

"Later. I have words to share, and I don't want to be confused by some confounded mixture to help me sleep. Go wait outside until I call you." He reached for Deidre's hand.

Fragile bones beneath thin flesh grasped her hand, the cold penetrating her skin.

"Your mother wrote home to your grandmother," he

said. "I read the letters but dismissed her concerns. She complained about being left alone much of the time. She was a social person who enjoyed being with other people, especially those her age. When she wrote about meeting Derek Pierce, your grandmother said Hannah was in love."

"I agree," Deidre said. "She wrote about him in her journal with the excitement and joy that was missing when she talked of Lewis. I believe they were happy for a little while."

"When your mother returned here after Derek's death, I let her stay. I thought Lewis would go to jail for murder, and she would need a home. Even though I didn't approve of her behavior, your grandmother defended her. When you were born, everything changed. I never held a baby before. You were the first."

She had always remembered her grandfather as being stern, but a distant memory surfaced. "Did you give me candy?"

He chuckled. "Against your mother's orders. When Lewis was acquitted, Hannah was afraid he'd claim you as his own."

"Could he?" She looked to Nate.

"He had a legal right since you were born while Hannah was married to him." Nate turned to her grandfather. "Did he try to take Deidre?"

"He showed up with a two-faced lawyer claiming he had a legal obligation to care for her under the law and should manage any money and property of the child's." Emerson looked at Deidre. "Your mother consulted with her own lawyer."

"My mother made it clear Lewis was not my father in the papers she gave Uncle Logan, and if that wasn't enough, I look like a Pierce."

"I fought to keep you for selfish reasons, which were wrong," he said. "Your grandmother had died the previous winter, and this dark and dreary mansion was hardly the place for a child. Then there was the incident where you fell down the stairs."

"I was pushed by Freddy."

He looked startled. "You know the boy's name?"

"Mother described him as a vicious little monster."

"His father's son." Emerson sighed and leaned back. "You and Hannah made this place a home for a brief time. Now it has become my tomb."

"It could come alive again," Deidre said.

"I have discovered two types of people in this world. Those who are hardworking and content as long as they have food on the table, a roof over their heads, and their loved ones are safe and free. Then there are the others who have wealth or crave it, who cheat, lie, and steal to attain more, and are never satisfied. I was the latter and fear my grandsons are cut from the same cloth." Emerson coughed and took several minutes to recover. "I know what your cousins will do with their share of the inheritance, but I haven't figured out what you will do."

She had thought long and hard about any inheritance she might receive. "I'd create a fund for Second Chance."

"What is Second Chance?" her grandfather asked.

"A friend of mine, Hazel, had to work in a saloon. Her father indentured her to the owner to pay off his debts. She was hired to serve drinks and clean tables, but the owner forced himself upon her and others…"

"I understand." Her grandfather shuddered. "He took advantage of her position as his employee, and you wanted to help her."

"She didn't complain until her father planned to sell her younger sister to the same man. Gwen was barely sixteen." She looked at Nate. "Hazel asked that we rescue her sister, but we rescued both. Now they have a second chance at a better life."

Her grandfather turned to Nate. "You helped?"

"I carried a ladder." Nate shrugged. "It was Deidre's plan. The sisters are safe now."

Emerson's head bobbed several times. "What would you need to give more women a second chance?"

"Well, we only have a few safe houses. It would be nice to afford a larger place where women could stay and recover from their ordeals. We couldn't help a woman who had three children because we didn't have the room." She fought back tears. "Her husband beat them. He threw the baby against the wall because she was crying." A sob escaped, and she fought to speak. "She died."

"He didn't go to jail?"

"He claimed it was an accident. The baby fell out of the loft."

"And the mother agreed with him?"

She shook her head. "I don't know."

"Was that the Thompson family?" Nate asked.

Deidre turned to face him. "Yes. How did you know?"

"I helped Mr. Montgomery with that case," Nate said. "The father had guardianship over the other two children. The wife agreed not to testify against him if she was granted sole custody."

"You work for this Second Chance group?" her grandfather asked Nate.

"I was recently recruited," Nate said.

"I didn't learn much from the sermons in church, but I realized sin is the love of violence," her grandfather said. "Men bully and hurt others for a variety of reasons. None justified. Your mother sought refuge, but I wasn't much of a father."

"Some fathers wouldn't have allowed her to return home." Deidre kissed his cheek. "We had shelter and food and love. That was enough."

"I spent my entire life accumulating wealth, and now I realize I can't take any of it with me. Those left alive will squander most of it. You have a generous plan to help others. Why?"

"My life would have been tragically different without the help of you, Uncle Logan, Aunt Jem, and even Nate Burroughs. I'm happiest when I help others. Life isn't always fair, and giving the unfortunate or unlucky a second chance is my dream."

Grandfather closed his eyes and grimaced.

"We should let you sleep," Deidre said.

"Tell Bruce to come in."

"How long has Bruce been your caretaker?" Nate asked.

"He arrived in March," her grandfather said. "He doesn't mind the dirty tasks, and I needed someone strong enough to lift me so I can get out of this bed instead of wasting away."

"He doesn't talk much," Nate said.

"He talks when he has something to say. It was his idea that I gather my grandchildren," her grandfather said. "He must know something I do not."

"It's best to be prepared for the worst." She grasped his hand. "And I think it's a wonderful idea to meet my cousins and you. Good night." She kissed his cheek.

Nate opened the door.

Bruce stood in the doorway.

Deidre swiped at a tear. "Take care of him."

Bruce grunted as they passed him.

All eyes turned to Nate and Deidre as they entered the parlor.

"What did Grandfather want?" Faith asked.

"He wanted to know what I would do with my inheritance. I told him about Second Chance."

"What's that?" Charlie asked.

Deidre explained about Hazel and Gwen. "Second Chance gives women an opportunity to escape abuse and start over again."

"But she was a prostitute," Bart said. "They don't deserve a second chance."

"She didn't choose the occupation." Nate didn't hide his displeasure.

"Women who work in brothels enjoy that sort of work," Bart said.

"How would you know?" Wilma asked. "When have you visited a brothel?"

"Before we were married, I had a life."

Wilma stood. "You never told me about your sordid past."

He chased after her as she left the room. "I was young."

Roland looked at Faith. "I did not compete with my brother in *that* way."

"Tell us more about Second Chance," Annabelle said.

"I believe that my father would be alive if my mother had some place to escape Lewis Smith," Deidre said.

"But didn't she come here?" Annabelle asked.

"My grandfather turned her away the first time." Deidre tried not to blame her grandfather. "He had believed, like many people, that a wife belonged to her husband."

"But the laws are changing," Nate said.

"Do you think it's a good thing to give women more power?" Roland asked.

"What are you afraid of?" Nate asked. "If women are inferior, we have nothing to fear."

As they headed upstairs, Deidre turned to Nate. "I liked what you said, but will it ever come true? Will women be respected enough to gain wealth and power on their own?"

"I don't know." Nate shook his head as he climbed the stairs. "Laws can't change the hearts of men who are afraid to fairly compete. They will do everything in their power to keep others from gaining wealth, influence, or an advantage."

"And as long as men don't think of women as equal, they won't treat them as their partners in life." Deidre sighed.

"Change can happen," he said. "Don't give up without a fight."

"I don't plan on surrendering, but how do we convince men we are created equal with the same rights and powers they take for granted? How do we gain respect for our own accomplishments?"

"One man at a time." He grinned.

"Don't use your charm on me, Nate Burroughs." Deidre went to his door. "I'll need the Bible back."

Nate unlocked his door. "Are you sure about this?"

"You can't catch a rat without bait."

He shook his head. "I wish you weren't so close to the bait."

Chapter Twenty-One

Nate sat in a chair near the fireplace, fully dressed, tapping his foot. Why had she set a trap without asking him? She didn't need his permission to reveal she had found the journal, but now he had to maintain a vigil if someone entered her room. The shared fireplace allowed him to hear any noise from next door. It was quiet. Had she gone to sleep? Wasn't she worried?

A woman screamed.

Nate jumped to his feet and dashed into the hallway.

Deidre opened her door. She wore a robe and slippers.

"Did you scream?"

"Not me." She looked down the hallway and pointed in the distance. "There's someone by the stairs."

Charlie had opened his door, a book in his hand. "What happened?"

"We don't know." Nate led as they hurried down the hall to investigate.

Faith stood on the top step of the staircase and gripped the railing with both hands. A broken plate lay in the hallway, and a slice of pie was overturned on the wooden floor along with an extinguished candle next to its brass holder. Her knees buckled, and she sat on the floor. "It was horrible." She looked around. "Roland, Roland, where are you?"

Roland, wearing a nightshirt and robe, exited his

room with a lit candle. "What are you doing out here? Why aren't you in bed?"

"I was hungry and wanted a slice of pie," Faith said between sobs. She grabbed her husband's hand, and he pulled her to her feet.

He patted her back. "It's pie. No need to scream about it."

Charlie waved his book in the air. "You disturbed my reading."

"I wasn't screaming about the pie." Faith's body heaved as she gulped mouthfuls of air. "I saw a ghost running down the hallway."

"A ghost?" Charlie's voice rose in pitch. "Are you sure?"

"It was horrible!" Faith clutched her husband as her body shook.

Roland raised his candle. "Anyone else see anything?"

James and Annabelle had emerged from their room in their robes. The door to Bart and Wilma's room remained closed.

"Where did you see this ghost?" Nate asked.

"I was coming up the stairs and saw it floating down the hallway." She pointed in the direction of Nate's room. "You had to have seen it. It went in your direction."

Nate shrugged. "We saw nothing."

"What did this ghost look like?" Deidre asked.

Charlie stepped closer. "Did it look like the ghosts in *A Christmas Carol*?"

"It wasn't a ghost," Roland said. "Ghosts aren't real."

"It was real and horrible," Faith screeched as she

pulled away from her husband. "This huge figure was dressed in a long coat and a huge hat as it floated down the hall. When he turned to look at me, I saw a hideous white face with empty holes for eyes and stitches across its mouth."

Annabelle clutched James's arm. "I'm frightened."

"Sounds like our scarecrow friend," Nate whispered. "I thought you might have imagined him, but it appears he's real."

"Imagined?" Deidre frowned. "You didn't believe me?"

He held up his forefinger and thumb with a small space between. "I had the slightest doubt. I needed evidence."

"You and your proof." Deidre crossed her arms.

"You've seen this ghost?" James asked.

"The scarecrow was the one who came into my room and took my book," Deidre said.

"I remember." Charlie clutched his novel as he looked around the dark hall.

"Do you think we should look for him?" Roland asked.

Faith tugged on his arm. "Don't leave me."

"He's long gone now." James yawned. "Or he only existed in the dreams of hysterical women."

"I was not asleep." Faith pointed at the candle on the floor. "And my candle was lit until I dropped it."

"I was not hysterical." Deidre turned to Nate. "Or imagining things."

"Which another witness supports." Nate hoped Deidre would understand his doubt.

"It could be another test of Mr. Kinsman," James said. "I think we should all go back to bed."

"Good idea." Charlie headed for his room.

"I don't think Grandfather planned this, but someone has a bizarre sense of humor," Roland said.

Deidre gathered the broken plate and pie from the floor. "I'll take this downstairs." She turned to Faith. "Do you need anything?"

"Could you bring me another piece?" Faith asked. "Please."

"Of course."

Nate gathered the discarded candle and holder. "Let me light this."

Roland offered his flame. "Thank you for replacing the pie."

"I wouldn't need something to eat if I wasn't so distressed." Faith clung to Roland as they returned to their room.

Nate held the candle aloft as they made their way down the staircase and hallway.

"Did you really doubt me when I told you about the man in the mask?"

"I was keeping an open mind and only doubted your description," Nate said. "Faith confirmed he looked like a scarecrow."

He led the way through the nook into the kitchen. Everything was in its place except for one item. Faith had left the tin with the remaining pie on the worktable.

Deidre cut another piece and placed it on a new plate. She dumped the dropped pie into the empty slop bucket and placed the broken plate next to the dry sink.

Nate returned the remaining pie to the pie safe and led the way with his candle while Deidre carried the plate. "Bart and Wilma did not appear with everyone else. Could he be pulling a prank?"

"To what end? Why would Bart try to frighten us?" she asked.

"Maybe he thinks if he scares the other heirs away, he'll inherit all."

She squared her shoulders. "Well, I'm not running."

"Your courage frightens me."

She paused on the steps. "Why?"

"Didn't you notice I was fully dressed? I was expecting someone to take the bait in your trap." He waited for her to continue up the stairs. "I'm earning every penny to protect you."

"I forgot you were paid to escort me." She didn't hide the anger in her voice.

"I was hired to be your lawyer, but I didn't take the job for the money." Didn't she know how he felt?

Deidre knocked on Roland and Faith's door.

He still had his robe on and took the pie. "Thank you."

"May I keep the candle?" Nate asked. "We're at the other end of the hall."

"We don't need it."

"How is she?" Deidre asked.

"Pretty shaken. She was plump as a child and horribly teased about it, so she hates to eat food in front of people."

"I bet Wilma's teasing doesn't help," Nate said.

"She's a lot like Bart when it comes to competing." Roland lifted the plate. "Thanks for bringing the pie. It will make her feel better."

Nate looked across the hall at the room belonging to Bart and Wilma. "How could they not have heard Faith scream?"

"No one but Charlie came out when I screamed,"

Deidre reminded him.

Nate pointed between the two doors. "Charlie was across from you like Roland is from Bart. They should have heard."

"That keeps Bart at the top of your list."

"Exactly."

They made their way to the other end of the hallway and stopped at Deidre's door. It was open.

"Didn't you lock your door?"

"Faith's scream made me forget." She stepped forward, but he grabbed her arm.

"Let me go first." He stepped inside. The bedcovers had been tossed on the floor to expose the mattress. Several drawers were pulled open and not closed.

She stood in the doorway. "It's been searched."

She hurried to the dresser but stopped midstride. The Bible was sprawled on the floor. She flipped it over. "It's gone." Her mother's journal was missing from its hiding place. "I shouldn't have told everyone I found it. I wanted to catch someone stealing it, but I left the bait unguarded." She burst into tears.

"It was a good way to flush out the thief." He patted her on the back. "The scarecrow came back but frightened Faith. He fled but must have hid until he saw his chance to take your mother's diary."

Tears coursed down her cheeks. Her hands shook as she swiped them away. "How could I have been so careless?"

"We were all distracted." He wanted to give her hope. "Maybe he wasn't after the diary, and it's still in the room."

Nate helped Deidre tidy scattered belongings and account for anything missing. Only the journal was gone.

She sniffled back more tears. "What if I never find it? My mother's thoughts are written in it. I can't lose her words."

"We'll find it." He placed the palms of his hands against her cheeks and gazed into her eyes. "We'll get it back."

She met his gaze, and the attraction was undeniable. "I don't understand what's so important in the journal that they would steal it. I'd show it to the thief if he asked."

"Maybe they'll realize there isn't anything of value in it except for you and return it." He pulled her close to comfort her, but as she snuggled against his chest, more amorous feelings stirred. "We can search for it tomorrow."

He reminded himself he had promised Logan Pierce he would maintain a professional relationship with Deidre, but his resolve was cracking. He needed to go to his room and splash cold water on his face, but he didn't move.

She stroked his cheek with her fingertips, her lips brushing close to his. "You're trying to make me feel better."

"What can I do to ease your pain?"

She gripped the fabric of his shirt tighter, refusing to allow him to pull away. "Kiss me, Nate."

The words were spoken in a low moan, begging him to comply.

He turned his head slightly and kissed her, plucking her soft lips with his own. He pulled away to keep it brief, but her hands held tight, and she kissed him back.

Every part of his body responded to the passion that boiled to the surface, and he fought to control the urge to do more than let their lips dance in delight. Her kiss ignited a spark that burned deep within and consumed every part of him.

When she pulled away, the warmth remained. He stepped backward, searching blindly for the doorknob. He opened the door. "Lock it after me."

"But there's nothing of importance left in the room."

"You're here."

Chapter Twenty-Two

Deidre turned the key in the lock and jumped on her bed. She buried her face into the pillow to smother the scream of pleasure that surged through her. She had asked for a kiss to satisfy her curiosity. A man of passion existed beneath the prim and proper lawyer Nate had presented since they left home. She had told him she would never consider him as a possible husband, but he was proving to meet all her standards for a spouse. Yet she had dedicated her life to helping other women escape the horrible circumstances like the ones Hazel and Gwen had suffered.

Would Nate consider a wife who helped the less fortunate instead of putting him first above all others? Was that too much to ask of any man? She couldn't let her feelings ruin her plans. She had chosen her path and needed to stay on course. Only spinsters taught school or worked as nurses. Married women had a responsibility to their husbands and children. A career and the role of wife did not mix.

After a restless night, Deidre dressed and climbed the stairs alone to the floor above. She searched through her mother's room, hoping the thief had discarded the journal in the same way as her book, but she found nothing.

"You should have waited for me to start your search." Nate leaned against the open doorway.

She jumped at the sound of his voice. She had rehearsed what she would say to him, but words failed her. She burst into tears instead.

He stepped toward her, and she held up her hand to stop him.

"I'm fine. It's just so final. The journal is gone."

"Why don't we search the hallway and then the library? That's where your other books turned up."

His logic made sense. She could count on Nate to be levelheaded. His need for facts and evidence helped to keep her from jumping to premature conclusions. They made a good team if only to uncover a thief. They spent an hour in the library, hoping the journal was hidden among the other books. No luck.

"You're upset about more than your mother's journal." Nate coughed and twisted the tie at his neck as they walked through the gallery. "Is it the passion we shared last night?"

He was adorable when he was uncomfortable. She wanted to kiss him and tell him how much she had enjoyed their brief lovemaking. But her own logic blocked her emotions. "I told you I wanted to help other women. I'm not ready to marry and give up my dreams. It wouldn't be fair to encourage you otherwise."

"I haven't been a lawyer for long," he said. "I can support my mother and myself with what I make, but it will be some time before I can afford a wife. Besides, I'm a member of the Second Chance secret organization, too. We could work together and see if we have a future together." He brushed his fingertips against her hand.

"You'd allow me to work?"

"Allow? That word is not in the vocabulary of a modern independent woman. My mother enjoyed working at the Ravens Roost. She only quit to take care of me. That was unfair."

"I don't think your mother has quit Second Chance completely."

"Neither do I," he said with a lopsided grin that made him look adorable.

"What have you two been up to?" Annabelle said as she came down the stairs.

"We've been looking for my mother's journal," Deidre said. "It was taken from my room last night. Have you seen it?"

"Me? Why would I have your journal?" Annabelle's voice squeaked, and her reply was rushed.

Nate looked up the staircase. "Where's James?"

"He's not feeling well." Annabelle twittered with a high shrill that made Nate wince. "All that excitement last night kept him awake." She headed for the dining room.

Deidre paused in the gallery. "Did you think her behavior odd?"

"I've seen enough guilty witnesses in court to know Annabelle was hiding something."

Most of the other cousins were eating a lunch of cheese, fruit, and sweet rolls.

Nate poured a cup of coffee and snatched a cinnamon bun from the sideboard. He took a bite and groaned. "This is good."

Deidre took one for herself.

Bruce wheeled Emerson in and placed him at the head of the table.

Annabelle brought him a cup of coffee and a roll.

Emerson looked around at his grandchildren. "I heard there was a ruckus last night."

"It was awful. I didn't sleep all night. I never encountered a ghost before." Faith held out her arm and hand. "I'm shaking just thinking about it."

Her grandfather shook his head. "This house has never had any ghost."

"I know what I saw," Faith defended.

"I don't think it's a ghost." Deidre studied her cousins. "Someone stole my mother's journal from my room while I was downstairs replacing Faith's slice of pie. It could have been the man in the mask."

"I'm sure it was." Annabelle sipped her tea.

"You think it was the same person Faith saw?" Charlie asked.

"He wore a scarecrow mask." Deidre didn't care if one of her relatives was guilty. "I would appreciate it, if any of you find my mother's journal, you return it."

"What does it look like?" Bart took another roll.

"It looks like a book with a brown leather cover," Deidre said. "My mother's name is on the first page."

"I can't believe nobody woke us." Wilma touched the necklace she wore. "We have a right to know there's a thief in the house."

"Don't be so dramatic," Bart said. "Nobody can wake you once you're asleep, and I have become deaf to any noise sleeping next to your snoring."

"I hope you don't think one of us stole your mother's journal." Faith clutched Roland's arm. "I was too frightened to do anything but scream."

"I don't think any of you took it." Deidre wanted to believe they were innocent. She looked at Faith. "You said the man in the scarecrow mask was running toward my end of the hall. He could have waited on the stairs until everyone left the hallway. During the commotion, I left my room unlocked. He could easily have entered and taken the journal."

"Why would someone want your mother's musings?" her grandfather asked.

"I don't know." Deidre shrugged. "I read through it and found little of interest to anyone but me."

"You said she wrote about Lewis Smith and Derek Pierce," Annabelle said. "Did she write about anyone else?"

"She mentioned a boy named Freddy."

"Freddy?" Charlie looked confused. "Who was he?"

"He was one of Lewis Smith's natural children," her grandfather said. "He was with him during his father's visit the week after Hannah's funeral. Lewis had read about her death in the newspaper and thought he could claim her money and personal belongings. While I tried to convince him I owed him nothing, Freddy snuck into the library and carved his name in the top of one of the tables with a knife he kept in a sheath on his belt."

"A knife?" Nate asked. "How old was he?"

"About fourteen. All arms and legs with a tangle of greasy hair. He liked throwing his blade," her grandfather said. "I found him in the garden where he stabbed a squirrel. He smiled as he watched it die. I warned Lewis the boy was strange, but he laughed. I refused to pay him anything, and I had some men escort them to town. That's when I had locks installed on most of the rooms, including the library."

"What happened to him?" Deidre asked.

"I don't know," her grandfather said. "I had no interest in the boy after Lewis died in '72. Do you think Freddy is here?"

His presence would eliminate her cousins as

suspects. "Would you recognize him if you saw him?"

"Been fourteen years," her grandfather said. "Mrs. Knox would remember. She could identify every person who stepped foot in Kinsman Manor."

"She remembered me." Had Mrs. Knox recognized Freddy in the library? Would Nate agree, or would he need more evidence? While the others moved to the parlor, Deidre pulled Nate aside. "I think he's here. Grandfather said he had a knife. The portrait was cut."

"It could have been torn," Nate said.

"It's difficult to tear canvas." She stomped her foot. "Why do you have to be so logical?"

"I don't convict criminals on hunches."

She moved her hand in a series of curved motions. "I'm surprised you convict anyone if you have to line up all your facts in a neat row."

"It's better than convicting an innocent man," Nate said. "Even if the portrait was cut with a knife, why would Freddy be here?"

"Grandfather said he wouldn't give Lewis Smith any more money. Maybe Freddy holds him responsible for his father's downfall. Revenge is a strong motive for causing trouble."

He tapped her forehead. "Now you're thinking like a lawyer."

"Please don't insult me." She crossed her arms. "But I'd like to have my mother's journal back."

He pointed toward the parlor. "If your relatives took it, you may have made them feel guilty enough to return it."

Deidre looked up to see James descending the staircase. "Are you feeling better?"

He looked confused. "Oh, yes."

"Everyone is in the parlor," Nate said. "Shall we join them?"

Annabelle jumped up from her seat and danced on her feet when she saw James, but he gave her a slight shake of his head. Annabelle suddenly froze and took her seat. He joined her on the sofa.

"The day has finally arrived," her grandfather announced. "Today is my birthday."

Everyone called out congratulations.

"Dinner will be roasted turkey with dressing with cake for dessert," he said. "This afternoon I have arranged a tour of the estate grounds. One of you will be inheriting Kinsman Manor someday."

"Will there be a carriage to tour the grounds?" Faith asked.

"The grounds are too rough for a carriage. Max is driving a wagon," her grandfather said. "He'll make it as comfortable as possible for the ladies. The men may ride horseback."

"I'll get my bonnet." Deidre headed for the door.

"I better find my hat." Nate followed.

"You won't need it, Mr. Burroughs," her grandfather said. "I'm meeting with my lawyer and would like you to join us."

Nate looked surprised. "I'd be honored."

"I'll try not to enjoy the sunshine too much while you're inside talking about boring laws." Deidre hurried up the stairs to find a bonnet. She locked her door even though the journal was gone. She passed the dining room where the doors had been closed. She could hear men talking. One of them was Nate. Why had Grandfather included him in the meeting?

The wagon had crates along the sides to serve as

seats. Max had provided cushions for the women and helped them climb aboard. Roland and James rode horseback. Bart sat next to Max on the driver's seat and asked the most questions. Did he think he would inherit the mansion and grounds? Charlie had brought a book, but the bumpy ride made it difficult to read. He set it aside and looked at the scenery.

Max drove the team of horses past the dairy barn. Most of the cows were in the field, gathered under trees to shield themselves from the hot sun. A building for making cheese from the milk was nearby. They passed chickens pecking the ground searching for food. A rooster guarded the plank leading to the chicken coop. Two large pigs cooled off in a mud bath in the shade of a small pen.

"What other animals do you have?" Bart asked.

"Sheep, goats, and horses in the other fields," Max said. "The geese and ducks stay near the ponds."

They passed a smokehouse marked with an *S* and a woodshed where firewood was stacked inside in neat piles. "That's the icehouse." Max pointed at a stone structure near a pond.

"Kinsman is a pretty place," Annabelle said.

"It's buggy if you ask me." Wilma swatted at gnats buzzing around her.

"It's your flowery perfume that's attracting them," Charlie said.

"How many acres are there?" Bart asked from the front seat.

"Nearly a thousand."

Bart whistled. "Isn't there a sawmill?"

"Yes, and plenty of trees," Max said.

"If you inherit this place, Bart, what would you do

with it?" Deidre asked.

"I'd sell it if the price was high enough." Bart looked around. "I certainly don't need to own this albatross. It's too big for a family. I don't know what Great-grandfather was thinking when he started building it."

"He saw the potential." Deidre saw the possibilities of a place like Kinsman Manor. Dormitories could be built in the open area, and the animals and gardens could provide plenty of food. It was perfect for a Second Chance refuge. The women could make cheese, weave wool rugs and blankets, and sell extra food at the local market. But Grandfather would never leave his home to her, and she didn't have the money to buy it from Bart or anyone else who inherited the place.

"Maybe Grandfather will give each of us a few acres to live on," Charlie said.

"Kinsman is in the middle of nowhere." Roland rode a mare beside the wagon. "I like living in the city."

"So do I," Faith said. "There's only one dress shop in Kinsman."

"I enjoy parties too much to live out in the middle of nowhere." Wilma swiped her palms. "Sell the place and be done with it."

Charlie lifted his book. "I would like to have Grandfather's library."

"It's yours when I inherit the place," Bart announced from the front seat.

"Thank you," Charlie said.

"You're so sure you'll inherit everything." Roland pulled on the reins of his horse. "It would serve you right if Grandfather gave it to someone else."

"He's too traditional to leave it to anyone but the eldest son of the eldest son," Bart said.

"We better head back." Max turned the team. "You don't want to be late for Mr. Kinsman's birthday party."

"I know he'll like my present." Bart looked at Roland. "I hope he's not too disappointed with what you're giving him."

"We'll see which gift he likes best." Roland urged his mount to gallop away.

Chapter Twenty-Three

Nate joined Emerson and Abraham Niles in the dining room. Bruce closed the door as he left. Abraham opened a satchel and began to remove papers.

"What are you normally paid, Mr. Burroughs?" Emerson asked.

"Three dollars a day plus expenses."

Emerson nodded at Abraham who placed three silver dollars on the table. "We have officially hired you for this meeting."

Nate stared at the money. "May I ask what my job will be?"

"Mr. Niles has drawn up the final draft of my will," Emerson said. "I need two witnesses."

Abraham showed him the latest will and allowed him time to review the contents.

"Do you think it is fair?" Emerson asked.

It wasn't his job to judge the decisions of Emerson. "I think it fulfills your wishes," Nate said.

"You will need to witness Mr. Kinsman's signature," Abraham said as he handed a pen to Emerson and pointed to the line he needed to sign on.

Nate added his signature, and Abraham signed below him.

"I feel I am being overpaid for my signature," Nate said.

"There is more," Emerson said. "As you can see

from the details of the will, the estate's executor will be an ongoing job."

Abraham withdrew another document from his satchel. "These are the businesses owned by Mr. Kinsman."

"I would like you to review my portfolio," Emerson said.

"I'm not a businessman, but I would be happy to share my opinion." Nate studied the documents. Emerson practiced diversity and had business dealings in shipping, manufacturing, and retail. He had visited his holdings personally until falling down a staircase at a boilermaker's plant. But each business was run by a capable manager, and quarterly reports were sent to Emerson to review. Abraham shared last quarter's financial reports, which proved he was a wealthy man.

"Your heirs should be well taken care of for many years," Nate said.

"I believe more than one person should oversee a business," Emerson said. "I want you to consider working for Mr. Niles and being my personal lawyer. You would visit my businesses and review reports from the managers. As you can see by the extent of my holdings, it will be a full-time job."

Nate had not expected the offer. "I have a job. I work for Mr. Montgomery."

"I'll double what he pays you," Emerson said. "In addition, I want you to be the executor of my will and carry out my wishes. Mr. Niles has other clients, and I need someone who will outlive me and take care of my heirs."

"Heirs?" Nate understood the gravity of the task he was being entrusted with and the pitfalls. "Why me?"

"Mr. Kinsman says you are a man of integrity," Abraham said. "He admires that in a lawyer. You're a lucky young man."

Nate wondered how this new position would affect Deidre and their future. He needed to be blunt. "Would I be able to retain my position if I married one of the heirs?"

"I thought your relationship with Deidre was professional," Emerson said.

So far. "What if I hoped for something more?"

"It would be a conflict of interest for a husband to represent his wife," Abraham said. "And I believe it would be a conflict of interest if you represented the estate and an heir, especially if she were your wife."

"I understand." Nate stood. "I appreciate your generous offer, but I cannot accept."

"What if she said no to marriage?" Emerson asked.

Was he testing him? "That is a risk I'm willing to take."

"Think on it," Emerson said. "You can give me your answer tonight."

Nate wandered the house, looking for Deidre and the others, but they had not returned from their tour. He walked along the road toward town to think. The generous offer by Emerson was a proposal any lawyer would seize. The estate's holdings and distribution would keep him employed for life. If he had the good fortune to marry Deidre, their relationship would be a conflict of interest. But what if Emerson was right? What if she said no to his proposal and married another? Would he want to be her lawyer and watch her with another man? But if he gave up hope of ever making Deidre his wife, could he enjoy his good fortune? Would money compensate for a lost love?

The clomping of a horse's hooves echoed in the covered bridge, and a rider emerged and rode toward him. He pulled on the reins. "I'm looking for Mr. Burroughs?"

"That's me."

"I have a telegram for you." He delivered the sealed note.

Nate tore open the message. It was from Tyler Montgomery. *Freddy lived with Lewis Smith until his death. Woman found dead in apartment from knife wounds. Freddy suspect. Never found.*

If Freddy was wanted for murder, he would be in hiding. Would he risk recognition by coming to Kinsman Manor? It was unlikely.

"Do you wish to send a reply?" the messenger asked.

"No." He tipped the man who turned his horse and left.

By the time he returned to the house, the others were in their rooms preparing for dinner. He did the same and knocked on Deidre's door.

Her gown was the one she had worn for the Fourth of July dance. He had played the events of that day and night over and over in his mind. If only he had not slandered her to Oscar. "Did you enjoy your tour?" He was dazzled by her smile.

"It was inspiring."

"What do you mean?"

"How did your legal meeting go with Grandfather's lawyer?" She had changed the subject.

"It was interesting." He could be just as mysterious.

She fussed with his tie. "Is that all?"

"They asked me to witness the will, but confidentiality rules keep me from saying more." Was he making a mistake? Should he declare his love and expose the sacrifice he was making for her? But he wanted her to come to him out of love not because he was willing to give up a lucrative position. But what if she didn't love him? What if she never loved him? Was he a fool?

"You seem so distant," Deidre said. "What's bothering you?"

He looked at the wrapped present in her hand. "I forgot to buy a gift."

"I think Grandfather will forgive you." She placed her hand on his arm, and he escorted her downstairs.

"I'll take that," Wendy offered as she pointed at the gift. "I'm putting them in the parlor."

They headed for the dining room. Emerson had assigned new seats, and Deidre was near her grandfather while Nate was on the opposite end. The cousins were more talkative, but he barely listened, his thoughts miles away.

Faith sneezed. "This is why I hate farms."

"How was your tour?" Nate asked, hoping she said something to explain Deidre's cryptic answer. *Inspiring.*

"Boring," she said. "Endless grass and smelly animals."

"I agree." Wilma pinched her nose. "I won't live anywhere but the city."

"Grandfather has some fine horseflesh," Roland said. "I've enjoyed riding this week."

Nothing they said helped him decipher Deidre's inspiration. He concentrated on his turkey and stuffing while James and Roland debated the different breeds of horses.

"Let's retire to the parlor for cake and champagne," Emerson said. Bruce wheeled him out of the dining room.

Wendy had placed the presents on a table, and Emerson surveyed the stack of gifts. "I finalized my last will and testament this afternoon, and my wealth will be distributed among you, my five grandchildren."

"Annabelle as well?" James asked with obvious excitement.

"Annabelle and Deidre are included," Emerson said. "You will have to wait until I die to know the exact distribution, but I would like to know what you plan to do with your inheritance. I will open each gift, and the giver can share their plans. Who wants to go first?"

Bart stood. "As the eldest, I think I should set the example." He retrieved a small box from the stack.

Emerson tore at the elaborate wrapping and uncovered a velvet box. Inside was a gold watch. He held it up to his ear. "Time passes too quickly for old men."

"Read the back." Wilma pointed. "It has an inscription."

"The best way to pass time is with others you love. Bart and Wilma." He put the watch in his vest pocket. "That's a lovely sentiment. Now tell me what you will do with your share of the inheritance."

Bart stood beside Emerson and looked out at the others. He cleared his throat. "I plan to invest it in new technology and multiply my wealth."

"You've had little success with your investments so far," Emerson said. "Do you think investing a larger amount will reap greater rewards?"

"New technology is the way of the future. A man must be willing to take risks in order to reap the benefits," Bart said.

"I advise you to invest in many different businesses as I have done," Emerson said. "When one fails, the others may succeed."

"If I inherit your businesses, then I will maintain them."

Bart was making promises he would have a hard time keeping if his current business dealings were any example. Nate leaned back in his chair, waiting for the next heir to impress Emerson.

Roland handed Grandfather a large box from the table. "I hope you like it."

Emerson struggled with the wrapping. "You're going to have to help me with this."

Roland ripped the fancy paper and opened the box. Inside was a silk and velvet robe.

Emerson ran his fingers along the expensive fabric. "I look forward to wearing it. Now what are your plans, Roland?"

"I plan to buy a house and start a family," Roland said. "Then you'll have great-grandchildren to carry on your legacy."

"Children?" Faith asked with a surprised gasp. "Must you compete with your brother about everything?"

Nate covered his mouth to halt a chuckle.

"Your wife seems surprised by your plans." Emerson studied her. "Don't you want children, Faith?"

"Someday, but I don't see the hurry to start a family. I'd like to travel and enjoy my youth before settling into a home and raising children."

"I doubt I will enjoy seeing my first great-grandchild, but I hope you are blessed in the future."

"If we are blessed with a son, we will name him Emerson." She gave her husband a sly glance.

"Your wife is right about competing with your brother. You need to live your own life, Roland." Emerson looked at Faith. "Men think their role is to make all the decisions, but you should value your wife's opinion. I learned too late to value my own wife's thoughts. It is one of my greatest regrets."

Roland and Faith sat down. They appeared deflated, but Nate thought Emerson's advice sound. He valued Deidre's ideas.

"Charlie, you're next," Emerson said.

Charlie handed him a long narrow box and chewed on his lip as he waited for Emerson to open it. "It's a cane to help you walk when you get out of your wheelchair."

"I'm glad you're optimistic, Charlie, but none of you will inherit if I don't die."

"That's not going to happen," Annabelle said with a catch in her voice.

He held up his hand, which shook from the effort. "Now tell me your plans, Charlie."

"I'm going to travel," he said. "And visit all the places I've only read about in my books."

"You'll likely be disappointed," Emerson said. "Better to live in a world of fantasy than the real one. But as an intellectual dreamer, you may figure out a way to make the world a better place."

Nate saw a softer side to Emerson. He had not crushed Charlie's dream.

Emerson turned to Annabelle who gave him a box and watched intently as he opened it.

He lifted a pair of slippers.

"I noticed your slippers were worn and wanted to

replace them to keep your feet warm."

"A useful gift," he said. "Would you like to put them on me?"

She knelt by his wheelchair. Bruce lifted the blanket covering his legs. His feet were swollen and discolored. She looked at James who helped her slide the slippers on.

Annabelle rose and kissed his cheek. "I also have a sentimental gift."

He unwrapped a music box.

He fumbled with the key. "Wind it up for me, Annabelle. These old hands are useless."

She turned the key, and it played a waltz. "I hope you think of me when you listen to it."

He closed the lid. "So what do you plan to do with my money?"

"I don't know yet." She looked at James.

"Annabelle seems to think you should decide what to do with her money, James. Do you have plans?"

"I could invest her funds in railroad stock," James said. "The little I own has done well."

"Annabelle is not that practical," Emerson said. "She will want pretty things when she has the money to buy them."

Annabelle blushed. "I like pretty things."

"There's no crime in that," Emerson said. "Deidre?"

Nate sat up, eager to see the gift.

Deidre handed her grandfather a wrapped package. He tore the paper and studied the framed picture.

"It's a photograph of me so you'll always remember what I look like."

Her beauty and smile had been captured for all time. Nate was envious of Emerson. What he wouldn't give to have her photograph by his bedside to greet him every morning.

Emerson placed it with the other gifts. "Now what are your dreams?"

"I would use my inheritance to buy this house and use it for a refuge for women," Deidre said. "A safe haven for those who want to escape abuse and start a new life. A place for second chances."

Bart jumped to his feet. "I may want to keep the house and lands for myself."

"You said it was an albatross," Roland reminded him.

Nate rose to his feet. "She can share her dreams."

Emerson turned to Deidre. "Why do you think this place would be a good choice for your plans?"

"There's plenty of land to grow food and raise animals for wool, cheese, butter, and eggs. The women could support themselves while healing," Deidre said. "Max showed us the pastures and outbuildings. There's so much potential here."

"She was inspired," Nate said, making her smile.

"Those types of women wouldn't know how to live in a place like this among decent folk," Wilma said.

"No one chooses to live in poverty and abuse." Deidre looked around at her cousins. "I would be ashamed if I didn't try to help those less fortunate than myself."

"They'll rob you blind," Bart said in a booming voice. "Charity is a con to part a rich man from his money for nothing in return."

"Helping others is about building relationships," Deidre argued. "You can't hug a coin."

"This is why women shouldn't make financial decisions." Bart gripped his lapels. "They're a grifter's easy mark."

"That's enough," Emerson said. "I know plenty of men who have parted with their hard-earned wealth to con men. I asked what your plans were to confirm my decisions. I think I made the right choices. I have added a clause to my will that if any of you object to the terms, you will be cut off completely. I'm glad to know you're thinking about your future, but I wish you were a little more compassionate to one another. Perhaps with time you'll realize family is more important than your petty squabbles. That is the advice of an old man."

Emerson looked at Nate. "And what have you decided?"

Nate cleared his throat. "I cannot accept your generous offer, but I am honored you considered me."

"I'm disappointed." Emerson looked at Deidre. "I hope the sacrifice is worth it."

Nate kept his gaze on Emerson. "I don't know what my future will bring, but I don't want any roadblocks to a chance at happiness no matter how slim."

Emerson signaled to Bruce. "Take me to my room. Enjoy the cake and champagne. Mr. Niles, we need to talk."

His lawyer had been silently watching from an armchair in the corner and rose. Abraham extended his hand to Nate. "It was a pleasure meeting you. I'm sorry things couldn't have worked out."

"I appreciate the opportunity." Nate felt a moment of regret when he was not invited to join Abraham and Emerson.

Deidre had a puzzled look on her face.

He coughed into his fist and turned to the others.

Everyone said good night to Emerson and watched

as Bruce pushed him out of the room.

"You were with him all afternoon." Bart stood in front of Nate with his hands on his hips. "Why didn't you tell us he finished his will?"

"It was not my right," Nate said.

Roland joined Bart. "How much will each of us inherit?"

The others crowded around him.

Nate took his oaths and responsibilities as a lawyer seriously. "I cannot reveal the contents."

"I bet he tells her." Wilma looked over her shoulder at Deidre.

"I'm not going to ask." Deidre helped Wendy gather the gifts Emerson hadn't taken with him.

Wendy adjusted her stack and carried the gifts out of the room.

"We'll find out soon enough." Faith shook her head. "Grandfather doesn't look well."

"We need to stop all this morbid talk." Charlie slammed shut the book in his hands. "Grandfather is going to live for a long time."

"But if he had the will finished before tonight, why did he want to know what we were going to do with our inheritance?" James asked.

"He enjoys playing with us." Roland paced back and forth.

"Grandfather said he wanted to know our plans to confirm his decisions," Deidre said. "I enjoyed hearing what everyone's dreams were."

Annabelle nodded. "He reminded us we're family and should try to get along."

They headed up the stairs to their rooms. Nate waited while Deidre unlocked her door.

"Charlie is wrong," she whispered as her cousin closed his door across the hall. "My cousins won't have to wait long to split up the spoils. But do they have to act like vultures on a tree branch waiting for Grandfather to die?"

"Try not to think too harshly about them. I think they're sincerely fond of him."

She rested her hand on his chest and smiled at him. "I know I am."

He tried to ignore how her touch made him feel. "Have you spent enough time with him and the others? You'll be leaving soon."

"I have their addresses so I can write. They're not so bad when they aren't fighting over Grandfather's money. We had fun riding around the estate."

He touched her nose. "You got sunburned."

She stepped closer, and he inhaled the scent of flowers and the fresh outdoors. Their time together was coming to an end, and he wondered if she had forgiven him.

"Can you tell me about the generous offer Grandfather spoke of?"

"I can say he offered me a job, but I turned him down."

She frowned and studied his face. "Why?"

"It would be a conflict of interest."

"If you're Grandfather's lawyer, how could it be a conflict of interest?" She stared at him. Her face changed from confusion to understanding. "Me. Grandfather said each of us would inherit. If I inherit anything, and you're the lawyer in charge of the estate, would that be a conflict?"

She had come to the conclusion faster than he had.

"You spend too much time with lawyers."

"Was it a good offer?"

"I would be grossly overpaid."

"Then you must take it. I don't need any inheritance."

She didn't know what she would be giving up. He did. "I will not allow you to sacrifice for me."

"But aren't you doing that?"

"I can make a good living as a lawyer for other clients. I don't need to work for your grandfather."

"I don't like the idea of you forfeiting a job because of me." Deidre's eyes widened. "Couldn't you work for Grandfather until…"

"You said that wouldn't be long. I thought about it. Even if I try to avoid any conflict of interest, your cousins could accuse me of showing favoritism. I have a good job with cases that help women and children. You've taught me that people not money are important. Don't worry about me."

She threw her arms around his neck. "Is it a conflict of interest if I thank you with a kiss?"

"I don't know if a kiss is the proper way to show gratitude for such a small sacrifice…"

Deidre silenced him with her lips. He pulled her tight, the warmth of her body pressed against his driving any doubts from his mind. He'd made the right choice.

Chapter Twenty-Four

Deidre took special care with her appearance in the morning. Last night's kiss proved Nate shared the same passion she felt. He had sacrificed a job, but for what purpose? She needed to understand why he had turned down the job. She could talk to Uncle Tyler to understand how Nate could work for her grandfather and avoid any conflict of interest. It wasn't as if they were married and he would be representing his wife. Or was that Nate's hope?

Deidre stared in the mirror of her dressing table as her shocked expression stared back. Nate had confessed he feared she would say yes to Oscar's proposal and had revealed her family secret to deter him. But to what end? She had made it clear her goal was to help other women with Second Chance. She hadn't taken his comments about helping with the cause seriously. Men promised the moon to impress a woman, but did he have plans to propose in the future?

A knock on the door interrupted her thoughts. Nate stood in the hallway. "Good morning."

The bruising on his handsome face had faded. He was intelligent and hardworking, but his books were too pristine, his wardrobe lacking, and he took the law too seriously. "Do you want to court me?"

"What?" He gulped and ran his fingers along his stiff paper collar. "Why do you ask?"

"It occurs to me that we'll be returning home Saturday. I usually receive callers on Sunday afternoon. Will you be calling?"

He looked surprised. "Do you want me to call?"

"I wouldn't slam the door in your face." She headed down the hall. Let him think on that.

He caught up to her. "You've forgiven me?"

"I'm not a vindictive person, and you've done plenty to redeem yourself, but I'm going to continue to write in my books, and Second Chance is my priority in life." She'd made herself clear but had left the door ajar.

"I'll call on Sunday, take your advice about packing and other things, and be your assistant on any Second Chance missions."

"You can hold the ladder next time." Deidre waved her hand in the air. "I'll be climbing."

He chuckled as they entered the nook for breakfast.

Wendy brought in their breakfast. "If you want something else, let me know."

"This looks great," Nate said.

"Do you know what Grandfather has planned for today?" Deidre asked Wendy.

"I don't know. Bruce said he's not to be disturbed."

"We'll have to wait until the others rise to find out," Nate said.

Wendy was gathering the breakfast dishes when Max entered and removed his flat top hat. "Patsy is having her pups. Would you like to see them?"

Deidre clapped her hands. "I'd love to see the puppies! Can we join you?"

"Let me remove these dishes, and we'll all go." Wendy took the stack into the kitchen, and they headed into the servants' quarters. Wendy removed her bonnet from a peg. "Look." She lifted a round ring of keys. "These were my grandmother's keys."

"What are they doing here?" Max asked.

"Someone must have found them." Wendy put them into her pocket. "I'm glad to have them back. I wanted to open a storage room and realized I didn't have the key."

Deidre stared at the peg. Whoever had returned the keys knew the bonnet belonged to Wendy. But why hadn't they returned them in person?

Nate waited for her. She followed the others down a hallway to the back door.

Deidre hadn't bothered with a bonnet and immediately regretted it. The sky was cloudless, and the sun heated the ground. "It's going to be hot today."

"The barn should be cool." Max took Wendy's hand. "The ground is uneven here."

Deidre put her hand in Nate's. He looked surprised. "Handholding is the first step in a long courtship." If Nate was serious about marrying her, he needed to understand she would need more than a week to make up her mind.

Max had shown them the carriage barn, the bank barn for the cows, and the stables that housed the horses.

She looked around. "Which barn is Patsy in?"

"In the stables." Max pointed to a large structure. "She's in one of the stalls."

The double doors were slung open in front and in the rear. The horses had been moved to the pasture. A man was busy mucking out a stall and looked in their direction before continuing the work of pitching the dirty straw and manure into a wheelbarrow.

Max stood by a stall that opened to the walkway that

ran the length of the barn. A light breeze blew through the open doors.

Patsy was a hound dog mix with light-brown fur and black markings. She rested in a pile of straw in the corner.

"I see two," Wendy said.

"Three." Max pointed to one hidden beneath the other two.

Patsy spasmed in a contraction, and a fourth was born. She licked the membrane covering it and ate the afterbirth before licking the pup. His eyes were closed, and she nudged him to a nipple.

They watched the pups squirm and claim a position.

Max rose to his feet. "We should leave them be."

"I need to return to the house. Your cousins will be rising soon." Wendy hurried outside and across the yard.

"I better see what's ripe in the garden." Max headed out the door.

Nate looked around. "This is a big barn. A dozen stalls."

"And prime horseflesh according to Bart," Deidre said. "Max showed us a separate barn for the cows. The Pierce farm has two draft horses for pulling a wagon and a horse for the buggy."

He examined a halter hanging from the trusses. "How many cows?"

"Four. We use a lot of milk." She laughed. "The number of chickens varies depending on what we're serving for dinner."

He stopped in front of a door and opened it. "What's this?" Inside were oat grain sacks stacked against walls made of fitted planking. A row of small windows ran along the top of the outside wall for light. He ran his hand along the smooth surface. "I've seen these. It's a grain locker. The walls have no gaps to keep out any rodents."

"I bet the mice would love to get their hands on the grain. We keep our oats in a spare tack box and employ barn cats."

He closed the door and latched it by turning a piece of wood that spun on a nail.

They made their way back to the house and found everyone gathered in the parlor.

"Where have you been?" Annabelle asked as she pulled straw from Deidre's hair. "Canoodling in the barn?"

Deidre ran her fingers over her hair to search for more straw. "Patsy had pups."

"I hope Patsy is a dog," Faith said.

"Bitch, dear," Roland corrected.

Faith looked shocked. "What?"

"A female dog is called a bitch," Charlie said.

Faith crossed her arms. "It sounds rather insulting."

Everyone turned their attention to her grandfather as Bruce brought him into the parlor.

"Time is running out with many of you leaving tomorrow. I have one final activity planned. A scavenger hunt. Five clues will be hidden on the property you toured yesterday. Each married couple will be a team with Charlie and Deidre a team."

"What about Nate?" Deidre asked.

"He and Max will place the clues."

"You wrote the clues?" Annabelle asked with surprise.

"As you have probably noticed, my hand isn't as steady as it was in the past. I dictated the clues to Bruce. He has excellent penmanship." He handed Nate a stack of envelopes. "The team names are written on the front and the location on the back. After you and Max place them, return here, and I will give each team their first clue." He looked at the others. "That should give you time to change clothing for hiking around the grounds."

Deidre wore her old bonnet and carried her new parasol. The other ladies were armed with bonnets and parasols as well. The men had discarded their coats and donned wide-brimmed hats.

Her grandfather handed Nate four envelopes, which he passed out. "Inside is your first clue. Even though the clues are the same, the order for each team is different, so don't think you can follow one another. And you must go on foot. When you arrive at the next location, take only your clue. It will have your names on it. Otherwise, you could end up at the wrong location." He began to cough and had trouble catching his breath.

"You should be in bed, Grandfather," Deidre said.

"I'll take care of him." Bruce pushed the wheelchair out the door.

"The others are leaving," Charlie said. "They'll have a head start."

Deidre opened the envelope, and Charlie read it over her shoulder. *"It goes around and around but no one can see what makes it move."*

"It's the windmill," she said. They went out the parlor's door. The others had scattered, heading in different directions. The windmill was to the south.

"Let's go," Charlie said.

When they arrived at the windmill, four clues were left on the bottom support, each one beneath a small rock. "This one is ours." Deidre tossed the rock while Charlie opened the envelope.

"The pecking order isn't by birth but lies on the ground." He shrugged. "I don't get it."

She read it again. "I think it means the chicken coop. They peck for food on the ground."

"That's on the other side of the farm."

"Then we better hurry." She picked up the hem of her skirt and ran.

He kept up but was breathing hard when they arrived at the chicken coop. He was bent over, his hands on his knees as he attempted to catch his breath.

She removed their clue, which was attached to the side of the wooden building with a string. Two remained. *"The sign of Leo has another name to greet the visitor."*

"Leo is a lion," Charlie said as he straightened. His face was flushed, but his breathing was easier.

"The next clue is the lions at the main gate. The name of Kinsman is above it."

He moaned. "That's in front of the house."

"Let's not run. I don't care if we win if you don't."

"Let someone else die from heatstroke." He wiped his brow with his handkerchief before replacing his hat.

One envelope remained at the paws of the carved lion. "I guess we don't have to worry about coming in first."

Charlie opened the clue. *"This barn is home to mares, geldings, fillies, and colts."*

"It's the stable." Deidre patted him on the back as he leaned over. It was obvious Charlie was not used to physical activity. "You can see the puppies."

The heat beat down, but the barn was cool inside. Charlie found the final clue resting on the front of the first stall. *"A cool drink awaits the weary traveler at home.* It takes us back to the house." He pointed outside.

"Looks like Bart and Wilma are heading that way."

"Our clues had us running all over the place," Deidre said. "I'm exhausted. Let's look at the pups before we go out in the sun again."

He joined her in the stall. "They're awfully small."

"They were born this morning." She removed her bonnet and placed it next to her parasol in the straw. She brushed back her damp hair. "It's gotten hotter in here."

He stood. "And darker."

She stepped out into the walkway and looked around. Light filtered through the cracks of the planking that ran vertically on the outside of the barn, but the double doors were closed.

"I could have sworn they were open when we entered," he said.

"They were," she recalled. The doors in the rear also were closed, and the lack of a breeze made the air stifling. She saw the shadow of a man heading toward them.

"Why did you close the doors?" Charlie shouted.

Something was familiar in his movements. A shaft of light illuminated a scarecrow mask instead of a face. "Run!" Deidre pushed Charlie toward the entrance. A rope was knotted around the handles to keep the doors closed.

She struggled to untie the knot. A large knife stabbed the board above her head. She screamed.

Charlie shrieked and pointed to an open door. They ran inside the grain storage locker, and he pulled it closed. "It doesn't lock from the inside."

She pulled on the wooden handle with him but felt no tugging from the other side. "Do you think it's safe to go out?"

He pushed on the door. "It won't open." He shoved with his shoulder, but the entrance didn't budge. "He's locked us in."

She looked through the thin crack of the opening. She used a hair comb to turn the piece of wood that locked the door. She shoved but met resistance. She saw a plank farther away and angled toward them. "I think a board is lodged against the door."

He looked around the room. "There must be another way out."

The windows were too small and tightly sealed with no other doorway. They were trapped inside.

He pounded on the door. "Maybe someone will look for a clue in the stable."

Their clue had been the only one remaining. Everyone had probably returned to the house, but she didn't abandon all hope. "Max comes into the barn all the time. He'll find us."

Charlie leaned against the door. "Was that the scarecrow ghost Faith saw?"

"Yes."

"I thought he was only trying to frighten people, but he threw that knife at us."

"How did he know we would be in this barn? It was our last clue, and everyone else had finished."

"Maybe he saw the others enter the barn." Charlie pushed against the door, but it didn't budge. "Do you think he'll let us out after scaring us?"

Deidre didn't think the scarecrow was coming back, but she didn't want to worry Charlie. How long would it take the others to miss them? The room was suffocating. Moisture beaded on her skin. She had worn a lightweight day dress, but her clothes were damp and clung to her skin. They needed to stay alive until they were found. "You better take off your hat, bow tie, and collar."

He obeyed and placed his clothing beside him on a stack of grain sacks. "What's in here?"

"Oats for the horses." She sat on a stack of bags. "Do you mind if I remove my shoes?"

"That's a good idea. Heat leaves the body from the head, hands, and feet."

She slipped off her shoes and rolled down her stockings. "I'm glad you're my partner, Charlie. You know so many things."

"I'm a wealth of useless information." He removed his shoes and socks.

"Knowledge is never useless." She made a seat with two grain sacks and placed her bare feet on the ground, her toes curling into the dirt, seeking the coolness of the earth. "If Grandfather gives you his books, what will you do with them?"

"I don't know." He created a seat beside her and kneaded the ground with his bare feet. "I don't have the space for all of them. The house our parents left us isn't large. I should get a better job. I work as a clerk at a store, but it doesn't pay much."

She digested his series of statements. "What would you like to do besides travel?"

"I'd like to write a book and share my knowledge."

"That's a good idea. I read that Mark Twain used a typewriter to write *The Adventures of Tom Sawyer*. It's much quicker than writing a book by hand."

"I love new inventions." Charlie found a stick and drew in the dirt. "I'll have to try typing my novel."

"What would you write?" She removed a comb and pinned her hair higher off her neck.

"I'm interested in writing something like Jules Verne. That's why I'd like to travel and explore the world."

"I was going to read *Around the World in Eighty Days* on my trip home. Have you read it?"

"Twice." Charlie drew a circle in the dirt. "You'll enjoy it."

Deidre felt weaker, the heat sapping the strength from her body. "How long does it take for the heat to kill someone?"

"I don't know, and we're not going to find out."

"I like your optimism."

Charlie unbuttoned his waistcoat. "We're first cousins. If you want to loosen your clothing, I'll turn the other way."

"I think I will loosen this corset." She turned her back and unbuttoned her blouse. She untied the strings to the corset and pulled them loose. She could feel air caress her damp skin beneath. "That helps."

He moved to the ground and formed a pillow from one of the grain sacks. "Who do you think the scarecrow is?"

She stretched out on the ground beside him. "My mother wrote about a boy named Freddy. He killed a squirrel by stabbing it with his knife, and he pushed me down the stairs."

"Were you hurt?"

"No, but my mother was terrified that he would do something worse."

"Sounds like a dreadful child."

"He'd be a man now." Deidre turned to her side so she could face him. "I think he killed Mrs. Knox."

His eyebrows rose. "I thought that was an accident."

"The sheriff ruled it an accident, but Mrs. Knox would never climb a ladder. I think the scarecrow killed her, but Nate only believes in facts."

"He's smart." Charlie sat up. "Let's think about this scientifically. What do we know about the scarecrow?"

Maybe talking about the masked man would help her sort out her imaginings from the facts. "He came into my room and took a book."

"And he broke your lamp," he added. "But I don't remember what book he took."

"*Little Women.*"

He laughed. "That must have been a mistake."

"I agree. Nate and I found the book discarded in the hallway on the third floor."

"Then we can hypothesize he was after another book. What was his next deed?"

"He scared Faith in the hallway and stole my mother's journal."

"You think the scarecrow stole your mother's journal?" His voice had a tone of disbelief.

"It was missing after Faith saw him. I don't know who else would have taken it."

He rolled his trousers to his knees. "And is this imprisonment the next incident?"

"Yes. I'm sorry you were caught with me."

"I ran in here first. I should have faced him."

"He threw a knife. If it's Freddy, he could be dangerous. I think this was safer than being stabbed." *Or killed.*

"Do you think he's waiting outside?" Charlie looked toward the door. "He wouldn't need to stay to watch us…"

"Don't think it." Deidre shuddered.

"We should write notes and let others know what happened. It would be the practical thing to do."

"You think like Nate." Deidre looked around. "Do you have any paper?"

"I have the clues. We can write on them." He handed her two clues and a pencil.

Deidre wrote a message to Nate and handed Charlie the pencil. "I told Nate about the scarecrow. He'll bring him to justice." She had written a more personal note on the other clue.

"I'm glad Annabelle has James to take care of her." He wrote a message on his clue. "I guess I won't write my book."

She felt as limp as a wet rag. She tucked her clues into her skirt pocket and embraced the cold earth. "We should rest."

Chapter Twenty-Five

Nate paced back and forth in the parlor, his anxiety rising as each minute passed. Everyone had returned from the scavenger hunt except Deidre and Charlie. Where could they be?

Faith fanned herself as she took another glass of lemonade from Wendy. "I don't know why we couldn't have done a scavenger hunt inside. The heat was unbearable."

He looked at the clock on the mantel. It had been nearly an hour since the last team returned. "Where's Max?" Nate looked at Wendy. "I think we should look for them."

"We'll help," James said. "One of them could be hurt."

The other cousins volunteered.

"Why don't Bart and Roland take the lions' gate and windmill?" Nate said. "They're in the east and south. James and I will take the stable barn and chicken coop."

"You have to find my brother. He's not very strong." Annabelle burst into tears, twisting at her handkerchief with her hands.

James hugged Annabelle. "We'll find them."

Wilma led her to the sofa.

"We'll take care of her," Faith said. "Go."

Wendy stood in the doorway. "I found Max."

"Have cold water to drink and gather medical

supplies," Nate said to Wendy. "We don't know if one of them is injured."

Nate joined Max in the flower garden.

He had a canteen in his hand. "Wendy mentioned water. I filled mine. I take it out in the field with me on hot days."

"Good idea," Nate said. "Let's search the stables first."

"I can take a horse and ride around the farm," James said. "They may have gotten lost. Charlie has no sense of direction."

The three men entered the barn. Nate allowed his eyes to adjust to the darkness. It was empty. The horses were outside, and the man mucking stalls had left.

"You'll have to get one of the horses from the pasture," Max told James.

Nate stopped when they came to the stall with the pups. He picked up Deidre's bonnet and parasol. "She wouldn't have gone out into the sun without these."

"Let's search the stalls," Max said.

"Split up." Nate headed back toward the front entrance. A bench had been jammed against the door to the grain locker. He dropped Deidre's belongings on a tack box. "Over here!"

James and Max helped him free the barricade. He pulled the door open. A wave of oppressive heat washed over him.

Deidre and Charlie were sprawled on the floor, their eyes closed, their bodies motionless in prone positions. Neither wore shoes nor stockings. They had loosened their clothing to escape the rising temperature. Nate knelt beside Deidre, afraid to touch her as heat radiated off her body.

"Are they dead?" James asked from the doorway.

Charlie groaned, his eyes flickering open. "Not yet."

Nate turned Deidre over, and her chest rose with a breath. He scooped her into his arms. She was drenched in sweat, and her gown clung like a second skin. Her face was red and her lips dry and cracked. Her mouth opened.

"Don't talk." He carried her outside into the shade. Max and James carried Charlie outside and placed him on the grass near Deidre.

Max had given Charlie water and handed the canteen to Nate.

"Sip this." He held the canteen to her lips and poured some on his handkerchief. Nate wiped her face, neck, and arms. Her breathing was shallow. He gave her another sip before handing the canteen to Charlie. "We need to get them back to the house."

"I'll hitch the wagon," Max said.

"That will take too long." Nate lifted Deidre. Her body drooped in his arms, and her hair had come loose and hung in wet tendrils. "Can you carry Charlie?"

"I can stand," Charlie said in a soft, strained voice.

Max gave him another sip of water and helped him rise.

James put his arm around him. "I've got you."

"My shoes." Charlie pointed at his bare feet.

"I'll get them." Max returned with their discarded clothing along with Deidre's bonnet and parasol. "The shoes are hot to the touch. You're going to want to go barefoot."

"Lean on me," James said.

Max supported the other side of Charlie as they kept pace with Nate.

"They could have died in there," James said.

"I think that was the goal." Nate didn't hide his anger.

"Who would do this?" Max asked.

"Scarecrow," Deidre whispered through parched lips.

The ghost and prankster had turned deadly in his intent. When he discovered he had failed, would he strike again?

Annabelle was waiting in the garden. "They found them!" She ran toward Charlie.

"Let's get them inside," Max said.

"We have cold water ready." Wilma held open the door to the parlor.

"Does anyone need bandages?" Faith lifted a piece of gauze.

"They don't appear hurt," James said. "Just overheated."

Wilma filled two glasses with water and handed one to Charlie.

His hand shook as he reached for it.

"Let me." Annabelle held it to his lips. He drank the entire glass.

Wilma brought the other glass to Deidre. "Try this, honey."

Deidre raised her hand but let it drop.

"I've got it." Nate held the glass to her lips, and she drank a little at a time.

Wendy removed wet rags from a bowl and wrung them out. "These should help." She handed one to Nate and the other to Annabelle.

Nate gently mopped Deidre's face as she drank another glass of water.

"What happened to them?" Wendy asked.

"They were barricaded in the grain locker," Max said. "They became overheated."

Faith looked around. "Who would do that?"

"The scarecrow." Nate took the empty glass from Deidre. "Can you tell us what happened?"

"The scarecrow was in the barn when we found our clue," Deidre said in a hoarse whisper. "He threw a knife at us. We ran into the grain locker, and he blocked the door."

"We could have died." Charlie put his head into his hands. "I have a headache."

"You drank too fast," Annabelle said. "Lean back and rest."

Deidre looked at her feet. "Where are my shoes?"

Max placed her belongings on her lap.

She poked her finger through a hole. "What happened to my parasol?"

"I think Patsy chewed on it," Nate said.

"Why don't we take you upstairs and give you a nice cool sponge bath?" Annabelle suggested.

Deidre tugged at the opening of her gown. "I'd like that."

"If I had any strength, I'd take a plunge into the pond." Charlie wiped his face with a wet cloth.

Annabelle examined her brother. "James can help bathe you."

"I'll bring up fresh water." Wendy hurried from the room.

"I better find Roland and Bart," Max said. "They're still looking for you."

"Thank you." Charlie looked around. "It's nice to know the family can pull together in a crisis."

"Come on, Charlie." James tugged him to his feet.

"I'll help you to your room."

"I've got Deidre." Nate lifted her off the couch.

"I can walk."

"Not until we reach your room."

Deidre relaxed in his arms until he put her down at her door.

She removed the key from her skirt pocket and unlocked the door. "It seems silly to lock it."

"No. I think we need to be more cautious." He didn't want to scare her, but if Freddy was the scarecrow, he had already killed a woman, and he wasn't counting Mrs. Knox. "The scarecrow is dangerous." He reluctantly let the women take over Deidre's care.

He found Bart and Roland in the parlor gulping glasses of lemonade.

"What happened?" Bart asked.

"The man in the scarecrow mask had a knife and chased Deidre and Charlie into the grain locker, trapping them inside." Nate ran his fingers through his hair. "They nearly died."

Roland looked confused. "I thought this fellow was only trying to scare the women."

"It appears he's raised the stakes," Nate said.

"I plan to leave tomorrow." Bart looked at his brother. "The sooner the better."

"Then we'll be traveling on the same train," Roland said. "I'm glad we had this time together, brother."

"I'm sorry I've been such a bossy braggart."

Nate looked from one brother to the other. "You two made up?"

"We've wasted too much time bickering." Roland put his arm around Bart's shoulders. "If we've learned anything this week, it's that family matters. We plan to stay in touch with the others."

"Deidre said she plans to write." Nate pointed at them. "You better write back."

"If we don't, the wives will," Bart said. "They've grown fond of each other."

Charlie and James appeared in the doorway. Charlie's hair was damp, and he wore a fresh shirt and trousers. Roland and Bart rushed toward them.

Bart gave him a hug. "You gave us a scare, Charlie."

"Come sit down." Roland had him sit on the sofa. "Nice bare feet, Charlie."

"My shoes stink. I may have to throw them out."

They talked about business, politics, and sporting events until the women appeared together, ready to dine.

Nate went to Deidre's side. "Are you sure you're feeling up to eating?"

"I'm starving," Deidre said.

Nate couldn't forget the image of Deidre prostrate on the dirt floor. He had thought she was dead. "I thought I had lost you."

"I wrote a note." She handed it to him.

Scarecrow locked us in. Find him. Tell my family I love them.

She handed him a second note. "I wrote this under duress."

Feelings change. I forgave you for the gossip a long time ago. I wish we had more time together.

"You do?"

"Facing death makes a person face the truth, especially about feelings they don't want to admit," she said. "Don't act so surprised. Haven't you been trying to win me over since the trip began?"

He ran his hand through his hair. "I didn't think I

was succeeding."

"You gave up the job Grandfather offered you. You risked your future for the possibility I might consider you for a suitor. I think you deserve that chance."

"I can always find a job as a lawyer. I could never find another woman I wanted to spend the rest of my life with but you. It wasn't a difficult decision."

She tugged on his coat and kissed him. The others made kissing noises.

"You know you're supposed to be cooling off," Faith said. "Not heating up."

Deidre laughed. "I'm showing my gratitude for Nate saving my life."

"I hope I don't have to kiss him," Charlie said, making the others laugh. He stepped toward her. "You're looking a lot better than the last time I saw you, cousin."

Deidre hugged him. "We made it."

They headed to the dining room. Emerson was absent. Nate tried not to think the worst.

"What's keeping Grandfather?" Annabelle asked.

"Dr. Jennings is with him," Wendy announced. "He said you were to dine without him."

Faith looked at the others. "That doesn't sound good."

Nate sat next to Deidre. She had grown fond of her grandfather, and he wanted to offer his support.

Wendy entered just as a dessert of peach cobbler and ice cream was served. "Mr. Kinsman is requesting you take turns and visit him in his room." She burst into tears.

"Is it serious?" Annabelle asked.

Wendy nodded, unable to speak.

Nate clutched Deidre's hand.

Roland looked at Bart. "I think you should go first.

You're the oldest."

Wilma stood. "I'll go with you."

"Then you and Faith." Bart looked around at the others. "We won't take more than fifteen minutes. Does that sound fair?"

They nodded in agreement.

They finished their dessert in silence and moved to the parlor to await their turn. Bart and Wilma had tears streaming down their cheeks when they entered.

"Is he dead?" Annabelle asked.

Bart shook his head. "He's holding his own. For now."

"Maybe fifteen minutes is too long," Faith said.

Roland took her hand. "It's our turn."

James and Annabelle took Charlie with them. Deidre was the last to go.

Nate stood. "Do you want me to go with you?"

Deidre nodded. She had been crying quietly while waiting her turn. He escorted her to the study. Bruce opened the door and took a stance near the headboard.

Dr. Jennings was examining her grandfather whose breathing was labored. His color was grayer if that was possible. The doctor pushed the covers aside and felt the man's ankles. His legs were more swollen than last night and had become darker in color.

Emerson's skin was taut against his skull, clinging to the cheekbones and erasing any lips. His eyes were sunken into deep pits. Overnight he had deteriorated. Death was lurking in the shadows.

"What's wrong with him?" Nate asked the doctor.

"His heart is struggling to pump blood," Dr. Jennings said.

"Can you do anything?" Deidre asked.

Dr. Jennings shook his head.

"Then make him comfortable," Deidre said.

"He said no morphine until the visits were completed," Dr. Jennings said.

"Mr. Burroughs," Emerson said as he struggled to sit up.

Bruce moved the pillows behind him to support his body.

Nate stepped forward. "I'm here, Mr. Kinsman."

"Help Mr. Niles make sure my wishes are fulfilled," he said.

Dr. Jennings took his pulse. "You need to rest."

"I can rest in the grave. I have one more grandchild to talk to." Emerson reached out his hand, and his misshapen fingers shook. "Deidre."

Tears flowed down her cheeks, but she smiled. "I'm here." She took his hand and rested her damp cheek against it.

"Have you found your mother's journal?"

"No, but I'm sure it will turn up." She released his hand, which fell limp to his side. "Then I'll read some passages to you. Would you like that, Grandfather?"

"I always enjoyed your mother's voice when she read to you as a child." He coughed with a rumbling echo in his chest. "Would you read to me now?"

She looked around the room. "What should I read?"

"Some psalms to lead me home."

Nate retrieved the Bible on the shelf and found the familiar passages.

She read for several minutes, her voice cracking with emotion.

Nate saw the doctor shake his head and lay Emerson's still hand on his chest. "He's gone."

Deidre put the Bible down, gazed at her grandfather, and kissed his forehead. "Good-bye, Grandfather. I love you."

Nate led her to the parlor. "He's gone," he told the others.

Deidre clung to him as her body racked with sobs. "I was just getting to know him. First Mrs. Knox and now Grandfather. I'm losing all the ties to my past."

Everyone cried out their grief together and shared memories of their grandfather until nightfall.

In the morning Nate escorted Deidre downstairs for breakfast. It had become their habit and one he would miss when they returned home. He noticed that the mirrors were covered and photographs turned face down. The household was in mourning.

Emerson Kinsman's funeral at the local church was attended by family, servants, and townsfolk Saturday afternoon. His body was laid to rest in the same cemetery as Mrs. Knox under a cloudy sky that threatened rain. Guests gathered at the Kinsman Manor, offered condolences, and partook of the food placed in the dining room.

It was evening when the last visitor departed, and Abraham arrived with a large leather briefcase. He summoned everyone to the parlor to read the will.

The doors were left open, and the servants gathered outside in the gallery. Abraham read the normal opening about being of sound mind and body before proceeding to the disbursement of his wealth. "*Each servant will receive one hundred dollars for every year he or she has served me*," he read. "I have a list and how much each payment will be."

It was a generous amount, especially for the older

servants. Nate handed a copy of the list to Wendy. "Share this with the other employees." He closed the doors.

Abraham turned to the next page of the will and read. *"I originally planned to give each of my heirs a fifth of my wealth upon my death minus the servants' pay, but after observing the foolishness and mendacity of my heirs, I have changed my mind."*

Bart stood. "What? He said we would inherit."

"Sit down," Nate ordered. "He kept his word." He remained standing and waited for the reaction the will's instructions would create.

Abraham continued. *"It has come to my attention that if I paid each of my grandchildren a lump sum, it would be gone within a year. Therefore I have established trusts for each of them with payments on a quarterly basis until the money is exhausted from my businesses. Hopefully, that will teach them how to manage their money, and they will not become penniless too soon."*

"Is that everyone?" Wilma asked. "What about the spouses?"

"I have specific gifts listed," Abraham said. *"To Bart, I am giving you fifty-percent ownership in a prosperous business with the hope you learn the skills from your partner that will help you run your own businesses. I also leave you the family Bible to record future generations. To Wilma, I leave a silver tea service and a ruby necklace to impress her friends. To Roland, I leave a carriage and a team of horses so he can appear as grand as his brother. To Faith, I leave six works of art my wife collected on our trip to Europe and an opal necklace. To Charlie, I leave a hundred books from my library of his choosing and my collection of maps. To*

Annabelle, I leave a dozen pieces of her grandmother's jewelry and the best dinnerware, silverware, and linens so she can entertain in elegance. To James, I leave my railroad stocks so Annabelle can manage her own funds and gain as much confidence to equal the amount of kindness she possesses in her heart. To Deidre, I leave the land and buildings minus the gifts I have mentioned."

"What?" Bart stood. "She gets it all?"

Nate stepped toward him, and Bart took his seat.

"Not all," Abraham said. "You'll receive your quarterly allowances from his numerous business interests once the will goes through probate. I've already begun the process and expect no delays. You can take the personal items listed immediately."

Bart pointed at Nate. "And what part did you have in this? Did Grandfather name you his executor? No wonder Deidre gets the estate."

Nate shook his head. "Mr. Kinsman offered me a job as his lawyer, but I turned him down. I didn't want there to be any appearance of a conflict of interest."

Deidre joined him. "Nate is an honorable man. He didn't receive anything from Grandfather."

James turned to Bart. "You said the estate was an albatross. Why would you want it anyway?"

"To sell for the money."

"I won't be selling it," Deidre said. "And you can visit anytime."

"He gave us each a generous allowance," Charlie said. "We should be grateful he gave us anything at all."

"How can you be happy about receiving a bunch of books and maps?"

"I like to read and plan to travel. Grandfather knew that. He based his gifts on how we behaved this week."

"We showed him our worst sides," Roland said. "We were lucky to receive what we did."

Bart turned to Deidre. "Were you honest? Are you really going to open this museum to unfortunate women?"

"Women and children," Deidre said. "Grandfather knew it was my dream, and he made it come true."

Charlie raised his glass. "To Grandfather. He knew us better than we knew ourselves."

Chapter Twenty-Six

When Mr. Niles had read the will, Deidre couldn't believe her ears. Her grandfather had left her the house and grounds to fulfill her dream. He had seemed so gruff and judgmental when she first met him, but he'd only wanted what was best for her and her cousins.

All of them had attended church services in the morning. They saw Bart, Wilma, Roland, and Faith off at the train depot. Everyone hugged and promised to stay in touch. The others were planning to leave Monday. Each one was a tie to her mother and the Kinsman branch of her family.

Deidre would have to wait for the will to finish the probate process in the court before taking possession of the property, but Mr. Niles had distributed the gifts mentioned in the will. Deidre sat at one of the tables in the library, making a list of what was available and what would be needed to create a Second Chance home.

Wendy delivered an inventory of rooms, furnishings, and smaller items inside the manor. "Max wrote a list of outbuildings and animals." She shifted from one foot to the other. "Will you be keeping any of the servants?"

"Yes. I'll need employees to help," Deidre reassured her. "Could you make a list of the employees who aren't retiring? I'll have to interview staff, but I'm sure we'll find a place for anyone who wants to work here."

"That's good news," Wendy said with a smile and a deep sigh. "I'll write that list up now."

"Wendy," Deidre called as she headed for the door. "Thank you for all your help."

Charlie was at the neighboring table, stacking and restacking books. He moved one publication from one pile to the next and searched for more from the shelves behind him. "There are so many wonderful titles. The first fifty were easy to choose, but I can't decide on the rest."

"Why don't you take one hundred books now, and when you've read them, you can bring them back and exchange them for different ones? I think that fits the description of your inheritance."

"That's a wonderful idea." He sorted through his choices and counted the number of books stacked before him. "I'm going to need trunks to pack them."

"Wendy has the keys to the storage rooms on the third floor. I'm sure you'll find something suitable up there."

"I can't wait to build shelves for them." He smiled and clapped his hands. "This was the best gift Grandfather could have given me."

"I'm glad he did. No one else would enjoy them more."

He paused by the door next to the table she sat at. "It took Grandfather's birthday to bring us together, and I can't believe he's gone, but I'm glad you're family. I think your Second Chance idea is a good one, and Grandfather made the right choice in giving you Kinsman Manor. I'd hate to see it sold and the money spent on useless things." Charlie whistled as he left the room.

Deidre gathered her papers into a stack and stored them in the drawer built into the table. She'd been sitting too long and rose, stretching her arms over her head. Above the fireplace was the empty space where her mother's portrait had hung. Before his death, her grandfather had sent it to be repaired. Another kind gesture for which she would be forever grateful.

She walked around the room, unable to believe this beautiful house was hers. She looked out on the garden and circled back to the table where Charlie had placed his books. She examined the titles. He had a wide variety of tastes.

"May I come in?" James stood in the doorway across from her. He stepped into the room and closed the door. "Are you alone?"

Deidre placed her hand on a stack of books. "Charlie left to search for trunks to transport his inheritance."

"I wanted to return this." He placed a familiar leather journal next to a stack of Charlie's books.

She stared at her mother's journal. "You took it?" Panic seized her. Was he the mysterious man in the scarecrow mask?

"After you and Nate took Faith's broken dish downstairs, I searched the other end of the hall for the masked stranger. I saw your door open and knew it was the perfect opportunity to search for your mother's journal." He gazed into her eyes. "I'd like to explain."

She looked toward the closed door behind him. She was alone with the man. He wasn't a blood relative. What did she know about him? Where was Nate? Would he hear her scream? She took a deep breath to calm her racing heart. "What could you possibly want with my mother's journal?" She edged slowly along the table, her hands touching the books stacked in front of her.

"Lewis Smith was my father."

What? Her knees shook, and she grabbed onto the back of the chair at the table to keep from collapsing in a faint. Was this Freddy? Did he have a knife?

He pulled a chair out and motioned with his hand. "You better sit down."

She stepped back against the bookcase and glanced toward the door. "Nate!" she screamed, panic in her voice.

"I'm not going to hurt you." James raised his hands, palms toward her.

"Are you Freddy?" she shrieked.

"No." He backed up, a look of pain in his expression. "He's another illegitimate son. My mother raised me, but I wanted to know more about my father and searched for his relatives. I knew Lewis Smith had married Hannah Kinsman. That's how I met Charlie Kinsman. He told me about the family scandal."

"Did you marry Annabelle to find me?" Her anger gave her courage, and she stepped to the end of the table. "How dare you use my cousin."

"No." He waved his hands in denial. "I fell in love with Annabelle. She was so sweet and honest. I told her and Charlie everything before I married her. We were a happy family. When the invitation for Mr. Kinsman's birthday arrived, I wasn't sure what to do. My father killed yours. I figured you would hate me if you knew of my ties to Smith. We agreed not to say anything about my parentage so you wouldn't misjudge me."

"Misjudge? I feel like I don't even know you. Why are you telling me this now?"

"You've been honest about your past, and I wanted

you to know the truth." He bowed his head and gripped his hands. "I'll understand if you never want to speak to me again."

He seemed sincere, but trust was earned. "How well did you know your father?"

"My mother left him when I was young. She never spoke of Smith except to say he was a dangerous man and not to look for him." He removed his coat and pushed up the sleeve of his shirt. "Someone cut me when I was a child."

A white line ran along his forearm. "Your father?"

"No. It was an older boy. He claimed it was an accident, but my mother and I left the next morning." James pushed the journal toward her. "I took the journal to learn more about Lewis Smith, but when you mentioned the name Freddy, I remembered he was the boy who cut me."

Deidre understood his thirst for answers. "You could have asked to read my mother's writings."

"Not without revealing who I was. I shouldn't have taken it, but your door was unlocked. I had every intention of returning it, but you were vigilant in locking your door after the theft. I couldn't get in to put it back."

She picked up her mother's journal and circled around the table. "Thank you for returning it."

"You said you wanted to find out more about your mother. Can you understand how I had questions about my father?"

"I do."

He pointed at the journal. "Your mother wrote enough about Smith to confirm what my mother warned me about. He was a cruel and selfish man, but I hoped he would have at least one redeeming trait."

"People called my father a fornicator, but he loved my mother." She flipped to the end of the entries. "This is where she wrote about Freddy. He pushed me down the stairs. What do you remember?"

"He had big hands." He made a fist. "He would hit me if I got in his way. And he always carried a knife and would toss it inches from me."

"The scarecrow barely missed me when he threw his knife in the barn." She ran her hands over the smooth leather of her mother's diary. "It doesn't matter who our parents were, James. It matters how we treat others."

Nate stood in the doorway. "Did you call me?"

She laughed. "You lost your chance at rescuing me, Nate, darling. Then I discovered I wasn't in any danger."

"Danger?" He stepped toward James. "Is there a problem?"

She saw no need to be subtle. "James is the son of Lewis Smith."

Nate stepped between her and James.

"He's harmless. He returned my mother's journal."

"He was the thief?" He turned toward James. "I'd like to ask you some questions."

"This isn't a courtroom, and James isn't on trial," she said.

"Then call it an investigation for the truth." Nate pointed at the chair James had pulled out.

James sat and placed his hands on the table. "I'll answer anything you want."

Nate paced back and forth between the empty table and the one stacked with books. "Were you the one who wore the scarecrow mask?"

James shook his head.

"But you took my journal the night Faith saw the

scarecrow." Deidre stood opposite James with the length of the table between them. "Did you see anyone in a mask?"

"The hallway was empty," James said. "I'm sorry I tossed things around, but I was in a hurry to find the journal before you returned from the kitchen. When I saw the Bible, I remembered Annabelle talking about it and looked inside."

"He took advantage of my carelessness." She turned from Nate to James. "Did you search my mother's room for the journal earlier in the week?"

James looked confused. "I don't know which room belonged to your mother. I didn't know about the journal until you mentioned it at dinner."

"You've never been on the third floor?" Nate asked.

"No."

"What about my mother's portrait?" She looked at the empty space. "Did you cut it?"

His brow wrinkled. "I thought Mrs. Knox damaged it when she fell."

"She couldn't climb a ladder let alone balance on one to destroy a painting," she said. "I think Freddy is responsible."

"You think Freddy is here?" James clutched his arm over the scar.

"Have you seen anyone who bears a resemblance to Freddy?" Nate asked.

James shook his head. "I was a child. I remember his cruelty, not his face."

Nate turned to Deidre. "If James wasn't the man in the mask, then someone else must be involved. But it doesn't mean it's Freddy. How would he even know about the birthday gathering?"

"If the man in the mask isn't a relative, he must be a servant," Deidre said. "Wendy is making a list of the staff. I plan to interview them for jobs for Second Chance."

"I'd like to see it," Nate said. "Do you know where she is?"

"Charlie was going to ask Wendy to unlock the third-floor storage rooms," Deidre said. "He needs trunks for his books."

"I'll find her." Nate pulled her close and kissed her in a way that tingled every nerve in her body and lingered after he released her. "I won't be long."

He looked at James. "Don't move from that seat. I want Charlie to confirm your story."

"We'll wait here." Deidre flipped through the pages of her mother's journal and turned to James. "When did you and your mother live with Lewis and Freddy?"

"I was five." He paused. "It would have been 1857."

She put the date on a timeline. "That would have been after the trial but before my mother died."

"Freddy was about ten. He would sneak up behind me to pinch, hit, or whisper a threat in my ear." He rubbed his arm. "Lewis was drunk most of the time and beat my mother. Freddy would watch while I hid in the corner, crying for him to stop. I remember the soul-gripping fear."

She had felt the same way in the barn.

His body shook. "That's why I wanted to know if the nightmares were real or only imagined. I wanted to put Lewis Smith to rest once and for all."

"Has Freddy tried to contact you since your father's death?"

"No. I read an obituary about Lewis Smith in the

paper. The writer made him sound like a good man even though I remembered otherwise."

"Grandfather didn't like Lewis or Freddy. Mrs. Knox didn't like them either." She looked at the floor where the elderly woman had died. "She may have recognized him."

"If Freddy Smith is here, he must be using a different name," James said.

Chapter Twenty-Seven

Deidre heard the door close and turned. Bruce stood in front of the door like a statue. How long had he been there? How much had he heard? He wore a long dark coat instead of his white medical jacket. He appeared larger. She hadn't thought about his position or future employment since her grandfather's death. "Are you hoping to continue working here?"

"No. I came to say good-bye." He turned a key to lock the door and stepped forward, a queer expression on his face. "Are you looking for a name? How about Freddy Bruce, Jimmy?"

James knocked over his chair as he stood and moved along the bookcase. His hand trembled as he pointed. "Nobody but Freddy called me Jimmy."

Freddy? This was the wicked boy in her mother's journal? She'd never noticed how cold his eyes were. *Cold as ice.* A chill ran down her spine. She stepped back until she was on the same side of the table as James. The stacks of books created a feeble wall of protection.

"My mother's name was Bruce." He looked above the fireplace. "This room looks so much better without that ugly woman's portrait."

"You cut my mother's painting!" She gripped the back of a chair. What else was he responsible for?

"I would have destroyed her image if that old woman hadn't wandered in to dust and become hysterical."

"I knew her death wasn't an accident." Deidre's voice trembled. "You killed Mrs. Knox."

He shrugged. "Funny how a bump on the head is blamed on a fall."

"Her keys were missing from her pocket," she recalled. "And returned underneath Wendy's hat."

"They were useless. None of them fit any of the doors I wanted to open."

Her hand shook when she pointed at the locked door behind him. "But you had the key to the library."

"Wendy gave me hers." He jingled the keys on the triangle ring before he shoved them into a pocket.

Bruce was a strong man. He had lifted her grandfather effortlessly from the wheelchair to his bed. He could easily overpower a woman and had confessed to murder. "What did you do to Wendy?" Her voice shook.

He looked at the ceiling. "She's tied up along with Charlie and Annabelle in a storage room upstairs."

"Then they've seen your face." Hope surged. They would know he was behind the crimes.

He removed a burlap bag from his coat pocket and tossed the scarecrow mask onto the empty table between them. "They saw this face."

He was the scarecrow. But why? "What do you want? Why did you lock Charlie and me in the grain locker?"

"I wanted to search Charlie's room." He pointed at the journal in her hands. "I thought he had your mother's diary, but I see Jimmy must have stolen it."

"He borrowed it," Deidre defended. "Why is it so important to you?"

"My father told me Hannah wrote lies about him in a journal." He pushed back his coat to reveal a knife on his belt. "When I began working here, I asked Emerson about the diary. He said your mother had given it to you."

"He was mistaken." He hadn't mentioned Nate. How long before he returned as promised? She needed to keep Bruce talking. "Did you steal my bag at the station?"

"Yes, but your mother's journal wasn't in it."

"But why did you return the books to this library?" She placed her hand on the table. Her skin was pale against the wood.

"Did that confuse you?" Bruce cackled.

The bestial noise sent shivers down her spine.

James shook as he rubbed the scar on his arm.

"Torture shouldn't be rushed. I wanted to see your reaction and enjoy the fear before the final act."

Fear. He fed on it like a predatory beast, and she was the defenseless creature trying to escape. Bruce had been listening and watching them behind the disguise of a servant. But why? What did he want? James had sought answers about his father. She tossed the journal on the empty table between them. "You can read it. My mother only wrote the truth about Lewis Smith. She mentioned your name once."

Bruce ignored the diary, stepped closer, and swept his arm across the stacks of books between them. He released a primal scream with each wave of his arm.

Deidre covered her ears with her hands but couldn't block out the savage cry.

The books flew through the air and thudded against the floor like beats of discord.

The thunderous crashes made her and James jump

back against the bookcases.

They needed to escape, but her heart beat against her chest in a rapid crescendo. Terror froze her in place.

Bruce blocked their exit through the door to the gallery, but another door on the far side of the room opened to the garden. Could they make a run for it? She signaled James to move toward the center of the room.

"You can believe the foolish musings of your mother. My father was the only person who spoke the truth." His voice was filled with pride. "But I was worried about my identity being revealed before I could put my plan into action. My real motive was to lure you and your uncle to Kinsman Manor."

"Uncle Logan?" She thought of his accident. "Did you roll the barrels down the hill that broke his leg?"

"Don't be stupid. I wanted him here to end the Pierce line. Your father and uncle made a fool of mine." Bruce hit his fist on the table, his face contorted in anger. "His presence would have made it easier to kill you both here. Now I'll have to travel to Ohio to finish the job."

"You leave my uncle alone!"

"You should be more concerned about your fate, Deidre." The corner of Bruce's mouth lifted in a snarl. "Do you think the cupid was meant for Mr. Burroughs?"

"Did Mr. Kinsman know who you were?" James asked in a high, trembling voice.

"I needed his trust for my plan. I encouraged Kinsman to invite his grandchildren to celebrate his birthday." Bruce removed the knife from his belt and stalked them in an arc to force them back into the corner. "I was glad when you all accepted."

Deidre wiped her wet palms against her skirt, which hid her shaking legs. All she could see was hate in the eyes of the man who had cared for her grandfather. "Did you kill him?"

"He was old, and the fall had taken his strength. It was more pleasurable to see him slowly die like my father. Do you know how it feels to see a strong man waste away?" His voice was angry. "I spent years washing my father's diseased body, forcing food down his throat, and cleaning up waste that spilled out of him. The only thing keeping him alive was hate for everyone who wronged him."

"I did nothing to you." James held up his hands, and his voice quivered.

"You were the catalyst for me, Jimmy. You could say this week has been a family reunion in more ways than one. After you and your mother ran out, I lost track of you. When I saw your wedding announcement to Annabelle in the paper, you gave me the idea of bringing everyone together. One. Big. Happy. Family." He stabbed the table with the blade of his knife with each word, gouging the smooth surface. "My knife was smaller then, but do you recall how I sliced open your arm?"

James grabbed his forearm.

"You screamed like a stuck pig. That's when your mother packed up and took you away. Just like I wanted. I had my father all to myself. I didn't have to share him with those who weren't worthy of his greatness."

"But he's dead now," James said.

"I praised Lewis Smith in his obituary. The least I could do was turn him into a hero instead of the pitiful joke he became. But that requires all those who spread lies about him to die."

"No one had to lie," she reasoned. "He caused his

own downfall."

"Derek Pierce and your mother ruined my father's life and mine." Bruce slashed the air with his knife. "He lost everything but me. I swore revenge against our enemies. But I was patient. I waited for an opportunity and seized it. No one notices a lowly servant. A sleeping potion and Emerson didn't know I had been gone hours. A scary mask and no one recognized me." He rapped his fist against the table. "Now death is knocking on your door."

Lewis Smith had killed her father and created Bruce in his evil image. "You won't get away with murder." Deidre's gasping voice betrayed her fear. "The sheriff won't believe in two accidents."

"That's why I'm going to put the blame on Jimmy." Bruce pointed at her mother's diary with his knife. "You discovered he took your mother's journal and confronted him here in the library. He became angry and killed you. When they find him wearing the coat and mask of the scarecrow, they'll blame him for everything that's happened."

James stared at the mask on the table. "I'll tell them the truth."

"You'll be dead, and I'll be the hero who stopped you." He made a sad face and sniffled. "Only not in time to save poor helpless Deidre."

Bruce moved so quickly neither Deidre nor James reacted. Bruce grabbed James by the back of his hair and slammed his forehead against the table. He slumped to the floor.

"James!" She stared at his limp body. Just like Mrs. Knox. Her lip trembled, and tears fell in spite of her resolve to be brave.

Bruce cracked his knuckles, and his laughter echoed in the room. "Your death will be more creative."

No one thought of dying. Everything about her future was on the edge of fulfillment with Nate and their lives together. *Don't let him end your dreams.*

Someone jiggled the doorknob. "Why is the door locked?"

It was Charlie.

"James, are you in there?" Annabelle called outside the door. "The scarecrow tied us up in a room upstairs, but Max found us."

A table separated her and Bruce. She dashed for the door and grabbed the knob, but the door wouldn't open. She needed to reveal Bruce's plan. "Bruce is the scarecrow!"

"Where is he?" Wendy shouted through the door.

"In here!" she screamed. "He wants to kill me! Help me," she begged as she tugged on the locked door.

"Help me," Bruce mocked as he crossed the floor. "You should have gone for the garden door." He locked it and strode toward her.

"Please open," she prayed, her hands clasped on the door handle.

He clamped his hand over her mouth and pushed her against the door. "Now I won't be able to blame James for your death, but it won't change the outcome."

His breath was foul, and his fingers bruised her face. She wrestled futilely to escape his grip as tears flowed down her face. She could taste her heartbeat in her throat.

"I'm not afraid to die to succeed, but if we're both going to meet the grim reaper, let's make your demise interesting." Bruce placed the blade of his knife against her throat.

She held her breath, afraid to move.

He turned her to face the room and tossed the ring of keys into the open space.

He stepped away from her, his knife held upright in the air. "Three tables, two locked doors, and a man with a knife stand between you and freedom. Can you reach the keys and escape? But there are so many keys on the ring. What will you do?"

His voice was taunting.

Her grandfather had said Freddy enjoyed torturing animals. Now she was the prey. Her entire body trembled. Bruce would show no mercy. She kept the door to her right and the bookcases behind her as she retreated slowly toward the corner to put the tables between them. "Why do you want to hurt me? I've never done anything to you."

"You were the reason my father needed to kill your parents."

Deidre wondered at his strange statement. "I wasn't born."

"He knew your mother was breeding. Why do you think he returned home in the afternoon to catch them together fornicating in his bed and end all three of your lives? But the other tenants heard the shots and came running. Your father took two bullets when he blocked your mother to save her and their unborn child. Lewis couldn't finish the job with witnesses. Now it's up to me."

Her father had loved her. He had died to save them. *Give me your courage*, she prayed. Bruce lunged forward, stabbing the air with his knife.

She jumped back.

IIc laughed.

She kept her eyes on Bruce, feeling her way along the bookcases. Her hand touched a ladder. She climbed the rungs, but he grabbed the back of her skirt and yanked. The fabric tore, and she scrambled higher.

He put his hand on the ladder rung. "There is no escape from death."

"Get away from me!" She kicked at his hand and pushed off. The ladder rolled along the floor and bumped into the corner. The jolt jostled her precarious position, but her tight grip kept her from falling.

She jumped to the next ladder and pushed before he could reach her. The ladder stopped at the fireplace. She was halfway to the windows and the door facing the garden, but the keys were in the middle of the floor.

"I can smell your fear," Bruce taunted as he raised his head and sniffed like an animal on the prowl. He positioned himself between the tables and an equal distance from the keys. "Go for them."

She clung to the ladder, unable to decide her next move. Her palms were sweaty, and her legs trembled beneath her skirt.

"Come down, Deidre. I'll make it quick. If not, your lover won't recognize your face." He lunged with his knife.

She screamed and scrambled higher to the top. The blade ripped through the thick folds of fabric on the back of her skirt. She felt no pain. He hadn't torn flesh. Not yet.

She was trapped on the ladder. She grabbed a leather-bound novel and threw it. She grabbed one volume after another and continued her onslaught as he cursed. Her arm throbbed, and she strained to reach more books on the shelves, but they were too far away.

He placed his hand on the rung below her. She stomped on his fingers, and he cursed a string of unfamiliar words. He retreated and waved his knife. "You little hellion. What makes you think you can escape?"

Her heart pounded in a staccato beat, and she blinked away tears so they wouldn't blind her to the enemy below. She wasn't going to surrender without a fight.

He began to climb.

She fought back the terror that shook her body and waited for the right moment to kick the hand holding the blade. She put her weight against the ladder, lifted her skirt, and swung her foot.

His knife flew from his grasp and slid across the wooden floor and under a table.

His face was contorted in anger. "I don't need a knife to break your fool neck." He grabbed a handful of fabric and pulled.

She screamed but clung to the rungs of the ladder as pain shot up her arms. He was stronger, and her grasp was slipping as gravity aided him. Sobs shook her body as she struggled to hold on to life. Her fingertips peeled away, and she fell. Her arms and legs thrashed about and hit Bruce.

He staggered and fell to the floor.

She lay beside him, stunned. *Move. Get away.*

Before she could make her body respond, he hovered over her, his soulless eyes staring into hers. He smiled in a way that chilled her blood.

"Deidre!" James staggered to them, blood dripping down the side of his face.

"Thank God you're alive." Her voice reflected relief

and hope.

Bruce pressed his fingers around her neck. "Don't expect him to save you."

She gasped for breath as his grip tightened.

James put his forearm around Bruce's neck. "Let her go!"

Bruce released his grip on her neck and flung James off. He left him in a heap and searched for his knife.

She sat up and gulped needed mouthfuls of air.

James was on his hands and knees and lifted his head to look at her.

She saw the ring of keys on the floor, but her body was exhausted with no strength to move and claim them. She looked at James and pointed.

He retrieved the keys and staggered toward the door.

A metal bench crashed through the windows overlooking the garden. Splintered wood and broken glass showered the floor. Nate followed through the opening.

Bruce had recovered his knife.

Nate wrapped his coat around his arm. He dodged the blade, using the thick fabric to avoid injury. He was at a disadvantage without a weapon. How long could he hold out before he was injured or killed?

James fumbled with the keys, unable to find the right one to unlock the door.

Deidre needed to help the man she loved. She slowly rose and gripped a chair for support. On the table in front of her was a tall brass candlestick. She discarded the candle and grabbed the top so the thick square base rose into the air. Bruce had his back to her, and she stepped toward him.

Nate met her gaze. After sidestepping the knife, he

jabbed with his fist, and Bruce jumped backward.

Deidre swung the thick base down on Bruce's head. He slumped to the floor, blood flowing from the wound.

"One swing to drive a nail. No tap-tapping from me."

James had unlocked the door. Charlie, Wendy, Annabelle, and Max crowded into the room.

Annabelle screamed when she saw her husband but helped Wendy lead him to a chair and apply a handkerchief to his wound.

Max retrieved Bruce's knife from the floor.

Nate gently removed the candlestick from Deidre's hands and handed it to Charlie. "Hit him again if he moves." He dropped his tattered coat to the floor and pulled her against his chest. "We couldn't get in. I went to the garden." He looked at the debris on the floor. "I was afraid I wouldn't reach you in time."

She melted against his strong body, feeling safe and warm in his arms. "I've always had a soft spot for a reformed scoundrel, my honorable Nate Burroughs."

He brushed his lips against hers, teasing her to match his passion. She clung to him, her mouth taking his in a possessive grip. Life never tasted so sweet, and desire grew with each kiss.

"I love you," he said between kisses. "I'll wait forever for you."

Deidre wanted Nate in her future, and she didn't need time to be confident of her decision. "I'm going to need a partner to help run Second Chance."

He paused, gazing into her eyes. "Business partners?"

"I was thinking personal partners." She ran her fingertips along the sides of his face and pressed her forehead against his. "I was so focused on helping others I forgot to seek my own happiness. Marriage wouldn't be a conflict of interests, would it?"

"Not for a clever lawyer," Nate said. "I'll figure out a way to make our partnership legal and lasting."

"I love you." She kissed him to seal the deal.

A word about the author...

Laura Freeman was a reporter for sixteen years for local papers and the Gannett national papers in Northeast Ohio. She won the Press Club of Cleveland's Ohio Excellence in Journalism award twice and the Ohio Newspaper Association award several times. Her novels include historical romances Impending Love and War, Impending Love and Death, Impending Love and Lies, Impending Love and Capture, Impending Love and Madness, Impending Love and Promise, a holiday novella Tackling Molasses Crinkles, a crime mystery Raining Tears, a mystery romance Tangling a Web of Deceit, and a women's lit Sailing into a Storm.

~*~

Find Laura online at:
https://twitter.com/laurafreeman_rp
https://www.facebook.com/laura.freeman.5648
https://authorfreeman.wordpress.com/